A KISS FOR MISS TRUELOVE

"Ah, Miss Truelove Beckons!"

It was Lord Drake. True stopped and turned, smiling up at him.

"What, hungry? Was dinner not enough? You shall be as plump as a pigeon if you take to late night meals this way."

His voice was rich and deep, and his tall, broad, presence looming above her set True's heart to thumping. "I . . . we needed hot water for our washing up, and the bread and jam . . ."

"Do not explain," Drake said. "I wonder if you are fetching and carrying for Miss Swinley. Are you really a companion then? Is that your secret?"

"I . . . well, we shall both make use of the water . . . I must go up . . ." True started up the stairs, but with surprising agility, Drake stepped up before her and barred her way.

"Now, you must know that the serving wenches at every inn must learn how to rebuff the attentions of their patrons who have had a little too much vino."

At first True did not think she had heard him correctly, but the next instant she felt his large hands spanning her waist and pulling her close to him. And before she had the time to gather her wandering wits, she felt his lips on her cheek . . .

Books by Donna Simpson

LORD ST. CLAIRE'S ANGEL
LADY DELAFONT'S DILEMMA
LADY MAY'S FOLLY
MISS TRUELOVE BECKONS

Published by Zebra Books

MISS TRUELOVE BECKONS

Donna Simpson

ZEBRA BOOKS

KENSINGTON PUBLISHING CORP.

http://www.zebrabooks.com

For my father, Alfred Andrew "Bud" Simpson, Lance Corporal of
the 27th Kent Regiment, and to all of the WWII veterans who sur-
vived the war, but carried the memory of it throughout their lives.
This is dedicated to them all with love, for their sacrifice.
Alfred Andrew "Bud" Simpson
1914–1996
Loved in Life, and greatly missed.

ZEBRA BOOKS are published by

Kensington Publishing Corp.
850 Third Avenue
New York, NY 10022

All Kensington titles, imprints, and distributed lines are available at special quantity discounts for bulk purchases for sales
promotion, premiums, fund-raising, educational or institutional
use.

Special book excerpts or customized printings can also be
created to fit specific needs. For details, write or phone the
office of the Kensington Special Sales Manager: Kensington
Publishing Corp., 850 Third Avenue, New York, NY 10022.
Attn. Special Sales Department. Phone: 1-800-221-2647.

Zebra and the Z logo Reg. U.S. Pat. & TM Off.

First Printing: June, 2001
10 9 8 7 6 5 4 3 2 1

Printed in the United States of America

One

Mud oozed up under the scarlet jacket of Drake's uniform as he was pushed down by the crushing weight of his horse, Andromeda. The cannonade thundered around him, and the stench of smoke and blood reeked in his nostrils, but that he could handle—*that* he was used to—it was the feeling of having all breath squeezed out of him that put him into a panic. His back felt as though it would snap, and he thought he could feel someone's knee in his groin. Andromeda was twisting and grunting, poor old girl, but then was ominously still, laying over him, her warm, heavy body limp.

He was buried, entombed alive beneath bodies of horses and men. Mother Earth vibrated under him as though she shrieked and writhed in misery at the abominable use men made of her surface, violating a once peaceful, green Belgian field. The air stank of death; the mud was bloodred and body parts and dead and dying men lay around him.

Drake knew he would die. Even now he felt his own blood pumping into the muck and mire from the saber wound in his thigh.

He would die. If not from loss of blood, then from this gargantuan weight, his poor dead mount, Andromeda, crushing the air from his fatigued lungs.

No, he would *not* die! He would fight and writhe

and scream—scream until someone found him and pulled him out of this bloody grave, this battlefield, this Waterloo.

"Sir! Major!"

Someone heard him; someone was coming to rescue him . . .

"My lord, wake up! You are all right, sir; you are home at Lea Park, and alive!"

Wycliffe Prescott, Viscount Drake, major general of the renowned Kent Light Dragoons, a cavalry unit of His Majesty's army, awoke, sweating and screaming, twisted in his bedclothes with the bolster on top of him. It was pitch dark and Horace Cooper leaned over him, candle in hand, his face twisted into a grimace of concern.

Drake threw aside the bedclothes, then sat on the edge of the bed and swept one long-fingered hand through his wild hair. He was home, or at least at the home of his parents, at Lea Park. The war had been over for months and he was alive, though injured. He buried his face in his hands. When would the horror leave him?

"Was I loud this time, Horace? Did I awaken anyone?"

"I don't think so, Major General, sir. . . . I mean, my lord." Horace straightened and set the candle on the table beside the large, ornately carved bed that dominated Drake's room. Flickering shadows of the heavy old furniture danced across the papered walls in ghastly silhouette.

"Good. I do not want to alarm Mother. Ever since I came back from Waterloo with this beastly leg wound and . . . and the nightmares, she worries about me."

"I know, sir," Horace said, his voice a gruff rumble in the quiet darkness. "That be a mother's chore, seems to me. No matter that you be full-

growed and thirty-two years, you still be her child.
It's nature, sir."

Drake glanced up at his former batman, now his
valet, in the wavering candlelight as the man
straightened the bedcovers. Everyone in the household called Horace "the sergeant," though it was
not a rank the man had attained. It was likely more
accurate, though, than calling him by his new position. As a valet he made a very good soldier.

"Don't you . . . don't you ever dream of that
day at Mont St. Jean, Horace?" He realized as he
spoke that he should have known he was deep in
another dream, for he had dreamt of Waterloo—
the place-name had sung in his ears like a Greek
chorus—and it did not become Waterloo until old
Nosey sent the dispatch announcing victory from
that town. The actual battleground was near Mont
St. Jean, some miles away.

The older man shook his head and bent to pick
up the candle once more. "No, sir, I reckon I leave
that part up to you. You was there through the
worst of it; I just came to pick up the pieces." He
handed his employer breeches that had been
draped over a nearby chair.

Drake grimaced and rose, stripping off his nightshirt and pulling on his breeches, feeling the familiar ache in his thigh. The wound had healed,
or at least it was no longer oozing or festering, but
the pain was still there, sometimes excruciating in
its intensity, slicing through him with every bit of
the agony of the first thrust. "You did more than
that and you know it, but even if that was the
truth, bad enough, old man. Bad enough. You saw
it all—the blood, the bodies, the small pieces of
humanity hacked to bits on that bloody battlefield.
And you saved my life—pulled me out from under
poor Andromeda and . . . and from beneath
young Captain Lewis, or what was left of him."

Horace held out a shirt to his master—that simple aid was the height of his valet skills, which were negligible—but would not meet his eyes, abashed as always in the face of praise. He had managed to raise self-deprecation to high art. "Just doin' my job, sir."

Drake smiled grimly and pulled the shirt over his head, then crossed to the bowl of water cradled in his elaborate mahogany and marble washstand. He dashed the cool, lavender-scented water on his brow, wiping away the sweat that filmed it with the soft cloth Horace handed him. There would be no more sleep for him that night. The only remedy for one of his nightmares was a few hours walking or on horseback. "And still are. You're the only one who understands, Horace, the only one who knows." He tossed the cloth down and straightened, trying to ignore the pain as he stretched. "I shall be gone for a few hours. Please let Lady Leathorne know that in the morning, will you?"

"I will, sir."

But there was no need, really, for that service. As Drake limped from the house, a plump, older woman stood at a window up on the third floor and watched her only son—her only *child*—crossing the grass toward the stables. A worried frown etched deep wrinkles on her forehead. Drake had not slept again, or at least had not slept for longer than a couple of hours, despite the quantity of brandy he had imbibed before retiring. Even through the thick walls of Lea Park she had heard his nightmare screams echoing down the old hallways, and knew that once more, his sleep was at an end for the night.

There was no anguish equal to that in a mother's heart when her child was so sorely in need of comfort, and she had none adequate to give him. It hurt so very deeply. When he had first come home she had been shocked at how pale and gaunt he was, and how very weak. She had been full of hopeful energy then, able to help him heal his body, not knowing the deeper laceration was to his soul.

Now he was getting better, physically at least. When would he recover in his mind and heart? And what exactly had happened to him that he could not sleep now, without waking screaming? She turned away from the window and returned to her bed, feeling helpless and old.

Miss True Becket gazed out of the carriage window with pleasure on the prospect of a bright, late-summer Hampshire day as they rolled steadily along good road between hedgerows and wooded copses. For miles now she had been riveted to the window, fascinated by the difference each mile made to the landscape. The landscape undulated around them, the vast beech "hangers," as the wooded slopes were called, a complete change from her own home, deep in Cornwall. The most exotic places she had been before now was the village of Polperro on the Cornish coast, and the occasional visit to her cousins in Devon.

The dense forests of Hampshire, the clear chalk streams, every pollarded beech and verdant village green, were fresh delights to her unjaded eyes. Even if she had to endure the sharp tempers of her cousins, Lady Swinley and her daughter, Arabella, it was worth it. Father would say she should thank God for giving her an opportunity such as this to see the world—or at least more of their own fair, green isle.

And she *was* thankful. The Swinleys were often surprisingly kind to her, especially Arabella—beautiful, blonde, willful Arabella. Despite a selfish streak that True was not blind to, she, at least, was usually affectionate toward her older cousin, a reminder of years gone by when True's humble home, the vicarage that housed her, her father and her younger sister, Faithful, had been Arabella's home, too. Arabella had no sisters, and True stood in that light, like an older sibling.

It did not stop the occasional cutting remark or petulant display of temper, but she thought that Arabella did hold her in genuine affection. If she had not believed that, nothing could have convinced her to be so available to them when they wanted a companion, for she certainly did not do it for Lady Swinley's convenience. She had never been able to be as fond of her elder cousin as she would have liked. The woman had a coldness about her that chilled any budding feelings of warmth or friendship.

The coachman turned the ancient, lumbering but well-maintained carriage off the road at a stone gate and onto a long, winding lane, following directions given them at their last stop, the Leaping Stag. The innkeeper had dispensed directions to Lea Park along with tea and marvelous biscuits from his wife. True had almost been tempted to creep down to the kitchen to ask the landlady for the receipt, but knew that would gain her a swift and angry reprisal from Cousin—no, her cousin preferred "Lady Swinley"—if she made them late by even a moment. It was not that she feared her cousin, but life was much more pleasant when everyone got along.

The lane broadened, from tree-lined into open parkland. They were laboring uphill, the carriage burdened with four adult women—Lady Swinley, Arabella, True and the maid, Annie—as well as the groom and driver, and a multitude of trunks and bandboxes, satchels and valises strapped to the roof. Lady Swinley did not have the resources for a cart or wagon with the second coachman it would have needed. But their slow pace had its reward as True gazed out the window over a gentle slope of verdant beauty, rolling down into a valley where a sparkling river, a tributary of the Itchen, wound through banks lined by overhanging willows, sturdy oaks and shallow inlets of rushes, full-blown in the late summer sunshine.

True's blue eyes sparkled just as the meandering river did; she delighted in natural beauty, though she was neither a painter nor a poet. Her enjoyment lay in the soothing rhythms of nature, the cycle of life and the abundance of creation. God's gift to man, her father always said.

"Tolerable park," Lady Swinley murmured laconically.

Arabella, her oval face alight with anticipation, glanced at her. "Surely more than tolerable, Mama? It is quite lovely, don't you think, True?"

"I do! I have never been to Hampshire, but have seen a book of plates, and it is just as I imagined, rolling hills, wooded copses . . . beautiful."

Arabella smiled. "Wait until you see the house! It is quite spectacular. When we were here last year it was a very wet spring, and so we could not get out much, but Lea Park has enough rooms and nooks and crannies to keep one busy through a month of wet Sundays! I am so glad you could come with us this time, True." She thrust her arm through her cousin's and hugged it to her slender body. "If I am engaged before we leave, maybe we can find a beau for you! Some dashing buck who has come to Hampshire for the autumnal hunt!"

True blushed and gazed out the window. "You know I do not look to marry, Bella. I am content to be in your shadow."

Arabella patted her blonde ringlets and smirked.

"I am speaking of after I am engaged, and can no longer be an object of flirtation, silly! I shall be very cold to any gentlemen who visit and say, 'La, my lord, you must not look at me as your flirt. Rather gaze upon my cousin. Is she not sweet, in a prim, vicar's-wife, kind of way?' I shall turn them all over to you."

True tried to keep herself from rolling her eyes. Arabella was spoilt by all the attention she had had over the last three London seasons. She had turned from a sweet young girl into a hardened flirt, and it took away some of the attraction of her vivacity, in True's mind.

But apparently the gentlemen found her as irresistible as ever, and that was all that counted in both mother and daughter's eyes. She decided a change of subject was warranted. "Is all this land Lord Drake's?"

Arabella's mother finally found the conversation of some interest and turned her gaze toward True. "His father's, the earl of Leathorne. But Drake will one day own it. For the time he has a pretty little estate not too far from here, I have been told." Lady Swinley's sources went deep into the nobility, and she had cultivated, over Arabella's three London seasons, acquaintances in every noble house of the realm. She likely knew Lord Drake's income down to a farthing.

Her green eyes wide, Arabella said, "Lady Drake . . . I shall like being called that, Mama."

"And you will be an enchanting viscountess, my dear. You will be an even more remarkable countess one day; you shall be Lady Leathorne."

"Not too soon, I hope," Arabella said. Her smile was natural and unforced as she added, "I very much like Lord and Lady Leathorne."

"Jessica is one of my oldest and dearest friends," Lady Swinley said with satisfaction. "And I have

long thought this match to be the happiest outcome for my darling daughter. It will serve to make
everyone happy." She sat up straight and peered
out the window. "Look! There is the house!"

True's gaze flew back to the window and her
mouth dropped open in an unladylike manner. Lea
Park was lovely, majestically rising above the
parkland in a series of terraced gardens that led
the eye up to the house—if one could call it by
such a homely name—its mellow gray walls turned
golden by the angle of the afternoon sun. From
the four stories of the main section of the house,
a conservatory, with high roman-arched windows,
stretched out to the left side, and a rounded library wing stretched out to the right. Formal gardens flanked the terraces and square boxwood
hedges lined the walkways.

Lady Swinley and Arabella had already looked
back down to gather their reticules and various ac-
coutrements, but then they had seen Lea Park before, and as recently as the year before when they
had made an extended visit there. True had no
such preparation, and she gazed in awe at the
lovely home she was to spend at least a fortnight,
and very likely a month or more in.

The carriage swung around a long approach that
coquettishly turned away from the house before
submitting and finally turning once more to bring
the carriage up to the front portico that stretched
over marble steps. The huge front doors swung
open, and two footmen descended the stairs as
Lady Swinley's groom leaped from his seat to put
the step down for the ladies.

Annie saw to the baggage, while Lady Swinley
regally sailed up the steps, followed by Arabella and
an abashed True.

She had never met a countess nor an earl. Would
they be dreadfully condescending? Lady Swinley was

just the widow of a baron, and she could be terribly intimidating at times, cousin or no cousin!

A butler ushered them in, led them through a cavernous hall and reception room to an equally enormous saloon, and announced them. "Lady Swinley, the Honorable Miss Arabella Swinley and . . . and Miss . . ." He waited for the name to be supplied to him.

Lady Swinley swept forward without giving it, but True didn't mind. In this one case she wanted to remain anonymous for just a while, until she got over her awe. It would not do to look like a moonling with these people, her hosts for a lengthy visit.

Like a formal portrait, Lord and Lady Leathorne sat in matching chairs at one end of the magnificent blue and white saloon. They stood as one, as Lady Swinley and Arabella approached them. Lord Leathorne was a plump, peevish-looking man with sparse hair swept back from a high-domed forehead. True thought he looked worried, but she could not fathom why a gentleman with everything in life would look worried.

Lady Leathorne was plump, too, but her erect carriage and uptilted chin hinted at pride and something else . . . defensiveness? True hung back and observed, as she was wont to do, not willing to interfere in the reunion of old friends. She drifted over to a painted screen near the fireplace and gazed out of the high-arched windows at the terraced gardens filled with late-blooming flowers, taking a moment to compose herself. This house was so very grand! She had visited her cousins at their home of course, in Devon, but Swinley Manor—the title had lapsed with the death of the baron four years before, and so the home was still Lady Swinley's—was smaller, a dark granite manse that did not compare to this enormous, bright . . . palace! To her, it was a palace.

"Isabella!" Lady Leathorne's greeting to her old friend was one of heartfelt welcome. Lord Leathorne hovered behind his wife, looking like he did not quite know what to do.

"Jessica!" Lady Swinley's face was wreathed in a genuine smile, as they exchanged brief hugs. Finally the plans she had made for her daughter in the cradle, a brilliant match with an old and monied house, looked to bear fruit. The two older ladies, bosom bows from their long ago London Season, embraced. They all settled down to a happy reunion, but still True held back, staying in the shadows, not willing to thrust herself on the notice of the gathering. She had been plagued with shyness as a child, and still struggled with that affliction on meeting new people for the first time.

The door to the saloon opened again, and she was conscious of a swirl of movement behind her. She turned, and a shaft of brilliant sunshine pierced the gloom of the farthest reaches of the room. Through it, from out of the darkness, came a young Galahad, a tall gentleman with a tumble of tawny, unruly hair swept back from a high white brow. He leaned on a cane and limped, favoring his left leg as the sunlight danced across golden streaks in his hair and lit up his golden eyes. True took in a deep breath. He was gorgeous, dressed in pale biscuit-colored pantaloons and a coat of dove gray. This *must* be Lord Drake.

He made his way across the expanse of marble floor as Lady Swinley and Arabella turned to greet him. Arabella blushed—with only a swift, frowning glance at the cane—showing a becoming sensibility for a girl who had come to Lea Park to be matched to the heir. True, unable to resist the magnetic pull of Lord Drake, was drawn across the floor, too, toward the grouping of elegant lords and ladies.

Lady Leathorne spoke. "Drake, you remember

Lady Swinley, and of course her lovely daughter, the Honorable Miss Arabella Swinley? They were visiting on your last leave, when that French upstart was first incarcerated."

Lord Drake bowed before the ladies. "Of course I remember, Mama. How could I forget?"

"I'm sorry," Lady Leathorne said, glancing at True and then turning to her friend. "I am afraid I did not catch your companion's name?"

Lady Swinley looked startled for a moment, then noticed True hovering just at the fringe of the group. "True? Oh, yes, of course. Lord Drake, may I introduce my cousin?"

Two

"Miss Truelove Beckons."

Drake, who had been barely listening and had turned automatically at some gesture Lady Swinley made toward her young cousin, was riveted. Miss Truelove Beckons! He smiled and gazed into eyes the color of periwinkle. Startled into gallantry, he said, "What a lovely name for a *lovely* lady! Miss Truelove Beckons."

Rising from a kiss laid on her gloved hand, he watched, fascinated, as a deep rose flush flooded her pale, softly rounded cheeks and a sweep of dark lashes veiled her eyes. My, but she was a pretty maiden, he thought, suddenly reminded by the color of her eyes of a dell near the woods, carpeted in periwinkle in the spring. She was not richly garbed as Miss Swinley was, but neat and sweet in a pale-blue day dress of some soft, clingy material. And her brown hair under her unfashionable bonnet looked like spun glass, soft as a catkin, probably. His fingers itched with a reprehensible and uncharacteristic urge to reach out and touch one drooping curl, to see if it could possibly be as soft as it looked.

"Not Beckons, my lord." Arabella tittered politely behind one slender gloved hand. "Her name is Miss Truelove *Becket!*"

Lord Leathorne let out a great shout of laughter and slapped his breeches-clad knees. "What a looby you are, m'boy! Nobody would name their gel Truelove, if their last name was Beckons! Like a written invitation, dontcha know!"

Lady Leathorne drew her son to her side with an affectionate glance and a maternal hug. "Understandable mistake; just an error in hearing."

"Too much cannon fire, dontcha know," Lord Leathorne added, with a smirk and a wink. "Frenchies fractured his eardrums! Ha!"

Lady Leathorne glared at him. "That is not true, Leathorne! His hearing is just fine."

"Still," Drake said, unfazed, staring at the young lady. "I think the name suits her down to her slippers, wouldn't you say?" He politely included Miss Swinley in his glance, and noted two sharp vertical lines between her arched brows, before she quickly smoothed her face to a pleasant calmness.

"I agree with his lordship, the earl," she said, with just a trace of petulance in her melodic voice. "It would be most unseemly if that were her name, Lord Drake. What *would* the gentlemen make of it?"

"Nothing if they were truly gentlemen, Miss Swinley," Drake returned, his rich voice cool with reproof. Normally he would not think of disagreeing with a lady, but really, who did she think she was to say such a thing?

True, uncomfortable under the scrutiny of the gathered company, wished she could just sink into the floor. She stared down at the figured Turkish rug, memorizing the intricate swirls and stylized flowers until she could have drawn it from memory. It was only when she heard the conversation resume, as Lady Swinley and Arabella were invited to sit—oh, and of course Miss Becket, too, someone added—that she dared raise her eyes. Another gentleman, Lord Nathan Conroy, a friend of Lord

Drake's, joined them, and was introduced to Lady
Swinley and Arabella. True took a seat, too, but a
little away and back of the main group.

How mortifying that was! To be stared at and
talked over as if she were not there! And yet, *he*
had come to her rescue, like a knight errant from
the old romances. . . . She turned her gaze back
to Lord Drake. He was tall and slim, but one got
the impression that he had not always been thin,
for his shoulders were broad and his legs muscular.
Despite the cane, his movements were elegant, his
mien noble. Her first impression of a young Galahad was not far from the mark. Voice, looks, character—all were of a knightly cast, despite a certain
carelessness of dress and hair that True found en-
dearing in so elevated a nobleman.

It was not that he was slovenly, but his hair was
longer than fashion decreed, a tumble of golden
curls that made her long to touch them, and he
was not clothed in high shirtpoints, nor was his
jacket so tight as to require aid to don it. He used
no quizzing glass, as Lord Conroy did to great effect, nor were there fobs dangling from his waistcoat. He either had no valet, or did not attend to
the commands of the one he did have.

Her confusion when he gazed upon her and uttered what he thought was her name had not come
merely from being the center of attention, but
from the strange feelings that had coursed through
her when she had first gazed deeply into his eyes.
They were amber, almost caramel, and they glowed
with a tawny light. There had been laughter and
sweetness deep within them and . . . and *hope*.
Hope? Yes, it was the only word to describe the
way they flared, as if a lamp had been lit within
them.

She sighed. It was her failing in life to see things
in people's eyes and expressions that she could

never quite be sure about. It was as if all of their hopes and dreams and wishes were alive in them, vibrating *through* them, and she picked up on emanations that expressed all of those deep feelings. Those about her often appeared to submerge their inner emotions under a veneer of civilized *ennui*, but their eyes did not lie, or at least she didn't think they did. Lady Swinley concealed a streak of vanity that came out in the haughty light in her frigid gray eyes. Arabella was unsure of herself far more often than her outer calm would ever reveal; it was there in the flick of her eyelid and contraction of her pupils.

And Lord Drake? He had felt something like a surge of hope, she had thought from a glimmer in his golden eyes, but as the minutes passed, she lost confidence in that initial perception. She could not now be sure. Perhaps she did not know him well enough to interpret, though in the past she had noted that her first impressions were sometimes more reliable than those gained when she became acquainted with someone, and somehow was coaxed into believing the facade they wished to present to the world.

Her gaze returned to Lord Drake. At first he had joined in the lively conversation with his friend and the others, but now he was gazing out the window, and his gaunt face had harsh shadows; his eyes had gone from golden and glowing to a muddy brown. What was bothering him, she wondered, watching pain flit across his face. Was it his leg? He had been wounded in the battle at Waterloo, she had heard from Arabella, who thought it a most romantic thing that he was a wounded war hero. He had attained the rank of major general two and a half years before at the stunningly young age of thirty, and had been commended by Wellington for his bravery, Arabella confided, after a letter had arrived confirming the long-standing invitation to Lea Park.

Pain could perhaps do that, etch those lines on his face and turn his bright eyes to dark. Her father, a vicar still active when able, was severely tested by his gout. When in the midst of a bad spell, his sweet, cherubic face became twisted with the pain and he laughed that the devil was prodding him with hot pokers. His laughter did not hide the agony. Perhaps Lord Drake felt the same and bore it just as bravely.

His gaze was fixed on the distant river visible, glistening, through the long windows of the saloon, but she didn't think he saw it at all. While Lord Conroy flirted and teased Arabella, who was glowing and beautiful under the skillful attention of the viscount's friend, Lord Drake pondered some painful thoughts.

Drake had become inured to the flow of polite conversation around him, and instead of the lovely scenery, he stared in despair into one of the many faces that haunted him day and night, the face of a Frenchman he had had no choice—or at least he had thought he had no choice—but to kill. It was many years ago now, on the Peninsula. Drake, a raw lieutenant with little actual battle experience, for until then he had been stationed in England, had been out foraging for the small game that would supplement his meager dinner, when up over the hilltop had come a young French officer. Drake saw the man's weapon and the glaze of desperation in the fellow's eyes, and had shot.

When he had checked his victim, it was to find that the poor sot had no ammunition. He was unarmed, in truth, though he carried a rifle. He carried, too, in his breast pocket, right above the red flower of blood that signaled Drake's deadly shot, a miniature of a young woman and a baby. His own? Likely. The woman was lovely, with elongated brown eyes and red-tinged chestnut tresses, and she held a baby of about one year on her lap.

Drake had sat down on the dusty hill and stared at the miniature for hours by the body of his first kill, a man not more than thirty and probably younger, a lieutenant like himself but with a family to support. What was the fellow doing unarmed away from his regiment? Deserting maybe? Or had he become detached from his regiment, lost in the unfamiliar Spanish wilderness? It did not matter. He was dead, and his wife and child would likely never know what happened to him. His body would rot in the blazing sunshine until scavengers pulled it apart.

Drake sighed as he came back to the present and gazed out the window toward the gardens. That poor lieutenant's was just one of the faces that haunted him, just one of the crimes he laid at his own door, made worse by the fact that when he remembered back he was almost certain the fellow shouted *"Ne tirez pas!"* just before falling. "Don't shoot." Would it have made a difference if Drake had understood or caught what he said? Could he have taken the chance that a Frenchman with a gun really would not—or *could* not—shoot him?

He shrugged and turned away from the window, trying to recapture the thread of the conversation. They were speaking of . . . of London, and the little season, just starting. Conroy, his dark Byronic locks falling over his forehead in studied grace—*his* valet was a genius who considered his master his work of art—was performing his magic again, and Miss Swinley was laughing, her lovely face and green eyes alight with pleasure. She cast him a mischievous glance and made some remark that set

Conroy into the whoops, but Drake didn't catch what it was. He had a headache coming on, the usual outcome of too much socializing. He would never survive a London ball at this rate, and did not intend to be bullied into going down to London for the little season, or any other season, until he felt like it.

What a gloomy Gus he had become, he thought, shifting and trying to ease the ache in his leg with a surreptitious rub. He was truly not fit for polite society. Horace had given it as his opinion that it was the lack of sleep that was making him a surly beast. Maybe, but maybe it was a thousand faces of the dead haunting him—from the first death he saw, a young man from an artillery regiment whose rifle exploded in his face, to young Lewis, the last body he had seen before passing out at Waterloo.

And there he went again, obsessed with death! It really was not healthy. He must find some way to get over the war, to get past all the men he had killed and seen killed. His mother worried, and he knew that she was anxious for him to move on with his life now that the wars were over. Arabella Swinley had been invited with the express intention of making a match with him; that he knew. He vaguely remembered that in the brief break, while Napoleon was incarcerated at Elba and he was given leave to visit his parents in May of the previous year, Arabella had seemed a pleasant enough diversion. She was lovely and witty and good company for an evening's flirtation. Had he raised expectations during that visit that he could not fulfill? He could not remember. Everything before Waterloo seemed like a hazy dream. But now . . .

She glanced at him again and cast him a flirtatious look, eyes downcast, and then slowly rising to meet his. There was a sweet expression of innocence and softness there, an invitation, a submission to his will. He *should* feel his blood race, his heart pound. The chase was on, and the doe was a willing victim. She was, as much as a young lady could, inviting him to pursue her. However, instead of the thrill of the hunt, all he felt was a vague distaste and the blooming of incipient dislike. It wasn't fair to her. He was sure she was a very nice young lady, but . . . and there was that deadly "but" again. *But* he could not like her. *But* her voice made him cringe. *But* her actions were so calculated as to leave him cold. *But* she seemed as fraudulent and superficial as his "hero's" welcome home had been in the streets of London. Perhaps he was manufacturing reasons to dislike her. If so, he could not help himself.

And he . . . well, he was not what she thought. If she only knew! He was no hero, he was a killer.

His roving gaze wandered the room and lit on Miss Truelove Becket, sitting just behind the others, in a shadow. She, too, was looking his way, but her eyes were calm and serious, with a hint of sweet understanding. There was no demand there, no expectation, nothing for him to live up to—blessed relief! He moved to a chair next to hers, and she observed him gravely.

"I hope you will be comfortable here at Lea Park, Miss Becket," he said.

She smiled. "Oh, I shall make the attempt," she said. "With a mere eighty or so rooms, three dozen servants, no doubt, or more, gardens to enjoy, a park to wander, a river . . . I shall *try* to be satisfied with that after the luxurious accommodation afforded me as the vicar's daughter in a very small Cornish village."

He laughed out loud at her droll comment and sober delivery, and felt the others' gaze collectively fasten on him. He nodded politely in their direction, but then bent his head toward Miss Becket, anxious to hear her lovely voice again. He had not expected from her slight stature that it would be so low, nor so achingly sweet. "When I first got back from a field hospital in Belgium and stayed briefly in our London house, I was almost overwhelmed by the opulence of my surroundings. I had been on the march for so long, and it seemed *obscene* how well-provisioned the average English aristocrat is."

"I can imagine that," Miss Becket said, her head on one side, "but the contrast is even more absurd when one realizes the chasm that yawns between the aristocracy and their own people, the people of England."

"Perhaps I have been used to taking that for granted. But at least our people have not had to deal with their homeland being invaded by marauding bands of foreign armies, all poorly provisioned, and so scavenging from the land anything they can take. I am afraid the country folk of Belgium will have little in the way of harvest this year, after the trampling we gave their crops."

Her brilliant eyes regarded him with interest. "I had been thinking, my lord, that I should like to learn more about your experiences in the war, but then I thought that was impertinent, to ask you to bring out stories that must be harrowing for you to remember, and merely for my edification."

"I have not spoken of it much. Too many people do not want the truth when they ask, and I will only ever tell the truth." He spoke from bitter experience. Conroy, his best friend, the companion of his youth, was a willing audience when Drake first arrived home. But he did not really want the truth, he wanted stories of valor and glory, a major general borne from the field of battle after a glorious victory. Conroy had stopped asking after the first ruthless tale of blood and misery. Drake was afraid he had lost forever the ability to make small talk. He was not fit for the drawing room, nor for polite company.

"That is ever the way of people though, my lord. In my village many of the gentry wish to help the poor, but they want it to be the picturesque poor— in rags, but *clean* rags, you see, despite the lack of firewood to heat the water to clean the clothes. They want to see clean, pretty children with bare feet and round rosy cheeks, not the half-starved babies of the abandoned wife, or the gin-soaked farm laborer who beats his family on Sunday, or the dirty little heathens children become when insufficient attention is paid to their upbringing." She sighed with a wry grimace. "To gain their help for the poor I must sometimes dress the truth, as well as the children, in prettier clothing."

He gazed down at her, frowning. She returned his fierce gaze with her steady blue eyes, wide but not alarmed. "I refuse to prettify war!" he growled. It had turned his stomach, when he returned, to hear some military men, men who knew better, turning the war into a glorious battle of good against evil, with the English and their allies as some kind of God-chosen heavenly army. The truth was so far removed from that, that to experienced ears their stories bordered on the ludicrous.

"And so you should, my lord," she replied calmly. "Refuse, I mean. You can do more good by telling the truth than ever you could by glorifying war. I saw so many boys from our village join, expecting glory and adventure, only to come home with no leg or arm, sad and poor, or . . . or not come home at all. The truth needs to be told by men who were there and suffered."

Drake swallowed hard past a lump, unable to reply to her calm, measured response. The quick rage that had arisen when he thought he was being counseled to lie, died. He must stop this defensiveness he had fallen into, this inability to allow people their own opinions about something he felt perhaps *too* strongly about. His own view of the war and the English military was hardly impartial.

Miss Becket looked down at her soft, worn gloves. "I—I am afraid I am one of those whom you will perhaps call foolish, having a tendency to hero-worship those of you who fought so hard for us. But I have since come to think that the burden of worship is not fair. You have done your duty and more. You should not have to live up to some myth of absolute goodness and heroism; no man could ever live up to that. I . . . I cannot imagine what you have seen, what you have lived through, but I do know that you must have seen friends, comrades-in-arms, die before you. And the awesome responsibility of command, of having all those soldiers looking to you for their next actions! How terrifying I would find that."

When True looked up, she saw a gleam of tears in the viscount's eyes, and wondered if she had gone too far, reminding him—as if he could forget!—of all that had occurred on the battlefields of Belgium, and so many battlefields before. But she had only said what she had thought as she sat there watching him. Despite his fierce demeanor, she knew somehow that she could say anything to him.

Drake felt his calm facade crumble. No one had ever asked him, or even mentioned, the friends he had lost, the men whose lives had been in his care and keeping. He had attained his elevated rank at Wellington's behest, for old Nosey complained that he was surrounded by fools and incompetents and he needed men with the ability to command. But the price paid for that ruthless ability to lead was a lifetime of sleepless nights and a weight that pressed on him always, the weight of the dead. He

could bear it—he *had* borne it all through the war
and even now—but it was wearing him down, he
feared. Now that the need to maintain a cool head
and a cold heart was gone, pain flooded in to fill
that hole in his soul.

He came back to his senses to find Miss Becket
gazing at him with ready sympathy in her lovely
eyes. Sympathy from some he could not bear; it
was too close to pity. But from her it seemed almost healing, a balm instead of a curse. He re-
called her last words, and said, "I have seen many
friends die, and had to write their wives and sweethearts letters of condolence. It was a most painful
duty. If I had known before I bought my colors
what I was in for, I do not know if I would have
had the courage."

"I think you would have always had the courage,
my lord. I believe that courage is facing fear, not
conquering it. Those with no fear die. We are only
human after all."

Her sweet voice washed over him. Only human.
Horace always said he was vain, thinking he ought
to have been better than all the others, all the ones
who also lost men under their command. Wellington himself bore the responsibility for all of them,
and carried his burden with grace and dignity.

"I . . . I suppose that is how I should look at
things, but I confess . . ."

"What are you two whisperin' about over there?"
Lord Leathorne's querulous voice was raised over
the conversation of the others.

Drake turned his cool glance toward his father,
resenting the way he had drawn attention to them,
interrupting what was a most interesting conversation. "We are not whispering, sir." He glanced at
his companion and saw her cheeks that pretty rose
shade again. Ah, she did not like attention drawn
to her, it seemed. "Miss Becket was asking me about

the war," he added. "We were conversing, not whispering." He saw the swift frown on Lady Swinley's pinched face. Was Miss Becket, spinster and vicar's daughter, truly a "companion" in the paid sense, he wondered, and did Lady Swinley hold that over the young lady?

"As a matter of fact, Miss Becket had just agreed to allow me to escort her on a tour of the gardens," he said, with sudden decision. He rose and held out his arm for Miss Becket, noting how the pink stain on her cheeks deepened.

Lady Leathorne watched them exit the saloon through the large doors between the sets of windows that lined one wall. On the one hand, it was good to see Drake being an obliging host, and drawing out that mousy companion of Arabella's, but he had not spent two minutes talking to Lady Swinley and her daughter. Isabella and Arabella had been invited with the express intention of matching the two young people in a marriage that would virtually guarantee the future of the Leathorne holdings through their progeny. It would also unite two old and proud families. This beginning did not bode well for the visit. Isabella's narrow, lined face was pinched into a frown, and even Arabella's lovely young visage was showing how much she would look like her mother in time.

Perhaps she should have canceled this visit, or at least postponed it, Lady Leathorne thought, knowing Drake was still ill, if not in body, then in his troubled mind. But the Swinleys had been invited the moment she had known when her son would be home. She couldn't very well have uninvited them without an explanation, and she supposed she did not want to admit even to herself how sick her son was. The servants were gossiping, she knew, about the "young master" being "not quite right in the head." One poor maid had found him dozing in the library, and as she had come to find him to deliver a message, had tried to awaken him. He had reacted most violently, striking out at her and shouting, whereupon the girl had gone into hysterics.

All of that would not be so bad if he did not fall into those brooding silences, often ignoring guests totally. If Lord Conroy were not there visiting—he was *so* skillful socially, and always had a way of deflecting attention away from his friend's moodiness—Drake's behavior would probably already have become common gossip in the neighborhood.

No, she would just have to have a talk with Drake about his behavior. Arabella had every right to be miffed that he appeared to prefer her companion, some poor relation, over her. It was terribly rude! At least Conroy, dear boy, had turned on his legendary charm and was turning her up sweet.

Lady Leathorne gazed out the window with troubled eyes to where her son was strolling arm in arm with Miss Becket. Miss Truelove Beckons, indeed!

Three

Oh, this was ridiculous, True scolded herself. Her emotions were a chaotic jumble of pleasure and nervousness and . . . well, and a silly feeling that she would swoon from the very touch of this devastatingly attractive man at her side. He held her arm close to his body as they strolled through the formal squares of gardens, lined with boxwood hedges and filled with chrysanthemums. Fragrant herbs spilled over the walkway in riotous profusion—lavender, rosemary, low globes of thyme and red-leaved basil that sent up their perfume when crushed inadvertently by a footstep. His hands were ungloved, and she was fascinated by the broad strength of them, the prominent veins, and how very different they were from her own small hands, encased in worn blue gloves a little too big for her, as they were Arabella's cast-offs.

Lord Drake was not a man to be taken lightly. Unwillingly, her mind turned to thoughts of Arthur Bottleby, her father's curate and soon to be vicar of his own parish, the man who had asked for her hand shortly before she had received the invitation from Lady Swinley and Arabella. Mr. Bottleby was not unattractive—in fact, many of the village maidens were entranced by his burning dark eyes and intense manner—but in comparison to Lord

Drake, this golden nobleman at her side . . . She
frowned, castigating herself once again. How could
she compare her suitor with Lord Drake—*Major
General* Lord Drake, one of Wellington's most
trusted leaders? It was not fair to Mr. Bottleby, and
another example of how silly and green she was
being. She knew better than to idolize a man based
on reputation, and really, Mr. Bottleby was a very
good man, very earnest. . . .

"Do you agree, Miss Becket?"

She had lost the thread of his lordship's conversation in contemplation of his lordship's magnifi-
cence! Just like the green schoolgirl she had not
been for many years now. She gazed up at him,
eyes wide. "I . . . I *am* sorry, my lord, I was not
attending. What did you ask?"

A grin lurking at the corners of his mouth, he
said, "Have I lost your attention so very easily?"

"No," True said, mortified that he would think
so. "No, really, I was just contemplating the beauty
of your home," she said, sweeping a hand out to
indicate their lovely garden surroundings. "It is
so—so beautiful." There; could she have sounded
more the widgeon? He would think her the veriest
half-wit, and deservedly so.

"It is. I thought of Lea Park often while I was
gone. And when I came back it was like stepping
into my own past, only I was so very different."
He paused at the edge of the terrace by a boxwood
hedge, and they gazed out over the valley, the hazy
distance to the west lit by the descending sun.

She relaxed again at his taking up of her subject.
It was kind of him to ignore her woolgathering.
Mr. Bottleby would have been stiff and angry with
her for that lapse in courtesy, for he did not like
to be ignored or not attended to. "That is the way
with all of life, though," True said, responding to
the viscount's comment. "When you revisit the

haunts of your youth, it is with the golden expectation that everything has remained the same. Sometimes it has, but you yourself are so changed that it seems—different. Smaller. Shabbier. It is the same with people that one has not seen in a long, long time."

"That is true. I spent some time in London when I got back, before I came down to Lea Park. I was injured, but still able to get around. I thought I would revisit my old haunts, visit with some of my cronies. We used to have such fun, going to mills, gambling until dawn, visiting the opera houses and—"

"And the opera dancers," True chuckled, and then flushed. Oh, her unruly tongue! A young lady was not supposed to know about opera dancers. She would not, but for Arabella's sometimes scandalous tales of London life. For a girl of twenty-two, her cousin had an extensive grounding in the affairs—sometimes quite *literally* the affairs—of the denizens of that great metropolis.

But Lord Drake squeezed her arm and chuckled with her. "That, too. Young men will have their amours. But . . ." His expression turned serious.

True gazed up at him, noting how the golden sun bathed his face in a ruddy glow. He was so very handsome, even with the lines of weariness and worry etched on his gaunt face. Something about him touched her deeply. Perhaps it was the sadness she saw in his golden eyes, or some longing she sensed from his soul, a longing for peace, she thought. "But?" A breeze swept up from the riverside and tugged at her curls. She swept them out of her eyes impatiently.

His voice, when he spoke again, was remote. He gazed into the distance and frowned. "Do you know, I never had to buy a single drink for myself those first weeks in London. And I was invited to

more parties celebrating our victory than I could
go to in a hundred lifetimes. But I was restless.
Something about it all seemed . . . fraudulent,
empty. I . . . I haven't been able to sleep well
since . . . since coming back. One night I was staring out the library window at the street outside . . ."

His voice trailed off and his eyes, misty with re-
membrance, showed a shadow of pain.

"You were staring out at the street?" True urged
him on. She gazed up at him, memorizing the high
arch of his rather beaky nose, the strong line of
his chin, noticing the faint sandy stubble. There
was something about this moment, standing on the
terrace of Lea Park with the scent of the herb garden drifting around her and the smell of him, a
musky, sandalwood scent, filling her nostrils, that
would stay with her forever, she thought. This day
was one of those days she would remember even
as a very old woman. The slanting sun filled his
curls with light and it was like a nimbus around
his head.

"There was a man," he continued, finally, "probably about forty or so, though he looked older, and
he was walking, or rather, limping. He was not
wealthy, and I figured that he must have been a
soldier in the war, for he was an amputee, as many
of our poor fellows are. He was struggling along
on homemade crutches; he was not used to them—
I deduced that he must have been injured late in
the war, at Waterloo or the run-up to it—and it
was painful to watch his slow progress. I did not
know what he was doing in Mayfair, but it didn't
really matter. I was going to run out the door and
'halloo' him, ask him if I could stand him a pint
somewhere. Horace—my batman, you know—was
off visiting his family and I was lonely for compan-

ionship with someone who would understand my . . . well, who would understand."

"I can imagine," True said, when Drake paused. "You must feel separated from your friends who were not in the war. You have not those shared experiences and they cannot know what it was like. None of us can."

He gave her a grateful glance and laid one long-fingered hand over her arm where it rested on his. His tawny eyes darkened to brown and his "halo" of gold faded as the sun was obscured behind a drifting cloud. "I was just coming out through the front door when I heard a clatter, and these young 'gentlemen' came racketing down the street on prime bits of blood and bone, whooping and hollering like savages." His voice had become bitter and the words dropped from his mouth like pebbles to pavement. "One of 'em had a cricket bat, and he leaned over as he rode and knocked one of the man's crutches right out from under him." Lord Drake made a swooping motion with his free arm, as if he held that cricket bat, then laid the hand back over hers again. "The fellow tumbled to the ground with an outcry of pain."

"Oh, no!" True cried, the vivid picture of the dark night and the soldier tumbling to the street making her heartsick.

"Yes!" Drake said, through gritted teeth, his lip curled. His eyes flashed with anger and bitter hatred. "At that moment I wanted to *kill* that young man! If I had had my pistol, I might have. As brutal as the offense was, it did not merit death, but I would have meted it out to that disgusting young demon without a second's thought." He glanced down at his companion and saw tears shining in Miss Becket's eyes.

"What happened to him? The fellow on crutches? Was he all right? Was he hurt? Did he get up?"

Unerringly she had struck to the very heart of the matter, Drake thought, humbled. She did not pause to reassure him or commend him for his reaction; she did not rush to condemn the young men for their actions. Her first thought was of the soldier, for the truly important part of his story was that man on crutches, not Drake's own anger and bitterness, nor his desire for revenge. And she had not lost sight of that for one second. His heart thumped and warmth flooded his soul to know there were still people who could judge so truly and care so much. It was the unerring instinct of true humanity.

"He is all right," he said, reassuring her with a half smile. He squeezed her small hand, wishing it were gloveless so he could feel the tender skin under his callused palm. "I went to him and helped him up. Poor fellow, I was right. He lost his foot at Quatre Bras, and counted himself lucky to be alive. He had been in Mayfair looking up his commanding officer, who had promised him work after the war; somehow he did not know that his captain was one of the unlucky ones. Died at La Haye Sainte. I knew him; he was a gallant fellow, one of the best, poor man."

He was silent for a moment, gazing off into the distance. "I could not see him just disappear on me. I took him to a tavern and we talked long into the night, about the war at first, but then the conversation turned to our intentions now that peace had finally arrived. He has a wife and children, but no one would hire a cripple, he said. It was all very well to celebrate the brave men who fought and died for this country, but what about the living? Do we not owe them something? At the very least, a job? I have hired him to do some work on my estate, Thorne House. He is a master carpenter; he hired himself out in his regiment to do carpentry that needed taking care of—made extra money to send home to his wife. He repaired wheels, carts, anything and everything. But he has a true brilliance when it comes to fine carpentry, and I have put him in charge of a crew of ex-soldiers; they are renovating my library."

True, tucked in to his side, so close to him she almost could not breathe, gazed up at Lord Drake. From her angle below him—she was not very tall, and the major general was—she could see the muscle that twitched in his jaw, signaling some inner tension that she was not privy to. She had just met this man, but she felt already that she knew him better than she would ever know Mr. Bottleby, and she was to marry that man! Or perhaps not. That was what she had come away to decide.

"Your anger against those thoughtless young men was understandable, you know," she said, and knew that she had read what his thoughts had returned to when his head swiveled and he gazed down at her with surprise in his changeable eyes. They strolled to a garden wall at one end of the terrace—she matched her gait to his limp—and leaned against it companionably.

He shook his head. "You have no idea how fierce that anger was, nor how close I was to killing someone. It made me wonder if I was fit to be around people anymore or if the war had made me . . . dangerous. I . . . I still dream of the killing, and the death."

Her heart ached for him, and for the edge of fear she heard in his deep voice. "You cannot know you would have shot the gentleman. Though the impulse was there, it does not mean you would have acted upon it. We all have impulses every day that we do not act upon." Like her own impulse to reach up and touch him, his face, his hair, the harsh lines of pain that marred his good looks, and yet gave him a depth of expression lacking in most young men. She wanted to strip off her gloves and lay her naked hands against his skin, and the impulse shocked her to the core.

"Perhaps you are right. I *hope* you are right. It was all so raw those first few weeks, the memories and the pain, and then to see that poor man mocked and bullied in that way! It was too much to take."

"But you did the right thing," she said, her tone bracing. She squeezed his arm. "And because of that incident the man has employment. You made a good end out of an unpromising beginning."

"Optimist," Drake laughed, gazing down into blue eyes that were surprisingly warm for so cool a color. He reached up and pinched her cheek, letting his fingers linger against the softness of her skin, feeling the warm flood of rosy color mount. "In another minute you will have me believing that it was meant to happen as it did, that young bastard—pardon me, devil—knocking poor Stanley down. I suppose you believe that God has a purpose for us all and that even bad things can have good repercussions."

True's whole body reacted from his careless caress, the gesture of a brother or friend. The touch of his naked hand on her skin, the warmth that pierced her, sent shivers through her body. "I . . . I do believe that we are given experiences and meet people for reasons, sometimes. Not all the time of course; but God sees what we need, and tries to help. Whether we are receptive to His help is another matter."

Drake pondered her words. It was certainly true that her arrival was helping him cope with a visit he had not looked forward to. He had not known how to break his mother's heart by telling her that he was not inclined to marry Miss Swinley, or anyone for that matter, especially after he had appar-

ently raised her hopes in that direction with his
thoughtless flirtation during the mother and
daughter's last visit, and so he had dreaded this
day.

Thoughts of matrimony raised a question in his
mind. He gazed down at the diminutive Miss
Becket, thinking what a cuddlesome armful she
made, tucked against him in the freshening breeze
of late afternoon.

"Why have you never married?" he asked, and
then cursed himself for his abruptness. And he
used to be at least an adequate hand at civilized
conversation!

If she was shocked by his forwardness, she did
not show it. "I . . . I was engaged some years
ago—seven to be exact—to an officer in the Royal
Navy. I lost Harry when his ship went down in an
engagement. He was never found."

There was silence between them. Miss Becket
gazed out at the river, and though there might
have been a gleam of tears in her eyes, it was
quickly conquered, though the blue was still shadowed with remembered pain, softened with the
passing of time. She must have loved him deeply
to be so affected by the memory after seven years.

"Seven years is a long time. You have never
found his equal since?" He was a cad for prodding
her, but he wanted to know. Miss Becket would
make an admirable wife for some lucky fellow, and
it would be a pity if she wore the willow for this
"Harry" her whole life. She seemed eminently
suited to the role of loving life partner.

"Love is not an everyday occurrence, Lord
Drake." It was an evasion, and True felt a fraud
for not revealing that she was even now considering a proposal. His words had pierced the armor
she had thrown up around her heart. Was Mr. Bottleby, her current suitor, Harry's equal? In fortune

and future, yes. The curate had gained a living in the north of England that though harsh, was a *good* living. And he had a small private fortune, which Harry never had. That was why they had not married while he was on leave the last time she saw him. Poor Harry had felt the need to make his fortune, and with the war raging had felt sufficient prize money was just a matter of months away, a year at the most. And so although in material goods her suitor was Harry's superior, Harry had a sweetness, a passion for life, that Mr. Bottleby could not match. Almost to herself, she said, "I have always thought that I would like to wait for love again, before marrying."

Her words were like a blow to Drake. Love? He had never thought about waiting for love, or perhaps, more accurately, had never believed that love was in his future. "I have thought about marrying. My mother would like me to, I know. But I have begun to wonder if it is fair to a young lady to marry, when I don't really believe in love, or any of that other rot that ladies seem to need before they consider themselves properly wooed." He had intended his words to be humorous, but to his ears it sounded false and bitter.

Miss Becket opened her mouth to reply, but just then, behind them, footsteps fell on the gravel walk.

"There you are, you naughty pair!" Arabella's dulcet voice fluted the words on the breeze with expert cadence. "We have been looking everywhere for you. Tea has been served, but you never came back, and you have been gone this *age!*"

Drake turned to find Miss Swinley on Conroy's arm, bearing down on them at a determined pace. "My apologies, Miss Swinley. You must lay such barbarous behavior at my door, for Miss Becket has been my captive audience. I have been boring her with war stories."

He could see from the corner of his eye Miss Becket's swift questioning glance, but he felt compelled to tell a half-truth. It would not do to say they were speaking of love and marriage; it made more of their conversation than there really was.

"Not the thing to do, old man," Conroy said, his voice smooth but his brown eyes full of questions. "The ladies prefer lighter subjects. Is that not so, Miss Swinley?"

Arabella cast him a side-glance and then swept her lashes down. "It is true. We are but frail creatures, and any talk of bloodshed is so . . . oh, terrifying! I can imagine a distinguished war hero like Lord Drake might not understand our feeble fears, being so courageous, but . . ." She trailed off and sighed, as though the subject were too painful to continue.

Drake felt a swift rise of the strange blend of ennui and anger bubble through him at her predictable and patently false deprecation of her own sex's fortitude. "I have always been under the impression that the fair sex was perhaps the more brave," he said, through gritted teeth. "After all, childbearing is surely the most frightening—"

Arabella gave a little scream, and swooned against Conroy in a convincing display of delicacy. Conroy cast him a reproachful look, and Miss Becket tore away from him to minister to her cousin.

"How could you, Drake?" Conroy said, his voice accusing, his dark eyes angry. "Have you no manners left? It is above time that you learned that you cannot trade on your war hero reputation to forgive your every rudeness. You are not in battle now, old man!"

Remorse coursed through him. Conroy was right; he was not fit for polite company. He bowed.

"Please excuse me, ladies. Conroy, I will leave them in your capable hands. My apologies for my beastly behavior." He turned to Miss Becket. "Your servant, miss."

True, supporting the still-swooning Arabella and thinking her cousin was doing it up much too brown, watched him limp away. What had caused that turn to bluntness when he had been the very soul of gentility with her? It just proved that though they had spoken for a half hour, and she had come to feel she was understanding some part of him, the inner man was still a mystery to her. And would remain that, for he was destined, if Lady Swinley and Lady Leathorne had their way, to wed Arabella.

How would the two go on as husband and wife? she wondered, as she helped Lord Conroy support Arabella back into the blue saloon. Arabella was lovely, and had taken well in London, but her own and her mother's aspirations had kept her from accepting any of the numerous offers she had, or so True had always believed. Nothing less than an eldest son would do, and a future earl was the best possibility. Both of them had held onto the notion that Bella would not marry anyone but Lord Drake—unless a duke or a marquess should ask, of course, but despite her success in London she had never been wooed by a gentleman with such a title. At twenty-two it was time she found a husband, her mother had said. One more season and she might be whispered of as "on the shelf." Lady Swinley was right about one thing; Arabella would make an admirable countess, if that elevated position required a measure of haughtiness, an outer calm, and a streak of stubbornness a mile wide.

But would she ever learn to love Lord Drake as he deserved? True worried that Arabella, determined to wed a coronet, would not stop to consider either her own, or her future husband's happiness. Of course, Lord Drake was a man, not a boy. He was used to command, and would surely not crumble in the face of feminine determination or wiles.

Or would he? He would not be the first man to be brought to his knees by feminine beauty or a mother's manipulation. True could only pray for both his and Arabella's sake, that they made the right choice.

Four

Drake, remorseful for his fit of pique, determined to behave himself at dinner. He devoted himself to Miss Swinley, his companion at the table, and had her laughing gaily and teasing him with coquettish glances. He found that he could detach himself from the scene and let his true thoughts and feelings run under his external behavior, and it helped him behave in a proper manner toward his mother's guests.

All the while, though, he kept glancing down the table to where Miss Becket, looking delicate and fragile in a deep gold gown of some glowing material, sat next to the vicar, who had been invited to dinner, too. Probably at the last minute and to balance the table, Drake thought wryly, knowing his mother's rigid adherence to the proprieties. Reverend Thomas was a fiftyish gentleman, learned and good-tempered. He had been Drake's first tutor, and had instilled in his pupil a love of good literature, along with the required Greek, Latin and mathematics. He and Miss Becket seemed to have much to talk about, but then the young lady was a vicar's daughter. It could be no more than that, that had them talking so intimately, with their heads together.

"I understand your own estate is close by Lea Park, my lord?"

Drake turned to his dinner companion. "Indeed, that is true, Miss Swinley. I am currently having some renovations done to make it more fit for habitation. It has been empty for some years and neglected terribly; there is much to do, but I am starting where my heart lies, I am afraid, rather than where common sense would dictate. The library is being entirely refitted with oak shelves by a carpenter, a fellow ex-soldier, actually. He was looking—"

"La, I never go near the library!" Miss Swinley laughed gaily, laying one bare white hand daringly over his, where it rested on the Irish lace tablecloth. "Mama says that too much reading leads to brain fevers!"

"You seem not at all at risk of that disease," Drake said, stifling his impatience.

That remark earned him a look of reproof from his mother.

"Were you not thinking of going to Thorne House to check on the progress of your renovation, my dear?" she said.

"I was," Drake replied. "I might go tomorrow. It appears that the weather will hold for at least a day or two more, and I want to check in with Stanley before too long; I have some new plans I want him to consider. And I want to see how far he and the other fellows have gotten."

"Tomorrow sounds like an ideal day," Lady Leathorne said. She glanced brightly around the table and said, as if it had just occurred to her, "Why do you young people, the four of you, not make a day of it? Take a picnic lunch and dine there. You could see the estate and still be back before dark. It is not above twenty-five or thirty miles."

"I would love that above all things, Lady

Leathorne," Miss Swinley said, her pretty face glowing in the candlelight. She turned to her mother. "May I, Mama?"

"Certainly, my dear. I long for a comfortable coze with Jessica," Lady Swinley said, casting a glance at her old friend with a delighted expression on her narrow face. "Just be sure to carry a parasol for your delicate complexion and stay out of the wind."

"It is settled then, if Lord Conroy does not object?" Lady Leathorne nodded toward the gentleman in question.

"I think it a marvelous plan!" he said, with a genial smile on his attractive face.

Drake's head whirled. From a comfortable day on his own, riding to and exploring his own estate, it had become a pleasure party for Miss Swinley. And they had included but had not asked Miss Becket! Whether she was a paid companion or not, she still deserved a say in the affair. He turned and looked down the table, and pointedly said, "Miss Becket, an outing tomorrow to my estate has been proposed. Would the anticipation of such a trip please you?"

Her cheeks suddenly rosy, the delightful blush that always seemed near flooding her face, she nodded, starting the soft ringlets around her face dancing merrily. "I . . . I would consider it a privilege, my lord."

True sat staring out the window at the moonlit grounds of Lea Park. It had been a long, tiring day, with traveling, and then the demands of company and dinner, and conversation in the drawing room after dinner. And yet she was wakeful, restless in a way that was not like her.

A gentle tap at her door, and True called out, "Come in."

Arabella swept into the room in her lacy night

rail, wrap and morocco slippers. "I'm so glad you are still awake, True. I cannot sleep! I feel so agitated, and I don't know why."

True patted the window seat beside her and Bella, as True called her in their private moments, assumed the other corner. Heavy green drapes curtained the window, but were pulled back and held in place by gold silk cord. True had not expected to be kept in such splendor, for when she visited Swinley Manor, her cousin—the mother not the daughter—always made sure that she got the smallest, darkest room that was still on the family floor. But here at Lea Park she was being treated not as a poor relation, but as an honored guest. It was a novel and welcome experience.

It was not that she really minded being often forgotten and seldom considered in people's plans. Good-humored resignation more accurately reflected her feelings on that matter. It did not affect her firm belief that as one of God's creatures she was the equal of any man or woman of any rank. That belief was radically different from the Church of England teachings she had grown up with, but she could think for herself, after all. That is why God gave her a brain. But she did understand the way of the world, and in that scheme she was a genteel but poor spinster lady. Which was why Lord Drake's deliberate asking of her feelings on the proposed trip had touched her so deeply. His was a nobility of the heart, not just of rank, and she had never met his equal, in *any* sense.

"Why are you agitated, dear?" True said, resorting to the endearment she had used when Arabella was a little girl, and True her older, wiser cousin. True had a younger sister near Arabella's age, and the three cousins had spent much time together, though that had not been so for four years or more, ever since Bella's removal from the vicarage in preparation for her come-out into London society. That debut was delayed a year after Lord Swinley's death, but Arabella had spent that year of mourning, True had always thought, in being drilled by her mother in all the ways to attract, flirt with and tease gentlemen.

Frowning, Arabella shed her slippers and tucked her feet up underneath her. "I do not know. I—what do you think of Lord Drake, True? Is he not handsome? But he seems so very ferocious, sometimes. He almost glares!"

"You're not afraid of him, are you?" True could not believe that of her cousin. Bella was up to any rig when she was a child, and True's younger sister, Faithful, would often have to run for help when their brave cousin got stuck up in a tree, or was being chased by a swarm of bees, or was surrounded in a field by a herd of cattle. It almost seemed impossible that that headstrong, independent child True had loved had become this elegant and sometimes icy young lady, but there were still occasional flashes of the impetuous girl she had been.

"N-no," Bella said, worrying at the skin that edged her thumbnail. When she realized what she was doing, she buried her hands in the frothy lace of her wrap. "I am certainly not afraid of him. He is just so different from when I first met him. You know, he bought his colors so young and is so much older than me that I never met him until last year, though our mothers have been friends this age. Mama and I have visited Lea Park before, but Lord Drake was always away." She clasped her hands together and looked starry-eyed for a moment. "Oh, True, if you think he is handsome now, you should have seen him in his scarlet regimentals, and without that repulsive cane and limp. Devastating! And not only that, but he was so gallant, and courteous

and—and I never saw anyone in London I liked half
so well. Except maybe Lord Sweetan, but even he—
well, he just was not like Lord Drake."

"And he is different this year?"

"Very. He is brooding and moody, and that distasteful remark about childbearing! Really, I was
shocked to my very core. Shocked and insulted."
Bella's narrow, pretty face took on the petulant expression that made her look much more like her
mother than she normally did.

"Really, Bella!" True was going to hold her
tongue, but could not resist falling into the mother
hen role she had played when her cousin was a little
girl. "He meant no harm, you know. It was just a
casual aside, and intended as a compliment to
women's strength. You had no reason to swoon, and
I do not believe you really did. I saw you peeking
when Lord Conroy was supporting you into the blue
saloon." True waggled her finger at her cousin, who
looked abashed for just a moment.

But Arabella was not one to remain so for long.
Her mother had drilled into her head that as the
Honorable Miss Arabella Swinley, she was entitled
to the best of treatment, and she would put up
with no other. After all, one must never let the
gentlemen have the upper hand, or they would
take one for granted, was that not true?

"Mother says that a young lady should appear
delicate and fragile at all times! What else was I to
do at such a remark? Lord Conroy was most gratifyingly attentive, and very angry with his friend. He
nearly called him a base brute for frightening me
that way." Her haughtiness dissolved in one of her
quicksilver mood changes, and she giggled.

It was the funniest thing she had ever seen, when
Lord Conroy had pressed her hand with his dark
eyes goggling slightly, and had said he would call
Drake out for the insult. She had had to do some

quick work to avoid being the cause of a rift between lifelong friends, which was not her intention at all. She had just wanted to show Lord Drake how frail and feminine she was. Her mother had *also* drilled it into her that her customary independence was anathema to the gentlemen, and she must conceal it until after marriage. There would be time enough then to assume the mantle of marital power.

So this courtship business seemed to be a careful walk on a thin wire, between dependence and independence. To gain the coveted title of Viscountess Drake, she had to establish that she was worthy—in other words, the epitome of a stylish, delicate young lady—and yet never let Lord Drake take her for granted.

She glanced over in the dim shadows at her cousin, True. For some reason Lord Drake and her had established a rapport, and as the viscount's future wife, it behooved her to find out how True had done it. She had felt just the teeniest bit jealous of her cousin when Lord Drake had invited her to walk in the gardens with him, but reflection had convinced her that it was just kindness on his part. He could not actually *prefer* True to her!

"True, what were you and Lord Drake really talking about on the terrace? It was not just about the war, I swan!"

"No, he . . . well, he asked me why I was not married, and I told him about Harry."

"And about Mr. Bottleby?" Arabella had heard evasion in her cousin's voice. She had known True all her life, and this was unlike her.

"I . . . I do not think I mentioned Mr. Bottleby's name, no."

"Why not?" Arabella said, sharply. Was True thinking of trying to steal her beau? She would be sorry if she did, because Arabella was a veteran of three London seasons and knew a thing or two about defeating feminine scheming. Lord Drake was her future husband, if she wanted him, and True had better not get any ideas! "Why would you not come right out and say you are considering an offer of marriage?"

True heard the sudden sharpness in Bella's voice. That was the trouble; London had changed her cousin. Or rather, a prolonged exposure to her mother had changed the girl. Until Arabella was ready to be presented, Lady Swinley had seldom deigned to notice that she even had a child. Bella had spent most school vacations at the vicarage, True's family home. But just before Bella turned eighteen, Lady Swinley had swept down, grasped her in her clutches and carried her off to London to be "finished," dressed, and presented. Lord Swinley's subsequent death had put off her presentation one year, but then at nineteen Arabella had been presented and London, or at least the male half, had been prostrate at her feet ever since, to hear her tell it.

And now, four years later, the sharp shrewishness of Lady Swinley was beginning to be evident in her daughter. Complimented, feted, adored, sought after as a diamond of the first water, Arabella was in a fair way to being spoiled.

"I did not mention Mr. Bottleby, because I need that to be private right now, until I make up my mind," True said.

"You had best say yes," Arabella said briskly. "It is likely to be the only offer you get at your age. I should not like to be a vicar's wife, but it will do very well for you."

A spurt of irritation flared within True. How like Arabella's new personality to presume to tell her what to do! "I will not marry because it is the last proposal I shall get. I told you, I had quite given up the idea of marriage, until Mr. Bottleby asked. I just am not sure what to do. I do not love him." And could not see herself *falling* in love with him.

"But he has a fortune; you said that yourself, even if it is a small one. What else is there to consider? You don't think to capture yourself a title do you?"

True was hurt by the scorn she heard in her cousin's voice. That was another unpleasant manifestation of the influence of Lady Swinley. "No, I do not think to capture a title." She saw Bella relax just a little and frowned in puzzlement. "But neither will I be rushed into making a decision that will change my life. I urge you to be just as cautious. Do not marry Lord Drake just because he is a viscount and will someday be an earl. You need to search your heart, as Father says, and decide if this is what God wants for you."

"God does not have to live with Lord Drake, I do!"

"Exactly right," True said. "All the more reason to be careful. Be sure that marrying him is what will ensure both of you happiness, because Father says that an unhappy marriage is painful to God, but devastating to a man or woman."

Arabella slipped from the window seat and started toward the door, carrying her slippers. She turned back, though, and said, "I have to marry, True. Why should it not be someone rich and handsome and titled? Mother says money and social position are the only things that do not depart in a marriage." She shrugged, then turned and exited quietly.

After Arabella left, True sat staring at the pane of glass in front of her. Bella's voice had held a note of . . . of what? Resignation? Yes, she rather thought it was that. But how sad to go into a marriage resigned to your fate. And how sad for Lord

Drake if that was what his bride brought to him. He deserved so much more, as did Bella.

Finally, True slipped from the window seat and into her bed, to sleep at long last. And to dream— to dream of strong hands and golden eyes and a voice that melted her heart.

Five

The next day dawned bright, and with baskets of luncheon, wine and fruit packed by the cook, the four started out in an open carriage through the Hampshire countryside. Drake, on his best behavior, maintained a flow of conversation about his estate, the orchards, the home farm, the timber, all of which Arabella Swinley seemed to find fascinating. She questioned him at length, with a shrewdness and perspicacity that was just a little unnerving in its intensity.

Miss Becket, he noticed, more often had eyes for the countryside, noting a covey of partridges flying up out of a thicket and a rabbit along the roadside. She commented on the chalk grasslands and the copses of hazel, oak, beech and ash trees they passed. No natural feature escaped her notice. Conroy regaled them with humorous stories of London life, a couple of which involved Drake, and with such a way to pass the time, they were soon at Thorne House.

As the carriage traversed the rutted lane, wending its way up to the manor, True eagerly gazed upon it. She thought that she had never seen anything so lovely in all her life. Lea Park was majestic, but Thorne House, a smallish manor house of rose brick, Elizabethan in design, was pretty, and she exclaimed out loud in pleasure.

Her eager eyes noted the shabby gardens, neglected and yet with so much promise, full-blown roses nodding in the September sunshine under diamond-paned windows, and she longed for an afternoon just to explore all the treasures that were hidden by years of neglect. Finding an untamed garden like the ones lining Thorne House was like finding a gold chalice smudged with years of soot; nothing could obscure true beauty to the attentive eye. Her fingers itched to take some pruning shears and go to work. But it was not her place; that job would fall to lucky Arabella, likely.

"It is beautiful," she cried, as the carriage stopped at the front door. She looked up at the house and had the oddest sensation of coming home, though she had never been there before.

Conroy leaped from the open carriage and handed Arabella down, as she dutifully said, "It is very sweet. Sweetly pretty. But . . ." She did not finish, but her eyes were traveling over the ragged gardens and cracked walkways.

Drake clambered down, cursing the infirmity that made him lumber like an injured bear rather than spring athletically, as his friend was able. He helped True down, it being a long step for someone so small, and somehow it was her arm he took as they entered Thorne House. Conroy followed with Miss Swinley.

"It has been uninhabited for so long," Drake said, apologetically, glancing around at the clean but dingy hallway. The furnishings looked tired and dilapidated, he realized, now that he saw it with others along. "And there has only been a caretaker and his wife living here. Inevitably, they could not take care of everything, and I am afraid it will need some work to bring it up to living standards. I have just started to take an interest in it, but now that I have, work will be quicker."

But True would not let him deprecate the manor. "Sir, you have a jewel in the rough here. With just a little love, Thorne House will repay you many times over with her beauty and tranquillity."

He squeezed her arm to his side in silent thanks, and they strolled on, through the hall and into a reception room overlooked by a high gallery. Shields of ancient design and crossed swords decorated the reception room walls, and there was a fully functional knight's suit of armor, harkening back to the history of the family. He showed them his home, answering questions as to its age and history, relating humorous ghost stories, and guiding them all to the top parapet, where a long ago ancestress of his was said to have leaped to her death out of love for a young man she was forbidden to see.

He then spoke about how the family title, Earl of Leathorne, had come about during the War of the Roses, and was the result of the amalgam of the two families, Lea and Thorne, which explained the house names of the two estates. Somehow, though he had started with Miss Becket on his arm, it was Miss Swinley he ended up escorting. She seemed to enjoy the tour, and Miss Becket was amply entertained by Conroy.

They then retired to the breakfast room for an informal luncheon, and consumed the pigeon pie, cold meat, fruit and apple pie with good appetite. All except for Arabella Swinley, that is, who seemed to pick at her food delicately. Drake excused himself for a half hour to consult with Stanley, his carpenter, and the crew of men he had hired to finish the library, and then rejoined his guests in the dining room.

"Now, what shall we do for a couple of hours

before it is time to start back to Lea Park?" He glanced around, asking them all.

"I should like to see the grounds of the estate," Arabella said, taking the task of answering for everyone onto herself. She thrust her arm through Drake's. "Shall we start with a walk down to the river?"

It was generally agreed that this was a good idea, and so they walked.

True found herself on Lord Conroy's arm again. He was a pleasant gentleman, and asked her about her home and her family as they strolled down a grassy slope to a wide stream dotted by willows that hung over the water, shedding tiny yellow leaves when a breeze stirred their languid limbs. It was late September; summer was almost over, and all of nature was preparing for the winter ahead. Lord Drake and Arabella seemed to be having a lively conversation, True noted, her eyes straying to the handsome couple more than once.

They all gathered on the bank and watched some ducks paddling upstream, nibbling at the weeds that grew at the edge and then sailing on together in a V-shaped formation. "Like a small fleet of ships sailing to a naval engagement," Lord Conroy observed, with a whimsical turn to his character True had not suspected.

Arabella laughed. "Or troops marching up a hill," she said, gazing up at Lord Drake adoringly. "Look," she said, pointing, "that big one at the front is Major General Drake!"

True did not join in the laughter, though it was a mildly funny jest. It disturbed her that Arabella was playing off her tricks on Lord Drake, using her undeniable beauty and saucy wit to attract a man she did not even know yet. What if he fell in love with her and she decided they would not suit? She had done that before. Every time she had put an

effort forth to attract a man, he had tumbled head-
long in love, only to be rejected for some flaw she
had decided was unbearable. Lord Bancroft was
found to snort when he laughed. Sir Lawrence
Gordon, a distant cousin of Lord Byron, made the
mistake of admiring another lady's beauty in Arabella's hearing. True knew all of this from reading
between the lines of Arabella's occasional letters.

Perhaps this time was different, because both
Arabella and Lady Swinley had decided that Lord
Drake was the one, the matrimonial prize beyond
any she had ever sought. True hoped her cousin
was serious this time, because for some reason, she
could not bear the thought of Lord Drake being
hurt. And for Bella's own sake, for her future happiness, True hoped that if she did wed Lord Drake
it was out of love and respect, not for the conse-
quence of his position.

Conversation had turned to more serious matters
while she had stood gazing at the stream.

"I think you must be the bravest man in England," Arabella was saying with an artful tremble
in her voice. Her lower lip quivered and she
caught it in her white, even teeth.

Lord Drake looked uncomfortable and cast a
helpless glance at True.

"There were many brave men both in the ranks
of the officers and among the foot soldiers," True
said. She wondered how Arabella could have so
misjudged Lord Drake as to think flattery of that
sort would win him. She had only talked with him
a half hour or so, but already knew that sycophants
would not please him.

"That lot of filthy rabble? The foot soldiers
wouldn't have lasted two seconds without a better
class of men to lead them," Lord Conroy stated.

"I suppose that was true of many, but how long
do you think a bunch of effete officers with little

experience and often no brains would have lasted without the seasoning and maturity of their sergeants?" Drake retorted, his voice hard.

True had the feeling he spoke from experience.

After a moment of silence—surprised and offended silence on Conroy's part—Drake continued. "They took fellows who thought they could fight because they had gone a couple of rounds at Gentleman Jackson's, and tossed them into battle with no preparation, as *officers*, for God's sake, expected to lead men! Some died because of their own stupidity. I know, I saw it happen. It almost happened to me, but one of those 'filthy rabble,' a sergeant by the name of Jack Lawrence, saved my life; he took a bullet in the arm because I was too stupid to duck at the right moment. If he hadn't pushed me down I would be dead."

True longed to go to Lord Drake, to soothe the ache she saw writ on his gaunt face. Arabella had drawn back and released his arm at his harsh speech. Her voice was cool with reproach. "I do not think this is fit conversation for a lady's ears, sir!"

Drake grimaced. "My apologies, Miss Swinley. What a dolt I am, nattering about such subjects in your and Miss Becket's company."

"The truth is always a fit subject, and I do not think we 'ladies' need as much sheltering as men seem to think," True said.

"I must disagree," Lord Conroy said, his voice serious. "It is our duty as gentlemen to shelter ladies, to protect their fragility and delicacy."

He won a smile from Arabella for that pretty speech.

Drake nodded. "Well said, my friend. I apologize for my unseemly outburst." He bowed, first to True, and then to Bella.

Graciously offering him a smile of forgiveness,

Arabella said, "I, for one, would like to see more of this pretty estate. Shall we walk?"

Drake's face was drawn, and True had seen him surreptitiously rub his left leg, the one he favored. He had left his cane back at Lea Park, but his injury was clearly bothering him. As long as Arabella wanted to walk, though, he would likely appease her. How to tactfully deflect her intention?

"I think a walk is a capital idea," Conroy was saying. "There is a very pretty vista overlooking the home farm. It is just a ways up that hill past the orchard, if the ladies feel able?" He pointed up a long, gentle incline that ended in a high ridge, with a row of trees along the top.

True hesitated. "I do not know how it is, but I feel a little tired. I would prefer to sit on the bank and watch the ducks, if you do not mind?"

Brightening perceptibly, Drake said, "Why don't you and Miss Swinley take that walk, Conroy, and I will sit this one out with Miss Becket."

"I would be delighted, if Miss Swinley will agree?" He offered his arm to Arabella.

She cast an uncertain glance at Lord Drake, but then looked longingly at the hill Conroy had indicated. True saw her dilemma. She knew that she should stay and continue in her campaign to attach Lord Drake, but Arabella was a restless sort, and liked to keep busy. She would much rather be moving—doing something, anything!—than just sitting and watching ducks. Her true desire won out, and she took Lord Conroy's offered arm.

"We shall not be long," she said over her shoulder. The two moved off, with Lord Conroy giving an explanation of how he came to know Thorne House and its environs so well.

With a sigh of relief, Drake shed his jacket, laid it on the ground and sat down beside it. "Tell me truthfully, Miss Becket; are you really weary, or did you just notice that I am?" He indicated the jacket, and she sat down beside him.

True felt the color flood her face. Oh, for a constitution that did not so readily betray her! "I . . . could not help but notice you favoring your wounded limb. I did not think you would be doing it any good by climbing hills."

"And so, would you rather be climbing hills yourself? My pride will not be hurt if you go after Miss Swinley and Conroy and join them on their walk. It truly is a delightful vista from the top of the hill."

Considering her answer for a moment, True discovered that a part of her motive, aside from giving Lord Drake a chance to rest, was that she so much enjoyed his company, she coveted a little more of it for herself. Selfish, she scolded herself! No good could come of such thinking. Any partiality she felt for him was doomed to lead to disappointment, and she would not deliberately make herself unhappy.

"I can be happy walking or sitting. There is food for thought in a lovely landscape, it is true, but quiet contemplation leads to a deeper introspection, I think."

"So do you look for a lesson in all you do, or is your motive ever just pleasure?"

Often just pleasure she thought, glancing over at the man beside her, riveted by the sight of powerful arms clad only in linen shirtsleeves. The warmth of the late summer sun had brought color to his pallor, and his golden curls were sun-kissed and glowing. "I am sometimes as frivolous and giddy as any girl can ever be," she said, and smiled at him, feeling a deep contentment wash over her. A gentle breeze tickled her curls and brought the fragrance of the stream and the grass to her. A flock of swallows swooped low over the stream and shot up, as one, into the blue of the sky. "This very moment I think I am happier than ever I have been in my life." She glanced anxiously over at the viscount, hoping he did not think her speech too particular in meaning.

"I am glad to hear it," he said, smiling back at her. "Everyone, I think, should have moments of pure joy, untrammeled by any moral lesson or deep thought. It makes up for those moments of pure tragedy, when you think you will never be able to go on, never be able to survive another day of being a human in this tragic world."

"You speak from experience," she said gently.

Drake grimaced. There he was, getting caught up in the darkness again, and on such a day! The sun beamed down and the grassy bank was soft and luxurious under them, and he brought a gray cloud to hang over this beauty. "I should not have said that."

"Nonsense," she said. "Though I believe it does no good to wallow in grief, nor give in to tragedy, neither do I think it helps to stifle those emotions and pretend they do not exist. I think you have to truly feel them before you can move on."

Frowning, Drake said, "I hope you are right. I have been having trouble banishing my moments of darkness."

"You were injured at Waterloo. Is that . . . is that a time you cannot forget?"

Drake plucked a stem of grass and tossed it into the water. A curious duck swam over to see if it was food, then paddled away again. "One of the many. I . . . I still have nightmares of that day, and I cannot get beyond them. Amidst all the carnage, all the death and destruction of that day, one moment still haunts me. One of the men in my regiment was killed, in all the confusion, by . . . by a cannonball from our own cannon. I was only feet from him, and saw the ball take his head clean off his shoulders . . . blood everywhere . . ."

He heard the soft gasp from his companion.

Aghast, he looked over at Miss Becket. "My God, how could I speak of such things to you?" He took her hand and felt her fingers trembling. "I am so sorry! What a cad I am—"

"No, Lord Drake," she said, unsteadily, her voice quavering. She took a deep breath. "I would know the truth of war. Remember, you spoke of only ever telling the truth about it all. The reports in the paper were full of patriotic speechifying, but I always knew there was more to it all than that."

"You are a brave young lady," Drake said, releasing her hand. "No one else wants to know the truth, not even the men. I think what bothers me most about that moment was that I never told his family how he really died. They think it was the result of French fire, but it was our own forces that killed him. Should I have told them the truth? Do I not owe them that?"

"Would the truth, in this instance, help or hurt?"

"If I put myself in their place, the place of his mother and father, I think it would hurt to know that my son was killed by a mistake on our force's part. I would be angry. I did tell his captain what happened, and I reported it to the War Office, as soon as I was coherent enough to remember. I almost died myself that day, so it was not until I was back in England that I had a chance to report the occurrence."

"Then I think," True said, watching a bee collect pollen from a nodding daisy, "that you have your answer. With such chaos in battle, surely this happened more than once, and pretending it doesn't does not help anyone. But his family will only be hurt by that knowledge, and it would be unnecessary pain."

A modicum of peace at her intelligent and ready sympathy settled over Drake. He had not been able to decide what to do, and he had not found anyone who was willing to talk about that horrible day in any depth. Her advice was sound, and was what he had felt deep inside. But he did not want to shirk his duty in any way, no matter how unpleasant, and was afraid that his desire to let it be was a cowardly side of him wishing to avoid a painful task.

He leaned back on the sloped bank and felt the warm sun on his face as he closed his eyes, just for a moment's rest. He had not had more than three or four hours sleep the night before. The nightmare had come again, but luckily this time he awoke before he started screaming. He felt a light touch to his hair and his cheek. The breeze? Or was it fingers, gentle, soothing fingers healing his troubled thoughts with a soft touch. That was his last thought before drifting off into a dream of sailing downstream in a rowboat with Miss Truelove Becket.

Six

As Lord Drake drifted off to sleep, True daringly smoothed the golden curls from his face and watched as care and worry loosened their hold, and his gaunt face relaxed into the healing balm of sleep. For a sweet hour she listened to his calm breathing, while she gazed down on the stream and felt the peace of Thorne House seep into her. A light breeze sprang up, and the willow branches languidly danced and waved over the water while the ducks busily cruised up and down the waterway.

How serene it was! And how very beautiful, with old stands of woods in the misty distance, over a small stone bridge that crossed the stream. They were in a valley, and she could see, rising on the other side of the narrow brook, fields broken up by hedgerows and copses of scrubby brush. Her companion had told them at lunch that no one had lived here for many years, though the home farm was still in use and the orchards tended, but that he intended to make it his home now that he had resigned his commission.

She didn't think she had ever found a place she liked so well. She could imagine Lord Drake in some hazy future, striding about the place with a brace of children and dogs following him as he came down to the stream to fish for the silvery trout that flashed and sparkled in the depths. In her daydream Drake was healthy and happy, all the gloom of his present convalescence dissipated by years of blissful and tranquil enjoyment of his home.

Their acquaintance was brief, but she had come to believe that gloom was not his normal state of mind. He had been deeply affected by the war, as every thinking, feeling man must have been, but he would recover, given time, and his lucky wife, whomever she was, would reap the benefit of being wed to a courageous, good-tempered and deeply moral man. Perhaps it was too soon for her to judge him thusly, but there were some things one knew from the first moment of meeting someone.

All too soon Arabella's high, excited voice floated on the breeze as she and Conroy came back from an invigorating walk. Drake awakened, stretching and yawning widely, just as she and Lord Conroy approached.

It was time to leave. Before they did, though, Arabella insisted, with a saucy toss to her blond curls, that they have a proper tea first, so they went back up to the house, consumed the rest of the basket of delicacies, and then packed up to go. They were rather later getting on the road than Lord Drake had anticipated. Dark clouds on the horizon gave an ominous hint that the weather was going to turn some time in the evening hours, and they had best make haste if they were going to beat the rain.

But at least Lord Drake looked rested, True thought, gazing at him from her seat with her back to the horses. His eyes were the color of amber, clear and bright, and his conversation was as light and witty as even Arabella could wish.

Experiences were given, True reflected, as they trundled along the road back to Lea Park, to teach one about life. For instance, meeting Lord Drake had helped her understand what she had only guessed at before. To her, the men who fought and died, or lived after risking their lives, were heroes. She had read every newspaper article, every dispatch she could find in her little village. But meeting the major general had truly shown her what a price the survivors paid for living through a long and bitter war. Physical impairment was the least of Lord Drake's wounds, True thought. The worst ones went deep into his soul, and cut up the peace of every waking moment.

And Lord Drake had hinted that even sleep did not "knit up the ravell'd sleave of care." For him, there were only nightmares and dreadful battle-fields waiting—lurking—in his slumber. How long could he expect to fight *this* battle, the battle of his conscience? She would send up a prayer every night, when she lay herself down to her peaceful sleep, in the hope that God would grant him serenity. At least the hour's nap on the riverbank had been peaceful and seemed to have lessened his exhaustion.

The drive back was proving to be quieter than the ride out that morning. When they started, the clouds were confined to the horizon, but soon the sky darkened. Minutes later, the driver gave a shout of alarm. One of the horses shied, and there were a few moments of stark terror as it appeared certain that they would upset as they careened toward the steep embankment at the edge of the road, bouncing and jouncing along the rutted surface. Lord Conroy put his arm around True, who clutched at the edge of the open carriage, and she felt some comfort in the steadiness of that gentleman, as Lord Drake did the same for Arabella. The skillful driver brought the carriage to a halt and leaped down with an oath, racing to the horses.

"Are you ladies all right?" Drake asked, concern etched in the grooves on his forehead.

True nodded though her heart pounded errati-
cally, and Arabella gamely said, "I think we shall
do, presently." There was a sharp edge of fear in
her voice, but no one could ever have accused Arabella of being cowardly, no matter that she liked
to pretend to more delicate sensibilities in front of
the gentlemen. True was relieved that at that moment Bella had not chosen to follow her mother's
dictates and appear the fainthearted widgeon.

The viscount clambered down from the carriage
and limped up to where the driver was checking the
horses. "What is wrong, Burt? What happened?"

"Damned rabbit," True heard the man complain. "Ran right across our path, and Dancer
didna like it one bit; shied, she did, and now she's
turned up lame." The driver swore and spat.

"Language, Burt. There are ladies present."
Drake's admonishment was offered in an absent-
minded fashion as he thrust his hand through his
gold-streaked curls.

True sympathized with his difficulty. They were
still over fifteen miles from Lea Park, at least, and
the day was darkening alarmingly, with the first few
spits of rain leaving spots on the skirt of her dark-
blue muslin gown and a rumble of thunder in the
distance ominously foretelling the immediate future. Even if they could find another horse to carry
them onward it would take a while, and night and
bad weather could easily catch up with them on
the road.

He limped back to the carriage and with a worried frown, said, "I am afraid Dancer is unable to
do more than hobble along. Looking at the sky, it
appears that we are in for some rain at the very
least, and quite possibly a storm. Burt remembers
an inn not very far up the road, and I think our
best alternative is to put up for the night at the

inn and finish our little journey in the morning. What say the rest of you?"

True was not surprised at his solution and nodded, but Arabella frowned and said, "Surely we could get another horse at this inn and continue."

"We could get another horse, yes, but I am concerned about the weather." He indicated the sky. "It is already starting. Did you not hear that thunder? I would not have you ladies getting a drenching in this open carriage."

"Quite right, Drake, I concur. We would best be served by putting up for the night at this inn," Conroy said. "I am sure you will agree, Miss Swinley, that it is far better to be prudent. It would not do to risk a downpour and have you get a chill."

Put in that light, Arabella agreed. There would be no impropriety, she said, frostily, with True as her chaperon.

It was a short walk to the inn, and when they entered it was just starting to drizzle. Burt was to follow with the carriage and lame horse, and the groom was dispatched to Lea Park to take a message to the sure-to-be-anxious Ladies Swinley and Leathorne.

The innkeeper's wife, Mrs. Lincoln, a rotund but neatly garbed woman with a snowy mobcap over equally white curls, welcomed them eagerly. She remembered Lord Drake from some past stop there, and was clearly overjoyed that she was to have the "Quality" staying the night. She showed Arabella and True to a small, clean room and left them with a basin of steaming hot water and towels. Lord Drake, she said, had ordered dinner in a private dining room. It would be served within the hour.

"This is just too bad," Arabella said, swishing her hands around in the water. She peered at it. "It does not look very clean. And these towels! Not soft at all. I am sure there must be a better inn somewhere than this . . . this hole in the wall!" With a disparaging look on her face she glanced around at the tiny room that though neat, was not of first quality.

"I think we should count ourselves lucky to have made it here before the weather turned. Come on, let us clean up and go downstairs." True was in no mood for any of her cousin's nitpicking, since it could be laid at Bella's door that they were stuck here. She had only been hungry for tea before they left Thorne House because she had just picked at her luncheon. If they had not stopped to have tea, they would not have been so late on the road, and would not have been stopped by their little accident and therefore would not have to put up at this inn overnight. So her cousin had really better not complain!

Dinner was not French cuisine, as they had eaten the night before at Lea Park, but it was very good English country cooking. Rabbit pie, mutton, and a roasted capon, with a ragout of vegetables, followed by apple pie, was gratefully consumed by all but Arabella, who just picked at the capon and ate a piece of bread and butter before pushing her plate away.

"Is anything wrong with the food, miss?" the landlady said, with an alarmed glance at Arabella's still-full plate.

"I am quite sure it is very well in its way," Arabella said with a gentle smile, as she pushed it away. "But I have a very delicate palate. Mama says I have a true aristocrat's constitution."

The landlady looked offended, though she clearly did not understand what Arabella was talking about. True understood, and sighed with resignation. What it meant was that no matter how hungry she was, Arabella would not eat her fill in front of a potential suitor. She would pick and claim a birdlike appetite, because Lady Swinley had drilled it into her that true ladies were frail and never ate more than a few bites. Of course Lady Swinley herself was a robust trencherwoman, and she did not regulate Arabella's eating as long as there were no gentlemen present.

Conroy nodded his approval, but Drake looked puzzled. True thought that he had probably, in his career, not spent a lot of time among *tonnish* ladies, for he had bought his colors at a young age and spent much time on the Peninsula, or he would have known that most young ladies claimed a poor appetite, and then feasted in private. Arabella was no different, though when she forgot herself she ate as any normal person. Her mother's influence was spotty, at best. True hoped she would escape the woman's influence before it became complete and Arabella became an unbearable snob and wholly false creature, governed by society's expectations rather than her own good sense and strong nature.

"I cannot imagine why an aristocratic lady should have a poor appetite," Drake said, as the landlady, in hurt silence, directed one of her daughters as she cleared the table. "My mother eats quite well, and I have always thought she was very regal."

Arabella, caught in the awkward position of seeming to impugn her would-be suitor's mother, wisely remained silent. True bit her lip to keep from laughing out loud at the absurd mannerisms ladies were forced to assume by ridiculous social dictates. She was grateful that in her world a young lady was only expected to be neat, modest, and to refrain from "putting on airs," as the local ladies of her father's parish called it.

After dining, the foursome played cards for a while in front of the great stone fireplace. Rain pattered against the windows, and the blaze made for a cozy atmosphere. True was entertained yet again by the lengths to which a very sharp-witted

Arabella would go to appear suitably dim in front of Lord Drake. She was the picture of pretty confusion when, partnered with him, she "forgot" a trump card, or needed to have the rules explained one more time, ignoring the fact that Drake was trying very hard to restrain his growing irritation.

True, with no such need to appear the lackwit, triumphantly claimed a win at the end of the game, despite the distinctly inferior play of Lord Conroy, her partner.

"Very well, you two win. You had a sharp partner, Conroy," Drake said, with a nod to True as he threw down his cards in defeat. "I will be sure who *my* partner shall be next time!" He glanced over at Arabella after he said that, and by the look on his face True could tell he had just realized the insult that implied to his partner.

Arabella had felt it, too. Her eyes widened, and she pouted prettily. "That was not chivalrous, sir."

"I say, Drake, that was too bad of you," Conroy chimed in. He stood and bowed before Arabella. "Miss Swinley, *I* will be your partner next time we play at whist. If you like, I can give you lessons when we return to Lea Park."

True groaned inwardly; Conroy, teach *her* to play? Arabella was a very clever girl, and could likely best Conroy in any game he chose to play. Her "game" was much deeper, and it was yet to be seen whether or not she would win with the stratagem she had laid out for herself. True did not think Lord Drake was one to be impressed by frailty or stupidity. He valued honesty, too, above all else. What would happen if he did fall in love with Arabella, marry her, and then find the woman he had been courting was not the woman he wed?

"I thank you, my lord," Arabella said, prettily, to Conroy. "That was the speech of a true gentleman."

"My apologies, Miss Swinley," Drake said, his

cheeks a deep red. "I meant no slight to your ability, I . . ."

"It is time we went up, True," Arabella said, rising gracefully. "I am fatigued."

Willingly, True rose. They ascended to their room, where Arabella dropped her facade of elegant simpleton.

"What is wrong with that man?" she fumed, regarding herself in the faded mirror and toying with one long ringlet. Though she had not been able to change her gown for the evening, she still looked elegant in a green carriage dress that brought out the color of her eyes. "I have never had a gentleman sneer at my intelligence in such an ungallant manner!"

"He did not mean it, Bella," True said, holding up the two night rails Mrs. Lincoln, the landlady, had provided for them. She picked the shorter of the two, and laid out the longer one for her cousin. "He is a competitive gentleman, and he did not think before he spoke. He likes to win and expects anyone with whom he is partnered to make the same effort."

"But he is not supposed to like to win over being partnered with me! I didn't act like a simpering fool for nothing! He should have been charmed and felt protective toward me, as Lord Conroy did. *That* is how a true gentleman behaves." She turned from the mirror. "And I suppose I have to wear that fright of a night rail, that has been worn by who knows who? And we have to take care of ourselves?"

"Yes, we have to look after ourselves," True said, letting down her hair and shaking it back over her shoulders. "It won't hurt us, you know. I am quite used to it, not having a maid at home." She picked up the brush from the vanity table.

"That is *you*," Arabella returned scornfully. "A

real lady does not even brush her own hair!" She
swished her fingers around in the bowl of water
provided for their ablutions. "And this is not hot!
It has not been touched, I swan, since before we
went down to dine!"

True, as fond of her cousin as she was, gritted
her teeth as she brushed out her long, soft hair,
untangling with her fingers the knots created by
the day's breeziness and a long carriage ride. Bella
was at her worst when she was forced to put up
with less than ideal conditions. True knew what was
coming, and she also knew she was helpless to pre-
vent it, cursed by her own liking for harmony.
"Mrs. Lincoln only has one girl to take care of
guests, her married daughter, and she has gone
home to her family already."

Scandalized, Arabella said, "But I need hot
water, and someone to brush my hair, and who will
help me undress? And I am absolutely *famished*. I
was going to ring for a little tray of cakes to tide
me over until morning."

"If you had eaten your dinner you would not
now be hungry," True pointed out, reasonably. She
tossed the hairbrush on the vanity table. If there
was an edge to her voice, she hoped her cousin
would not hear it, but it made her angry that the
cousin she grew up with, the child who willingly
put up with the Spartan living conditions of the
vicarage—Spartan compared with Swinley Manor,
anyway—to be with her cousins, was now so
spoiled.

"But I wasn't hungry then; I am now," Arabella
fretted, crossly. She glanced sideways at her cousin
and her expression softened. "Will you go down
and get me something, True?"

Her tone had changed to wheedling, and True
knew she would end up doing it. She sighed. "Look,
I will go down and get a tray and bring a pitcher of

hot water, but you must brush your own hair and
don your own night rail. And no more complaints!''

"All right," Arabella said, satisfied. She began to
pull the pins out of her hair even as True headed
for the door. True smiled at the flashes of the
happy child she used to be, the child who had followed her cousin True like a shadow. If only Arabella would show that sunny side more often! But
it did not seem to injure her credit in London that
she was petulant and pouting at times. If all the
gentlemen were like Lord Conroy, it was not surprising that young ladies were indulged and
spoiled. That gentleman seemed to think a female
was a delicate flower, incapable of doing the slightest thing for herself. True shuddered. She did not
think she could stand to be treated that way, like
a Staffordshire shepherdess, likely to shatter at the
merest bump.

The halls were dark as True ventured down to
the kitchen, where Mrs. Lincoln bustled around in
a voluminous white apron, setting pans of bread
dough to proof by the fire while a scullery maid
scrubbed pots at the huge sink. The landlady
glanced up, and dropped a swift curtsy. "And what
service may I do for ya, miss?" she said.

"I dislike bothering you, Mrs. Lincoln, but if it
would not be too much trouble, may I get a pitcher
of hot water for our room?"

"Certainly, miss." She wrapped a towel around
the handle of a kettle hanging on a hook over the
fire and poured steaming water into an ewer.
"Woulda done this myself, if I had known you was
finished with the card-playing and were wishin' to
retire. Is there anything else?"

True flushed. How to say this? "I . . . I wonder if
we might, that is, if I could ask . . . could we trouble
you for a plate of biscuits, or bread and jam? We—
my cousin and I—are just the slightest bit—"

"Ah, lass, do not think to cozen me," the woman said, with a smirk. "That beanpole you say is your cousin is nigh unto famished, as she didna have the courtesy to eat what was set before her. And good sturdy food it were, too, naught wrong with it. Miss High-an'-Mighty stuck her nose in th' air, an' now her belly be growlin'."

True shrugged and nodded. She would neither conceal nor try to put a good face on Arabella's petulance.

"For you, I will do this, because you had the goodness to come down an' ask, prettylike, unlike Miss Nose-in-the-Air." She cut some slices of soft bread and slathered butter out of a crockery dish, then coated the pieces with apricot preserves. She cut the bread into triangles and arranged them on a plate. "And if the missy does not like our plain country fare, then she can expect no breakfast in the morn! You tell her that, lass! I'll send her off starvin' afore she says nay to my cookin' another time. I'll not give her another chance to slight me kitchen! Do you need a hand taking that up?"

"No, Mrs. Lincoln," True said, grinning. "I can manage." She tossed her hair back over her shoulder, thinking she should not have taken it down so soon, and then took the plate in one hand and the ewer of hot water in the other. "Shall I bring the dishes down after?"

"Nay! Set them outside th' door, lass, and Jane will take them in the morning."

True made her way up the hall from the kitchen, toward the stairs, thinking that Mrs. Lincoln and Arabella would have a rare battle of wills if they were forced to stay there another night. Still balancing the plate in one hand and carrying the jug in the other, she opened one door with her foot, and then found she had taken a wrong turn and was headed down the dim hallway toward what was presumably the taproom, from the sound of patrons talking loudly and the smell of pipe smoke.

She was just headed back the way she came when the door behind her opened, and someone came down the hall toward her. She bustled toward the stairs and made it to the first step, not willing to be accosted by a patron on his way to the "necessary" out in back.

"Ah, Miss Truelove Beckons!"

It was Lord Drake. True stopped and turned, smiling up at him. She was glad it was one of their party and not a stranger.

"What, hungry? Was dinner not enough? You shall be as plump as a pigeon if you take to late-night meals this way. Not that I object to a little plumpness in so *pretty* a pigeon."

His voice was rich and deep, and his tall, broad presence looming above her set True's heart to thumping. "I . . . we needed some hot water for our washing up, and the bread and jam—"

"Do not explain," Drake said, his voice just a little thick from a glass or two too much of ale. "I wonder if you are fetching and carrying for Miss Swinley. Are you really a companion then? Is that your secret? And is she using you as her handmaid?"

"I . . . well, we shall both make use of the water. . . . I must go up. . . ." True started up the stairs, but with surprising agility, Drake stepped up before her and barred her way.

"Now, you must know that the serving wenches at every inn must learn how to rebuff the attentions of their patrons who have had a little too much vino."

At first True did not think she had heard him correctly, but the next instant she felt his large hands spanning her waist and pulling her close to him. She could smell the ale on his breath and the tobacco smoke on his clothes, but before she had the time to gather her wandering wits, she felt his lips on her cheek.

Drake bussed her quickly and stepped back. She would slap him now, and rightly, too! No matter if she was acting as a serving wench, she was a lady down to her toes. But in the dim light offered by the candles in wall sconces, he could see her bright blue eyes opened wide in shock. The look in her eyes was not one of revulsion or alarm, but of question and sweet confusion.

Drawn by that innocent expression, entranced by the delicate softness of her skin and the tumbling dark waves of fine, silky hair, he pulled her back to him, resting her against his length and gazing down at her in the dim light of the stairwell. She clung to the ewer, and the plate of bread and jam threatened to slide from her grasp, but he didn't care. He was aware of her softly rounded breasts against his waistcoat, and the slim outline of her legs against his breeches. He raised one hand to caress the catkin velvet of her brown hair and he spanned the back of her head, holding it firm while he lowered his face toward hers. Her eyes fluttered closed, and when his lips touched hers and they parted beneath him, he felt a surge of dizzying desire he had not experienced in years.

It seemed an eternity, but he awoke to the feeling of her struggling in his arms, and he released her carefully, not wanting her to tumble down from the force.

"Miss Becket . . . Truelove, I am sorry, I forgot myself."

Face flaming, she turned from him and raced up the stairs, losing a jam-smeared triangle of bread in her haste.

Seven

"What took you so long?" Arabella snapped.

She was always like that when hungry, and True resisted the urge to snap back. Laying the plate of bread and butter on the vanity table, she crossed to the wash basin, dumped the cold water into a pail by the door and refilled the china bowl with steaming water from the ewer. It would do neither of them good to quarrel, and she wanted quiet and solitude to ponder what had just happened. It had been seven years since she had kissed a man, and God help her, but even Harry's kisses had never *ever* made her feel as though her body was aflame, or like her bones were turning to gruel.

Fussing with the hot water, and then washing her face, she kept her back to Bella, sure her cheeks must be bright scarlet. Her cousin was occasionally selfish and always self-involved, but she was also surprisingly shrewd about some things. True would not risk being questioned.

"I have brought bread and jam," she said, patting at her face with a cloth. "It was all Mrs. Lincoln had. I am tired. I . . . I will leave the candle for you." True undressed in the shadows, laid her clothing neatly over the chair by the bedside and slipped the night rail on over her shift, shivering a little in the damp chill of their room. She didn't really think she would sleep, but neither did she want to talk. "Good night, Bella." She slid under the covers and turned on one side, facing the wall.

Arabella stood staring at the dark hump in the bed that was her cousin. She bit her lip. Had she been peevish enough that she had offended True? Not possible! If there was one thing in her world that was a rock, one person whom she could trust, it was Truelove Becket. True was gentle, complaisant, sweet-tempered to a fault. Arabella tried not to take out her peevish humors on her cousin, but the trouble was, she knew True would forgive her after, and so she did not always guard her tongue as she ought. She considered apologizing, but it looked as if True was asleep already, and she supposed she shouldn't disturb her.

Perhaps she wasn't feeling well.

Sitting at the vanity table, Arabella picked up one of the slices of bread and jam and bit into it. Instantly, the homey taste brought back vivid memories of childhood stays at the vicarage, and of True smuggling from the kitchen late night feasts of bread and jam as they giggled and gossiped with Faithful, True's younger sister. Tears started in her eyes.

It was strange that even though she had spent three glittering seasons enjoying London, the memories of the vicarage were still sharp and clear, and could still raise a lump in her throat. For all those years she had never thought that her mother really loved her; she *could* not and abandon her daughter at the vicarage for every school holiday with excuses of travel and commitments. And, yet, with True and Faithful as her friends, and the gentle vicar as a substitute father, she was not the lonely little girl who had first arrived there at eight years of age.

She would never stop loving her cousin for that,

even though now her mother seemed to value Arabella as she should. True had made the vicarage what she would always think of as her childhood home. Arabella glanced over at the bed, took a deep breath and whispered, "I'm sorry, True, for . . . for being snappish. Good night."

She really would have to learn to curb her tongue. Sometimes she longed for the old days, the simpler days, when she lived at the vicarage between school terms with her cousins, romping in the country meadows and exploring winding lanes. But that part of her life was over. Now she was engaged in the serious business of finding a husband, a wealthy, titled, and hopefully attractive husband, and it must absorb all of her concentration. Her mother had been unusually insistent about the necessity of attracting Lord Drake and getting a proposal out of him. She would have to watch the man, and decide how best to flatter and tease him into love.

Meal done, she blew out the candle and crept into bed beside her cousin. Within minutes she was deeply asleep.

Drake, recovered fully from the slight tipsiness he had experienced, was in a mood for solitude, and so he strolled the stableyard "blowing a cloud" as his fellow officers called smoking a cigar. He had become addicted to the weed in Spain, where small, dark, slender cigars were plentiful. Smoking calmed his frayed nerves and gave him something to do, he supposed.

Truelove Becket. What on earth had possessed him to grab her in the stairway and kiss her as if she were a serving wench? Drunkenness was not an adequate excuse, though some men chose to employ it. It was usually what men in his regiment used as an explanation if they were caught being unchivalrous to the local ladies in Spain or Portugal or Belgium. It did not matter to him if they were drunk or stone-cold sober, he told them. He expected them to treat the local ladies as they would English ladies, with chivalry and good manners.

So he would not use his drinking to explain that lapse from propriety. The first kiss had been meant to tease her, as a jest. He had fully expected a slap across the face for his efforts. Of course her hands were occupied. . . .

But then, that bewildered expression of—of what? What had that look meant? Her blue eyes had widened and she had gazed up at him, her plump lips parted, and he, urged on by insidious desire, had taken that berry-sweet mouth with a ravenous kiss, feeling even as he did it that he was very much in the wrong to take advantage of her surprise in such a caddish manner.

That second kiss . . . if he was very lucky he would dream of it, feel again her soft mouth under his, the pounding of his blood through his veins, the powerful surge of desire. And he would experience the delicious sensation of his fingers sliding through fine hair as soft as a cloud. He did not think he would be so lucky. He had dreamt of nothing but battlefields since "That Day," as Waterloo had become in his memory. He turned to pace the length of the stable yard again.

Arabella was snoring softly. It had taken her only minutes to fall into her usual deep sleep, but True had not even been able to close her eyes. She had heard her cousin's whispered apology and soft good night but had not replied, fearing Arabella would want to talk if she knew True was awake.

She slipped from the bed they shared and crept around it to the window, curling up in the narrow window seat and tucking her bare toes under the hem of her borrowed nightrail. Their room looked down into the stableyard—Arabella had complained, but it was all that was to be had—and even at this late hour someone was awake and strolling the yard.

Lanterns mounted on the archways that led into the yard lit the area with an eerie yellow glow, and the lone occupant was wreathed in a cloud of smoke. True watched with interest as he emerged from the cloud like a phantom. It was Lord Drake! As recent as their acquaintance was, she could still tell him by the set of his shoulders, his halting gait, and the aureole of tawny hair that glowed golden in the light.

True touched the window, wishing against all sense, all propriety, that he was close enough that she could touch those tawny curls, run her fingers through them, feel him close again, his breath against her ear, or his lips touching hers. Reprehensible desires! She was in Hampshire to consider an honorable offer of marriage from a man of God, a good and pure man who had chosen her from all the ladies of his acquaintance as his helpmeet, his completing half, his wife.

But Mr. Bottleby had never set her afire with the merest touch of his fingers, nor had he ever let his lips do more than brush her fingertips. Cursed desires of the flesh! Surely it was not suitable for a woman almost betrothed to a vicar to be having these feelings, these wanton thoughts?

Just at that moment, as though he felt the touch of her gaze, Lord Drake looked up and smiled to see her tucked up in the window seat like a naughty child, or so True felt. He bowed, gesturing as though he were swishing a cockaded hat in an elegant motion.

She stifled a giggle.

His smile died, and he gestured for her to come down and join him in his restless perambulation.

No. She could not do that. She was far too fond of him already, in just one day, considering that she had an offer of marriage to think about and decide upon. No good could come of further intimacy between them, no matter how sweet the moments when they had touched had been. Until she knew her own heart and had made up her mind, she must avoid him.

She shook her head and turned away from the window, slipping from the window seat, tiptoeing around the bed and sliding under the covers beside her slumbering cousin.

The ride back to Lea Park the next day was silent and uneventful. Arabella complained fretfully that she did not sleep a single second, and that her bed was musty and lumpy. True did not contradict her, though she was in a position to know from her own sleeplessness that her cousin had slept the entire night, and very deeply if the slight snuffling sound of a ladylike snore was any indication.

Drake, haggard from another restless night, glanced over at Arabella and said, "Perhaps if you ate your dinner and did not gorge on bread and jam late at night, you would have slept better."

Arabella stiffened and shot True an annoyed look. True just shrugged, not sure if she should say that she did *not* tell his lordship who the bread and jam was for, and that she had met him in the hall by accident; no, better to keep that part to herself. It was difficult enough to forget the intimacy of her last encounter with Lord Drake without having to explain it to Arabella.

"I say, Drake, another unchivalrous comment. If

you ever had a way with ladies you have lost it."
Conroy shot him a reproving glance.

His friend was right yet again, Drake thought. It
was unpardonable to take out his peevishness on
Miss Swinley, and so he apologized handsomely for
his ill-tempered remark and the foursome fell silent.

The slight drizzle of the night before was followed by a day of dark clouds and an enervating
humidity that made the air feel charged with elec-
tricity. Drake felt the weather in his aching leg,
which made him even more gloomy. It was not
Miss Swinley that he was angry with, but himself,
he realized. Even though he had puzzled out the
plate of bread and jam Miss Becket had been carrying as Miss Swinley's replacement for the meal
she did not eat, and he did find it annoying that
she should send her sweet cousin to fetch and
carry for her, it was still himself and his own treatment of Miss Becket—Truelove—that was preying
on his mind.

He had taken liberties, and that was likely why
she had not come down to walk with him the night
before, though she was evidently as sleepless as he.
Or it could have simply been that she had no desire to be near him. Why should she? He would
not delude himself that the kiss they had shared
had meant anything more to her than a puzzling
departure from courtesy by a gentleman she barely
knew. He had never treated any lady of his acquaintance in that manner, though while in uniform he had had his share of relationships with
women of easy virtue that included the more physical aspects of male-female interaction, the giving
and taking of passion hopefully enjoyed by both
parties. But a *lady* deserved his restraint.

He did not understand himself anymore. While
still in uniform, he had seemed protected from

moodiness by the exigency of his position. He had
worked hard, slept soundly, and approached every
fresh battle as a situation that required his full attention. Now with the war over, his commission resigned, he had become as sour as an unripe apple.

He was never so grateful as when the river and
the long lane up to Lea Park came into view. He
needed time to think, and he could not do that
in company.

The next week passed uneventfully, though True
found her resolution to stay away from Lord Drake
impossible to keep. Arabella was restless often, and
Lord Conroy was best able to walk with her and
show her the points of interest around Lea Park,
which he was familiar with, having been a school-
mate of Drake's and spending a good portion of
his school holidays there.

This day found them determined to explore the
home woods, which Conroy declared had the best
hickory nuts to offer. Arabella, in a pair of stout
jean half-boots and with a woven basket in her
hand, took his arm and they strolled off. They
made a handsome pair, well-matched in size, and
with his dark head bent to her golden one as he
listened to her prattle with mannerly indulgence.

Mid September was a lovely time in Hampshire,
True found, as she strolled in the opposite direction from her cousin, down a gentle decline into
a grassy meadow with Lord Drake. Her companion
was silent as he often was, though his eyes became
a glowing golden as he picked a delicate pink wild-
flower and presented it to her with a flourish.

"Thank you, sir," she said, with a formal curtsy.
"It has been a long time since a gentleman gave
me a flower."

"Since your gallant seaman fiancé was lost?" he

asked, taking her arm and gazing down at her as
they walked on.

Matching her gait to his, she said, "Yes. He was
the last." She held the dainty pink flower up to
her nose. "My . . . current suitor is not much for
flowers." A shudder passed through him and she
glanced up at him, alarmed.

"Your current suitor?"

His voice was slightly wheezing, and True wondered if they were going too fast for his injury. She
stopped and broke away from him. Why had she
never mentioned Mr. Bottleby before this? Was it
because the subject was private and personal, or was
it more because she did not want to waste her time
in Lord Drake's company speaking of real life? It
was lovely to walk with him through enchanting val-
leys, down wooded lanes and along verdant river-
banks, pretending that life was different, that the
world was different. She could make believe that an
impoverished vicar's daughter and a future earl
could meet on equal ground, and maybe even fall
in love among the wildflowers. It was a fairy-tale, but
then she had always loved fairy-tales, particularly the
one of the cinder girl and her prince.

"Mr. Bottleby," she said, determined to "put
away childish things," as admonished in Corin-
thians, "is, or was, my father's curate. He has ob-
tained a living in the north, and has . . . has asked
me to go with him, as his wife." She could not
look into his eyes, and instead spread one hand
out flat, running it over the tops of the long weeds
around them. She watched them sway and tangle
under her hand and felt the tickling sensation on
her bare palm. In the last week she had come to
feel much more at home, even amidst such luxury,
and had taken to leaving her gloves behind when
walking. Nature could not be experienced with the
artificial barrier of cloth.

"And you are considering it," Drake said, in a voice curiously devoid of inflection.

"I am considering it."

Drake picked up a stick and swished it through the long grass, decapitating some of the feathery daisies that grew wild. "I wish you happy, then. You will make an eminently *suitable* vicar's wife."

The way he said it made it sound like an insult, and True gazed at him in puzzlement. She did not wish to quarrel, especially when she did not know what he was angry about. "That is just what Mr. Bottleby said when he proposed marriage. He goes as vicar to a poor parish, one that needs an energetic and good man, which is what Mr. Bottleby is. He genuinely cares about the less fortunate, and I honor him for it." *Honor him, but cannot love him,* she added to herself. Why could she not love so good a man?

Drake stabbed his stick into the ground and kicked at it. As usual he was carelessly dressed, and his boots were already badly scuffed, so a few more scratches would not even be noticed. "Sounds like your perfect match, Miss Becket. What are you hesitating for?"

True could not answer, taken aback by the dryness of his tone and the violence of his jerky actions. They had become used to talking with a degree of comfort and amity, but at that moment she felt separated from him, in feeling as well as in actuality.

"All I have ever done with the less fortunate is kill them in battle," he said, morosely, the dark mood that was never far away descending upon him.

Ah, now *this* she understood. She moved back to his side and took his arm. "My lord—"

"Can you not call me something other than 'my lord'?" he said. His eyes were dark and his expression moody. "Call me Drake, or even better, call me by my name."

"Which is?"

"Wycliffe. My mother was used to call me 'Wy' when I was a boy. She said it was an appropriate name for a child who was always asking 'why.' "

She was grateful to hear him under control of his voice again. The wry tone had returned. "We are both blessed with unusual names," True said. "Wy and True. I . . . I shall call you Wy, but only when we are in private like this. It would not be seemly in public. Will you call me True, in private?"

"I will. Though I have come to think of you as Truelove, in my mind, you know. Such a perfect name for you, I thought, the minute I met you."

Drake covered her hand, which rested on his arm, with his other hand, and she felt the warmth of him flood her as his broad hand engulfed her small one. He gazed down at her, his eyes fixed on her lips, and for one dizzying moment she felt that he meant to kiss her again, but he did not. She should have been grateful for his restraint. He guided her to a large tree, stripped off his jacket and laid it on the ground for her to sit on.

"We ought to find the others," True said, hesitating. "They may come back from their walk at any time."

"We shall. Soon."

They sat down. The grasses and wildflowers around them were tall, and it felt like they were sheltered from the world.

"Do you really see yourself that way, Wy? As a killer, and nothing more?" True shed her bonnet and drew her knees up, putting her arms around them.

Wy reclined under the tree and gazed up into the green leafy boughs, his curls tangling with the weeds around his head. "I was in the army for fourteen years. Do you know how many battles I have been in, and how many men I have killed?" A lark fluted a trilling song somewhere nearby. Stretching his full, long length out, he cupped his hands and put them behind his head. "How far away it all seems now, but it was only months ago that I was butchering men—men who had done nothing but take a side opposite my own. I dream about them, you know, all the dead soldiers. They howl, in my nightmares, for my blood. And then I awaken, screaming, sure that I am once more on the battlefield at Mont St. Jean, and I am dying."

The dark subject matter was ill-suited for such a brilliant day, but True did not notice. Heartsick, she gazed down at the handsome man reclined so close to her. This explained some of the strange noises she had heard during the night on a couple of occasions in the last week, the wild keening. How she longed to gather him to her and soothe the anxious lines from his gaunt, noble face. "And so you do not sleep."

"No. I do not sleep. Or at least I do, but only for a time. That is why I was pacing the stable yard that night at the inn. I knew I would not sleep."

"And you dream of dying?"

He nodded. "I . . . dream I am back there, where I almost did die. I fell, you see, wounded by a saber cut to the thigh, given me by a gallant Frenchman whom I then slaughtered. Andromeda, my horse, was blasted by artillery fire just then and fell on top of me as I went down, and then Captain Lewis, one of my men, *also* fell on me, dead before he hit the ground, poor lad. The field was muddy. It had rained all night the night before, and the battlefield had been cut up by horses' hooves. Andromeda's weight was squeezing the life out of me, and the mud . . ."

He rolled onto his side and covered his eyes with one hand, but continued talking. "I knew I would die. I lost consciousness a couple of times. You cannot imagine the noise, the sound of thousands dying, horses groaning, cannonade, artillery fire, and everywhere the black pall of gunpowder burning, stinging the eyes. I don't know how long it was that I lay there, but the fighting was over and it was beginning to get dark when I heard Horace, my batman, the most stubborn man alive; he was calling my name. I managed to cry out, and he found me.

"It is a miracle that he heard and recognized my voice, because around me hundreds were crying out for water, and moaning, and . . . I hear it still, in my sleep. I don't remember the rest, because I blacked out again, but he pulled me out and carried me—you must see Horace to understand the ludicrous picture we must have made, for I am six foot and fourteen stone, or at least I *was* fourteen stone, while he is barely five foot five—he managed to pull me out from under my mare and carried me to safety! I still do not know how he did it, but I will forever be grateful. I had been taken for dead, and would have been, if not for him."

True swallowed back tears. He did not need her becoming a waterpot. "And you dream you are back there, and dying?"

He moved restlessly onto his back again. "That is the usual dream. It starts with faces, the faces of the dead. Those I have killed, and those who were my responsibility and died under my command. Hundreds of faces. *Thousands* of faces."

It was too much for any man, and even more so for a sensitive man as Wy evidently was, True thought. He was caught reliving the past nightly, and if it did not stop it would break him, drive him mad from lack of sleep and anguish. Amazing that it had not already. He was punishing himself, she thought, punishing himself for surviving what had killed so many.

"I do not understand why I lived," he said, his eyes closed and his face twisted in a frown, "while so many better men, men with wives, children, died. Why did I live?"

"Perhaps that is what your dream is about; it is your way of sentencing yourself to death on the battlefield, where you think you should have died. But every man has a destiny, you know; yours was to live. You must not regret that."

"I don't regret it. I just don't know how to live now, how to go on." He opened his eyes and gazed up at her, then reached up and cradled her cheek in his warm palm. He sighed deeply. "The vicar is a very lucky man," he said, then swung himself to his feet and limped off toward Lea Park. "Come along, Miss Becket. The others will wonder what has become of us."

They strolled back arm in arm, with golden sun beating down on their heads. True looped her bonnet over her free arm, too entranced with the feel of sunlight on her hair to worry about her complexion becoming brown. Likewise, Wy carried his jacket. They didn't speak, each lost in their own thoughts and completely comfortable together even in silence.

If only, True thought; if only Wy thought he was spared for something, or found something worthwhile to do with his time, he might forget the nightmares. The day they visited his estate she had met Stanley, the soldier/carpenter/amputee Wy had hired to work on Thorne House. The man was openly grateful for the work, and the chance to provide for his family. He was happy, it seemed, perhaps because he was busy and fulfilled, and had no time to brood on the war. Sometimes work healed in a way no amount of contemplation could.

Was that the answer to Wy's pain, simple busyness, a full life? Would marriage and children heal him? Perhaps, then, marriage to Arabella would be the best thing for him. True tried to picture Bella soothing Wy's nightmares, working at his side to refurbish Thorne House, giving him children, laughing with him, loving him. Somehow it was a picture that just would not form, but was that because it was unrealistic, or just because True did not want to believe it could work?

Eight

This matchmaking effort was not at all going as planned, Lady Leathorne thought as she politely kept her eyes trained on Arabella, who was executing a rather difficult piece on the piano. The girl was skillful and graceful, everything a future viscountess—and later, countess—should be. So why did Drake not see it? Why was he not pursuing her as he had the year before?

When the young people had come back from a walk that afternoon, she had been overjoyed to see a modicum of peace on Drake's face, his brow smoother than it had been of late. It pleased her that walking with Arabella should have that effect on her son, for she believed that marriage and family were what he needed to help him recover from the horrors he had witnessed, horrors she could only guess at, as Drake never spoke of them. If Arabella could help him find his way back to himself, to the man he used to be, they could have a good life together; Lady Leathorne was convinced of it.

But then she found that she had been mistaken. Arabella Swinley had spent the afternoon walking with Conroy, while Drake strolled in another direction with Miss Becket. And so if anyone was to be congratulated on her son's more peaceful countenance, it was the vicar's daughter. It was not that she did not want him happier, but she wanted him happier for the right reasons.

With a mother's shrewd gaze she examined Miss Becket, who sat serenely doing some needlework by the light of a lamp. Was the girl a fortune hunter? Long in the tooth, at least twenty-five or so years of age, she would hazard a guess, and poor as a church mouse, judging from her tidy but out-of-fashion dresses. Lady Leathorne could see many neat darns along the cuff and collar of her gown, where worn spots had been turned under and mended. She was not a *real* companion; she did not take payment for accompanying the Swinleys, Isabella had explained, or for occasionally visiting them at Swinley Manor. She was not so poor, apparently, that she needed to find work. But for some unfathomable—to Lady Swinley, anyway—reason, Arabella enjoyed Miss Becket's company, and so the widow had given in this time when her daughter had asked if her cousin could join them.

Lady Leathorne examined Miss Becket closely. She thought she could understand why the restless and active Arabella enjoyed the young woman's company. She exuded peace and tranquillity, as though she was completely happy within herself, and those around her absorbed some of that serenity. Perhaps that was why Drake looked calmer, almost rested, after spending the afternoon with her.

But it just would not do! Miss Becket was all very well, and likely a nice enough young lady, but she was just not a suitable match for Drake, and so it was not good for him to spend so much time in her company, rather than with Arabella. Propinquity could lead to Drake thinking he was in love, or something equally ridiculous, especially in his weakened mental and physical state.

No, the Honorable Miss Arabella Swinley was the

perfect match for him. Certainly a baron's daughter was not as high as he could go; with his lineage and his looks, an unencumbered estate of his own and the earldom in his future, he could likely have looked even to a duke's daughter. But the Swinley barony was very old, older than the Leathorne name, even, existing back in the mythic past from the time just after the Norman Conquest, in the eleventh century. And it would unite the families of two old friends. She and Isabella had planned this match from the moment Arabella squawked her first cry. Well, perhaps "planned" was too strong a word. They had hoped for it, wished for it, talked of it.

Perhaps they should have put the two together more as young people, but Drake bought his colors at such a young age that Arabella was still a little child. One did not announce to a headstrong lad of eighteen that he is to marry a little girl who is just learning her ABC's. If he had in the meantime chosen another young lady of equal birth and fortune, Lady Leathorne would not have objected. After all, Arabella had spent a few seasons in London, to see if *she* found someone more to her taste. Nobody knew, then, how long the war would last, or when Drake would come home, and so both mothers had agreed it was hardly fair to tie Arabella to a man she had met only once.

But neither had wed, and so they would make a match of it, if the mothers had anything to say in the matter. He would *not* wed a nobody. He was a powerful young man, and he needed a girl of equal strength. He and Arabella would make magnificent children together.

In Lady Leathorne's imagination, a hazy, golden future opened up of tawny-haired Apollos and Athenas, the flower of English youth, her grandchildren. She had waited so long, and she was not getting any younger. She wanted time to enjoy those grandchildren, hold them on her knee, spoil them with sweets, coddle them. But if Drake was not pushed a little he might never make the move that would ensure the Leathorne legacy. Miss Arabella Swinley, young, beautiful, well-born, was his perfect match in every way. Miss Becket was all very well, and a pretty girl, but no more than a dab-chick compared to the brilliant Miss Swinley.

She glanced over at her son to see if he was taking proper note of Arabella's superior performance. He certainly was looking her way, but she knew her boy too well. He was thinking of something—or someone—else. Even as she watched, he glanced over at Miss Becket, and his golden eyes held a soft look, an expression of . . . was it yearning? Not good. Not good at *all.* When she and Lady Swinley had planned this visit, it had been understood between them that Drake and Arabella would likely be betrothed before two weeks were up, judging from the flirtation they had enjoyed when last they met in the spring of '14. It was over a week already, and though polite to each other, there were no intimate little glances, no rush to be together, no stealing away to be private.

Arabella appeared to be doing her best. When with him she played the coquette, and found little ways to touch him, or get close to him; Lady Leathorne had seen and approved of her campaign. She was using every trick she had learned through three London seasons littered with men prostrate at her feet. Drake should be head over ears by now; Lord Conroy certainly appeared be a fair way in love with her, and she wasn't even trying with him! And, yet, Drake remained unmoved.

Well, it looked like she and Isabella would have to put their heads together and come up with something. They must be doing something wrong,

or maybe it was just that they were letting the
young people alone too much. Maybe they should
take a firmer hand on the reins and steer a course
to matrimony for Drake and Miss Swinley. She
wanted what was best for her son, and marriage
and family were what was right and proper at this
point of his life.

His life!

Once more, she sent up a prayer of thanks that
his life had been spared, because if Drake had died,
she would have, too. Her body might have lived on
for years, but her soul would have been buried on
that awful battlefield alongside her beloved son.

He was alive, and he would have the life he deserved, and the *wife* he deserved! She motioned to
her bosom bow, Isabella Swinley, or Isabella Trent
as she had been before marrying the baron, and the
two women slipped out of the room for a council
of war.

September melted away, an unusual string of hot,
sunny days and warm evenings filled with visiting,
picnics, a *fête champêtre* dinner for the neighbors on
the lawn, games of battledore and shuttlecock, im-
promptu dances for the young people of the neighboring town—all manner of social activities. It did
not seem to Drake that he had a single moment
to himself. Wherever he went, Arabella Swinley was
there, his partner in whist, on his arm as they
walked, alone with him in the garden . . . everywhere. He saw his mother's controlling hand in it,
but was helpless in the face of her and Lady Swinley's clever maneuvering. And really, was it so bad,
he wondered? He had gotten over his initial distaste for Miss Swinley's company and conversation,
and found that, all things considered, she was an
entertaining companion for an afternoon.

She might be a little spoiled, she might be high-handed and demanding, but she was more clever than she let on, and her conversation, when she forgot to be coquettish, was intelligent. She played games with vigor and good-sportsmanship and was a spirited competitor when her mother was not there to dampen her vivacity. Lady Swinley appeared to have the idea that gentlemen preferred a spiritless widgeon to an intelligent woman, and perhaps that was true of many. Conroy, for example, looked rather put out when Miss Swinley bested him in battledore and shuttlecock, despite the impediment of her long skirts.

Miss Swinley, in other words, had every potential for a charming wife for some lucky gentleman; if his mother had her way, it would be him. But was he the gentleman who would say his vows with Miss Swinley and mean them? He did not love Arabella Swinley, but she seemed good-natured—when she got her own way—and intelligent, when she allowed herself to be. He could do worse. It was not as if he really thought he could "wait for love," as Truelove put it.

Truelove. Though they had spent little time together that week, he had been aware of her always, strolling with Conroy, or talking with the ladies. Sometimes there was a pensive look on her pretty face, an abstracted air of indecision about her. He was not usually good at reading people's expressions, especially ladies, but he rather thought she was thinking about her offer of marriage. Had she made up her mind? Would she marry her earnest, good vicar and move away to the north? It would be a life of toil, but he could see that she would not mind that. Did she perhaps love her Mr. Bottleby just a little? He didn't know, and he shouldn't care. But he did.

The days wore on, the heat and humidity in their

valley building. The relentless activity his mother enforced among the company was meant to keep his mind off his troubles, no doubt, but it was wearing him down, with no sleep at night to give him back his strength. How could he sleep when he was straining every nerve and sinew in the attempt to awaken himself before he entered the hideous dreams? It was too humiliating to think that everyone in the household might know about his affliction. Most nights he was successful and snatched a couple of hours sleep before waking up, but there had been once or twice when Horace had had to awaken him in the throes of his agony.

And he was longing for some solitude. Doing the pretty to the ladies had never been his strongest suit—even when they had been stationed in England and there were balls and parties and dinners held for the officers every night, or so it seemed, in the town nearest their encampment. Someone such as Conroy would have been in his element, but Drake was a sore disappointment even to Wellington. The duke himself was a gracious and gallant guest at balls and dinners, and Drake had tried to emulate the great man, even altering his habitual relaxed manner of dress to conform with the expectations that every officer would be perfectly attired. When he had come back to stay at Lea Park during Napoleon's incarceration on Elba, he had tried his best with his mother's guests, Lady Swinley and her daughter. Apparently he had been more successful than he had given himself credit for, as was evidenced by his mother's persuasion that he and Miss Swinley would suit as marriage partners.

The constant pressure to be charming was becoming more and more difficult, though, in his present state of mind. He needed to escape, at least for a few hours. The sultry weather had reached a peak, finally, ending with a day that was so stultifying that most of the company were spending the day napping or reading in their own rooms.

Drake took advantage of the quiet house and crept out alone to a shed off the stables, retrieving a beat-up hat and canvas bag. He was going to go fishing, and he was going *alone*.

True was glad Lady Leathorne had declared a day of inactivity. It was hot and humid, and she did not want to spend the day in enforced games or sports. The sky was lowering and dark after luncheon; Arabella had gone back upstairs to lay down—humidity always gave her a headache—but True needed to get out of the house, needed to be alone for once. She was aware that she still had come to no decision regarding Mr. Bottleby's proposal, and she must decide soon. He was leaving for the north in a little over a month and a half, and he wanted to marry before that. They would need three Sundays for the banns to be read, but other than that she did not anticipate much in the way of a wedding celebration.

Marriage! True slipped from the house with her oldest bonnet—or at least the oldest one she had brought with her—on her head and a basket on her bare arm. She had come to know Lea Park, and took a shortcut toward the river where she had promised to gather some cress for the cook. Would she really marry after all these years?

Mr. Bottleby—Arthur she would have to call him if she accepted his proposal—was a good man. He genuinely felt the call of the church. Her father had been impressed, in the time the young man had been his curate, by his fervor and true devotion to the downtrodden. His methodistical leanings had disturbed Mr. Becket, but still, both father and daughter had agreed that Mr. Bottleby was the best kind of man of God, one who really believed in Him and wanted to do His work.

And did his proposal mean that she was chosen by God, as he was, to do His work? She didn't know. She enjoyed helping the people of her village, doctoring the sick when they couldn't afford medicine, teaching the children when the teacher of the village charity school was sick, visiting the elderly. As her mother had died when True was just twelve, she had taken the duties of the vicar's wife upon herself, and now it felt like second nature to her. Marrying Mr. Bottleby and going north would mean new challenges, new people to care for, by the side of a man she truly respected, but it was a familiar role, one she knew herself to be capable of and trained for. But in thinking of marriage to Mr. Bottleby she found herself focusing almost entirely on the challenges of the job ahead and ignoring what marriage to the man would mean. She liked him. She esteemed him. She *respected* him.

Was it wrong to want love and . . . and passion, too?

Inevitably, thoughts of passion led her back to Lord Drake. He was everything Mr. Bottleby was not; gallant, handsome, a soldier who had proven his courage on the battlefield. His kiss had left her feeling weak in the knees. She was drawn to him, and wanted so very badly to soothe his troubled brow.

But it was not her place. Even if, by some miracle, he fell in love with her, they were socially so far apart as to be on opposite sides of a stone wall. Well, perhaps not *opposite* sides. Her father was a gentleman, an Oxford man, and though not rich, was a member of the landed gentry, and her mother had been related to a baron and a marquess. So she was not completely removed from his social sphere, though she was certainly his inferior in standing.

It did not change her upbringing, though. Wycliffe Prescott, Viscount Drake, needed a wife of breeding, a woman who had been raised to grace the position of countess after Lady Leathorne was gone. He did not need a vicar's daughter who knew about making preserves, haggling with the butcher, and doctoring villagers with her own herbal remedies. True knew how to run a household—a very small household—but she would be lost if she had to plan a party for two hundred!

She had been wandering through the meadow on a meandering route toward the river. Her destination was in sight, and she headed down the sloping bank toward the sluggish, winding waterway. From a previous walk she knew there was an old oak tree that overhung the bank, and on the other side of that a narrow rushing stream was where the best cress, tender, green and fresh, could be found.

But who was that reclined on the bank under the oak? If it was some local gentleman, a stranger, she did not want to disturb him. And yet, this was Lea Park land. It would not be a stranger unless he was trespassing.

She swished through the weedy grass, quietly approaching until she saw that the gentleman dozing on the bank, a fishing rod discarded beside him, was Lord Drake. She crept closer and stood gazing down at him, serene in sleep. Even more casual than usual, he was dressed in a pair of disreputable breeches and a shirt with no cravat, and had a slouchy hat pulled down over his eyes. To her he looked perfectly splendid, stretched out at his ease, his long muscular legs crossed at the ankle. His open shirt exposed a triangle of pale skin with a swirl of golden hair, the most of any gentleman's body she had ever seen, and she felt a heated flush rise in her cheeks.

And she had no right to be standing there gawking at him like a lackwit. She longed to join him, to sit down at his side on the peaceful riverbank, watch him sleep and think of all of the tomorrows she would never have with him, all the tomorrows they *could* have if their situations were more equal. And yet . . .

Lord Drake's hand twitched, and it was as though an electric surge pulsed through him. He cried out and flailed, shouting, "Up the hill, gentlemen, we must take the hill!"

He thrashed from side to side as True stood wondering what to do.

And then he stiffened, his whole body arching as though he suffered some incredible pain, and he wailed, a keening so mournful that the small hairs on the back of True's neck stood up.

"Dead, I am . . . oh, God! Dead . . ."

With a cry, True dropped her basket and rushed to Drake, horrified to know that he was in the depths of one of his hideous nightmares. What to do? Oh, Lord, what should she do? She dropped to her knees beside him and pulled off his hat, now wildly askew. Drake's gaunt face was twisted in a grimace and tears rolled down his cheeks as he moaned and thrashed.

Gentle; one should be gentle with someone in a nightmare and not awaken them too abruptly, True remembered. "Oh, Lord," she prayed, "Let me help him, let me do the right thing."

Awkwardly, she put her arms around him, but he savagely fought her. He struggled in a nightmare battle with phantom enemies, clutching at her arms with a powerful, bruising grip. She was suddenly afraid; what did she know about this, about how to bring someone out of this kind of a state? But she would do what she could. She would surround him with her peace, she thought desperately, trying to twist her arms out of his grip. He released her. "Hush, Wy, hush. You are safe," she murmured as he settled somewhat. She stroked his face and talked, pulling him closer as he stilled, cradling him in her arms. It was awkward. He was so very large compared to her, but her arms were long enough and she would let love comfort him.

With a great sigh, he went limp. And then, as quickly as it started, the nightmare ended and his eyes opened.

Nine

His eyes bleary and clouded, he stared up at her from his place in her arms and the drying tears on his cheek were joined by a fresh stream. He reached up and touched her face, his hand gentle, his touch wondering. True thought that he might not know where he was, or even who she was, his eyes were so unfocused.

And then he wept, great gusty sobs that wracked his body. He encircled her waist with his powerful arms and laid his head on her bosom and cried, murmuring incoherently at first, mumbling. But then she could make out words, and it was like a prayer for forgiveness, she thought, rocking him and soothing him.

"I killed him, poor f-fellow," he cried. "He didn't even have ammunition but I shot him, watched him die. And . . . and he had a little picture, wife and baby, I think, and she n-never saw him again. Never saw her poor hus-husband again! Not right! Not fair."

True felt a surge of tenderness course through her as she held him and rocked him and listened to his confession while she stroked his face and ran her fingers through his golden curls. "But you didn't know that, didn't know that he had no ammunition," she murmured, hazarding a guess.

"N-no. . . . didn't know it, but still, he was dead, and his poor wife and fatherless babe . . . not right . . ." He wept again, his whole body shuddering with a searing pain that had been suppressed for years under the needs of battle, the exterior of a warrior. "And all the others . . . sons, husbands, fathers, all! Dead. I k-killed them."

His tears were soaking the bodice of her gown; she could feel the wetness on her skin. She rubbed and massaged his shaking shoulders, kneading the knotted muscles of his neck, holding him to her. No one had ever been so close to her before, not even Harry, but this felt utterly right, holding him like this. She wondered at the welter of confused emotions that were pelting through her brain and heart as she stroked and touched him, but then she turned away from her own feelings. There would be time to think, to contemplate, later. Right now, he needed her.

If she could just infuse him with some of her faith and peace, it would be worth any price, even . . . even the destruction of her reputation if they were found like this.

She glanced around, up the riverbank and across to the other side. No one in sight. Not that it would make any difference to her actions if there was someone, for she felt needed in a way she had never felt before. She was overwhelmed by her desire to give this man in her arms whatever she had that would ease his acute suffering. His heart pain was so deep it was almost like a physical wound, she thought. What do we do to our men and boys, she wondered, murmuring comforting words as she gazed tenderly down at the sobbing, clinging man in her arms. How can we send them off to kill or be killed? And, yet, when they return, we expect them to be fine, to suffer not at all, to not feel all the fear and horror and pain of what they have

had to do. We call them heroes, but expect them
to be the same young men we sent off to war, un-
tainted by all the violence and death that surrounded them for so long. It was not right, she
thought. After the celebration was over these men
were sent back to their families to resume their
lives as if nothing had happened in the interim.

"Wy, you could do nothing but what you did."
She spoke in her gentlest tone, and smoothed the
hair back from his damp brow, laying a kiss there,
a kiss such as a mother might offer her child. "As
long as governments start wars, they will send their
best and brightest men out to fight, to kill or be
killed, and you were one of them. You went out a
boy, eager for the glory, and came back a man,
saddened by all you had witnessed. But you could
do nothing less, once on that battlefield. You could
do nothing less."

She talked on for a few minutes, sharing what
she had just been thinking, and then realized that
his tight grip around her waist had loosened and
he slept, peacefully and with a look of sweet relief
on his handsome face.

The afternoon advanced. The lowering skies
cleared, eventually, and the sun came out, though
they sat in deep shade under the old oak tree. A
breeze, cleaner and cooler than any in the past
days, riffled over the top of the long grass in the
meadow, setting the daisies to dance. And Wy slept
on, a deep, dreamless sleep of a relaxed and un-
burdened heart.

Through the long afternoon True felt her limbs
numb from staying in one place so long, but she
would not move for the world. Her mind wandered
far afield at first, over her own dilemma. To marry
or not to marry? But it was a subject that curiously
could not hold her attention. Instead, she thought
of Wy, and his pain. What could she do to soothe

the ache in his heart? The one thing that had given him the most joy, it seemed, since he had been back, was helping Stanley, the ex-soldier amputee, and the other former soldiers he had hired to rebuild his library. Perhaps if he found others to help—and he did have the resources to do it—he could find solace in the lives he was helping to mend.

He needed something to look forward to. He had been a soldier for so long, it was hard for him to be idle, she thought. As he was rebuilding his library, so he needed to rebuild his life, from the very basics, tear it all apart and start over again. He had long defined himself as a soldier, and he was not that anymore. What was he? *Who* was he? He would need to answer those questions before he could find comfort.

The shadows lengthened. Those at the house must be wondering where they were. Could she say she lost her way? She did not think a lie was a sin in a case like this. She knew in her heart that she had done nothing but what she ought, so there was no guilt associated with her actions. But no one else would understand, least of all her cousin. Arabella was there to win Lord Drake's hand, and she would either swoon or go into a rage to see Drake and True at that moment. As much as she loved her younger cousin, she still knew Arabella well enough to know that she would see it as True poaching in her woods. Ah, well, True thought. There was nothing she could do about that.

Drake stirred, stretched and yawned. He nuzzled his pillow, feeling like he had slept better than any time since he had come home. It was a foreign feeling, this sensation of rested wellness. Turning slightly, he looked up . . . directly into the smiling eyes of Miss Truelove Becket!

He scrambled away from her. Her cheeks were pink, but her blue eyes were calm, as though it was quite an everyday occurrence to cradle a gentleman in her lap while he slept. "True! Er, Miss Becket, what—?"

She stretched her legs out awkwardly, her movements as clumsy as a newborn calf. With a rueful grimace, she rubbed her legs. "I am afraid it was not just you who fell asleep, Wy. My legs seem to have done the same."

Memory flooded back to him. Another tortured nightmare! He had started to dream of the first advance of the day—of *that* day, Sunday, June 18, 1815—but it had swiftly turned into the old nightmare of pain and death, and hands clutching at him, pulling him, demons dragging him down to hell for his misdeeds. Mortified, he remembered it all, remembered awakening to find her gazing down at him with a look of tenderness and pity so powerfully sweet that he had burst into tears, as half-asleep as he was at that moment. And on her bosom he . . . God help him, he had babbled all his pain and torment, all his shameful weakness, all his dark hatred of what he had become on the battlefields of Europe.

"I . . . I suppose I owe you an apology," he said, stiffly. He was horribly embarrassed to be caught in such weakness, and by a woman for whom he had an enormous amount of respect and . . . yes, and care. No one had ever seen him cry. It was unmanly, as his father had impressed upon him when he was just three years old. Men did not cry!

"Apology?" she said, as she staggered to her feet.

"For babbling like an idiot; for crying like a *woman!*"

"Why is it that men always compare themselves to women when they feel they have been weak and stupid?" True said, frowning. "My father says that God weeps when He looks down on the world. When I was a child, that is what I thought rain was—God's tears. If God can weep from sorrow, then I do not suppose that men are above such a thing."

He had to smile, so adorable did she look, doing her best to appear the scowling harpy and only succeeding in appearing even more enchanting, with her hair disarranged and grass clinging to the skirts of her ugly brown dress. She had scolded him as she would a child, and a curious lightheartedness stole through him, his embarrassment disappearing in the face of her resolute sanity. "And who does God tell His troubles to?" he teased.

She chuckled and her eyes widened. Hers was a face made for smiling, and not for scowling. "Why, I suppose St. Peter. Or perhaps the angels."

"St. Peter has always struck me as being just the slightest bit judgmental. He would have to be to guard the gates, I suppose, only letting the right people in."

She cocked her head to one side. "Perhaps you are right. Archangel Gabriel, then. That is who God would tell His worries to." She watched him for a minute, as her hands brushed at her skirts in a doomed attempt to get rid of all the twigs and grass. She stood just at the edge of the shade of the tree, and the sun glanced off sparkling reddish highlights in her brown hair. "I—I hope you are feeling better, Wy."

"Do you know, I think I do." Wonderingly, he realized that it felt as though his *soul* had slept for a while, and was refreshed, cleansed just a little. All of the pain was not gone, but he had given away a little of it, just by telling True. He glanced around and gathered his hat, fishing pole and jacket. The shadows were long and the breeze was becoming chilly, refreshing after the heat they had suffered lately. Suddenly he wondered just how late it was. "How long did I sleep?" he asked.

"For a few hours," she answered calmly, picking up her discarded basket and bonnet.

"A few . . . my God, True!" He had compromised her, utterly and completely! They had been alone for hours, and he had actually slept on her bosom. Staring at her, aghast at the implications she appeared to be completely unaware of, he said, "True, we have been gone for hours. People will wonder. I think we should say . . ." He gulped and moved toward her, but stopped before touching her. "I think we should tell them that we are to marry."

"Marry?"

Her expression was an unreadable mix of incomprehension and something else. If only he was more adept at reading faces, but he had never had that knack, especially with ladies. He could not tell if she was disturbed, incredulous, or disbelieving. As for himself, he was a little shocked at such an outcome, but he felt certain that it was not only right and necessary, but that it would not be the worst thing that could happen. Having Miss Truelove Becket around every day and every night would be . . . well . . . pleasant? That word did not do justice to his feelings on the subject, but he could think of no other.

"Why should we marry, Wy?" Her voice trembled just a little, betraying some strong emotion, but her stance was straight and her expression serious.

Was she thinking of her vicar? Damn, but he had forgotten the bothersome man. "We have been alone together for hours. If anyone found out, you would be ruined! I cannot let that happen to you because you were so kind to me. It would not be right."

She sighed and shifted her empty basket so it was looped over her arm along with her bonnet.

"No one needs to know that we have been to-gether. As far as anyone knows you went out for an afternoon of fishing, and I went for a walk. I simply lost track of time and lost my way. I have a habit of absently wandering, and so I have been gone for hours before; Arabella knows that." She stepped toward him and laid her hand on his arm, looking up at him with a smile touching her pink lips. "It will be all right, Wy. There is no need for us to marry."

He glanced down at her small brown hand on his arm and wondered if he most felt relief or disap-pointment. He had the oddest impulse to pull her to him and kiss her, like he did that night at the inn. But this time the reason for doing so was not desire—or at least not wholly desire. The warmth of the day, the sweetness of her face, the delectable curves under her soft, worn dress; any man would have to be mad not to want her in that way.

But there was something more, and he could not for the life of him name it. He wanted to hold her, to surround her, to enclose her in his arms and stand just where they were until the shadows became twilight and the night noises of owls and wee creeping animals started. Ridiculous flight of fancy for a soldier! He cleared his throat. "Yes, well, if you think there is no need, then I suppose we should be getting back."

She stepped away from him with that same un-readable expression on her unfashionably brown face. "I think we ought to arrive back at Lea Park separately, though, or there *will* be talk." She smiled, turned and started up the bank and across the meadow, stopping to pick some wildflowers as she went, swinging her basket and shabby bonnet on one arm. He watched her until she was out of sight.

* * *

Lady Leathorne presided over the tea table, filling cups for the ladies while Lord Conroy, her husband and her son drank port. This day had been an unfortunate one—or had it? Miss Becket had been gone all afternoon, hunting for watercress she *said*, though she came back with nothing but some wildflowers. And Drake had been gone even longer. He had fallen asleep while fishing, he said—she'd met him in the hall coming back with his fishing pole over his shoulder—and slept most of the afternoon.

"It is true, Mother, so do not give me that suspicious look. I fell asleep." He smiled down at her from his absurd height—where he had got that from she did not know, for neither his father nor herself were tall—and challenged her to disbelieve him. He wore a shabby hat and carried his jacket on one arm.

She was loath to bring it up, but curiosity would prevail. "And you did not . . . did not have one of your nightmares?"

His eyes became hooded, shadowed, but with a shrug and a deep sigh he seemed to release whatever brooding thought had arisen to plague him. "I did have a nightmare, but I awoke, and . . . and then I fell back to sleep and slept the rest of the afternoon without incident."

Why did she have the feeling he was leaving something out? She knew him. Not from time spent together, for he had been gone most of the last fifteen years or so, and before that had been at school. When, at seventeen, he said he was buying his cornetcy in the Kent Light Dragoons, she had raged and stormed and wept. She had not borne a son, her only child, to have him perish on some distant battlefield alone. She had tried every strategy in her bag of mother's tricks, but stubborn, willful—and, yes, strong and manly—he had resisted all argument, and calmly done what he wanted. He was a boy when he left, but through the years, on his occasional visits home, she had seen him grow into a handsome, intelligent man. But when he came back from that dreadful Waterloo, he was a *different* man. Regardless of all the changes in him, though, she knew him as a mother knows, from her heart. And there was something he was not telling her.

She knew that Isabella and her daughter thought so, too. Their suspicions were of their cousin, Miss Becket. She had overheard their whispered conference as she was just entering the saloon for tea.

Isabella had told her daughter that no matter what True and Lord Drake were doing together, to not make a fuss. "For he is only having his bit of fun, you know, Arabella. Men do. They are creatures of lust, and when they find a willing lady. . . . But he does not intend to marry her, you know, and that is all that is important. It is you he will wed, I would bet my diamond tiara. We must not force him to admit that they were together, or he will feel compelled to offer for her. What a disaster that would be! There will be plenty of time to curtail his . . . well, his outside interests, once you are married. There are ways to ensure a man's good behavior, and I will teach you them all."

It was a chilling conversation in a way. Arabella had said not a word, but with such counsel! Isabella seemed to be saying that after marriage there would be plenty of time to apply the yoke of fidelity on Drake, that he could be brought to heel soon enough.

It was enough to make her wonder, Lady Leathorne thought, if Arabella were truly the right mate for him, if that was what her mother had been feeding her. She glanced across the saloon at Drake, so tall next to his father. They were discussing something, horses likely, their one point of common ground. Since Drake had come back in mid July, it was as though a piece of him were missing. Had he found that missing piece—or rather, *peace*—he had been missing, down by the river, alone . . . or with someone else?

And was Miss Truelove Becket the kind of young woman who would lay with a man outside of marriage? She was a vicar's daughter, but that did not guarantee morality or innocence. More than one maiden had given away her virtue, hoping to snare something of infinitely more value. But was Miss Becket one of those? She would not have thought so. In the two weeks or so the guests had been at Lea Park she had never seen the young woman act immodestly or say a thing that could be taken as flirtation. Was it all an act? Did she scheme secretly to seduce and capture Lady Leathorne's son?

He glanced across the room and smiled at her, and she felt her heart jolt with joyous recognition. So had he looked as a boy, her son, her child. She stiffened against the swell of tenderness in her heart. She would rein in her emotion, for if she did not, tears would come to her eyes, and she would not look like a foolish old woman in front of the man she loved more even than her husband. Her love for Lord Leathorne was for what *was*, and for the kindness he had shown her throughout their married life despite the fact that he had never understood one tiny portion of what she thought or felt or needed; but her love for her son was fierce and deep, the most powerful emotion she had ever felt.

Drake came across the room to the tea table and sat down beside her. "Father is talking about getting rid of his hunters, and I have said I will purchase them for my stables at Thorne House."

"He has been talking about getting rid of his hunters for two years, ever since he took that fall off Strider during the Quorn, and nothing has come of it," she said dryly.

Drake chuckled. "Well, when he is ready to sell, I will be ready to buy. I hope to have Thorne livable by Christmas; I think I will go even if it is not quite done. I want to move into it. You will have to see it, Mother; it is coming along well. It will be odd to have a home of my own, after so many years as a soldier, but I look forward to it."

Did that mean he intended to marry? Lady Leathorne wondered. He had never said so, though she was sure he knew the reason Arabella Swinley had been invited. "I . . . if there is anything you need, just let us know. We are so happy to have you back." And whole and alive, she thought, unable and unwilling to put all of that into words.

"I begin to be glad I am back," he mused. "I know it was like I was in a fog for a time, but I think it is a difficult adjustment to civilian life. I wonder if others are finding it as difficult as I. There may be some reason I was spared. Perhaps I can help somebody else."

"I know you were, Wy; I know you were spared for a reason." She allowed herself the luxury of running her fingers through his unruly hair, the curls that during his time as a soldier had been closely shorn; it was a caress that had been habitual between them when he was a child. He had gone from Lea Park a boy, anxious to don scarlet regimentals, and had come back finally, at the end of it all, a stranger—a tall, brooding mystery man with sad eyes, haunted by horrors she could not even imagine. What had changed in one afternoon that made her feel able to touch him as she did when he was a boy? She sensed a . . . what was it? Healing? Was he truly beginning the road to wellness?

If she thought for one minute that Miss Truelove Becket was responsible for this change, she would have kissed her and called her daughter. If he had spent the afternoon with her, as the Swinleys seemed to suspect, and he came back looking so rested, then the young woman must have some magic no one else possessed. But it was not the kind of thing she could ask him, and so she would bide her time and wait and watch. Vigilance would be her watchword.

Annie, the Swinleys' maid, was combing out Arabella's long, silvery-blonde tresses when Lady Swinley marched into the room.

"Leave us, Annie."

"She is not done, Mother," Arabella said crossly. She was not in the mood for another of her mother's lectures on what a young lady should do to entrap a man into marriage. "I like her to do one hundred strokes and she was only to eighty-three."

"Then she can come back and do the other seventeen later. Off with you, Annie. My dressing table needs tidying."

The girl curtsyed and left, quietly closing the door behind her. Arabella gave a martyred sigh and resigned herself to her fate. She flounced over to her bed and climbed up on it, using the little stool beside to mount the high mattress. Her mother followed her and stood at the bedside.

Arabella watched her mother, waiting for the lecture to begin. What was she doing wrong now? Had she eaten too much dinner? Had she laughed too loudly at Lord Conroy's jokes? Had she not held her back straight enough, or her nose high enough or . . . there seemed to be a never-ending stream of things she was doing wrong, all of which could be fatal errors in the calculated campaign to win Lord Drake's attention and secure a proposal.

Which was ridiculous. After all, she was a veteran of three London seasons, she knew how to charm a man, and had had her share of proposals.

But nothing was good enough for her mother, it seemed. Never did Arabella reach the height of perfection her mother sought. It was exhausting being on one's guard all the time, never able to truly be oneself.

Lady Swinley paced up and down the length of the gold and green counterpaned bed, her pinched face drawn with a harried expression.

"What is it, Mother?" Arabella asked, feeling a stirring of dread; she was afraid some unknown disaster had her mother panicked.

"How do you think it goes between you and Lord Drake?"

Deciding on honesty, Arabella said, "I think not well. He is polite, and kind enough, but he has those frightful moods when he just stares into space, and . . . and I have heard his nightmares at night. Have you not? His screams?" It all came spilling out, then, all the worries she had been fretting about over the past weeks. "And the servants whisper that he is not quite right in the head, that Waterloo left him damaged somehow," she said, finally. "Mama, what if I do not want to marry him?"

Lady Swinley halted and stared at her daughter, her eyes starting like boiled gooseberries from her face. "Do not talk like that! Do you want your cousin to snatch this coronet right out of your hand?"

Arabella plucked at the bed cover. "No, I do not want her to marry Lord Drake! She would become a viscountess, and it should not suit me to have to follow her in to dinner, nor to give way to her. And she would be presented at court! Lord, what a mull she would make of that! Can you see little True swamped in court dress and diamonds?"

If she had thought to bring a smile to her

mother's face, as a little ridicule of True usually did, it was not to be. Lady Swinley frowned, still, and patted the bed cover absently while she stared at her daughter.

"You *must* marry Lord Drake, Arabella. If you find him distasteful, then do what I did with your father; close your eyes while he has his way and count to one hundred, or fashion a new dress in your imagination, or think of new wallpaper for the dining room."

Arabella gasped at the indelicacy of her mother's speech. Never had her mother spoken of the intimate side of marriage, and really, Arabella knew very little, other than what ridiculous posturings she had witnessed among the animals on the farm near True's home as they did their business. If that was what humans did, she would be hard-pressed to keep her mind on wallcoverings and not burst out laughing . . . or crying.

"It is not that I find him . . . distasteful, exactly," Arabella said, trying to put into words her fear of being tied for life to a man of such dour moods. He wasn't like that all the time, but occasionally he would have one of his, what she called privately "spasms," and then he would stare off into space with no notice of the company. And his shrieks in the night! She shivered and crawled under the covers. "I don't want to talk about it, Mother. I am doing my best, and if I do not get him, I will get someone when we go to London in the spring. I promise."

"There will be no season in London next year, if you do not marry Lord Drake," Lady Swinley said harshly.

"What . . . what do you mean?" In the flickering candlelight of her room, Arabella could see her mother's expression, and it was terrifying to her.

There was despair in her eyes, and fear. She looked quite old.

Lady Swinley twisted her hands together and stared down at them. "We have no money," she said. "We are well and truly in the suds."

Ten

Lady Leathorne decided not to force a closeness between her son and the girl she had thought would make him a suitable bride—no more picnics or games arranged to show Arabella to her best advantage, no more planning or scheming. Though she still thought them well-suited when she saw them together—both were tall, remarkably good-looking, and intelligent—she had begun to feel that perhaps Drake would make his own choice in time and be happy in a way Lady Leathorne had never considered possible in marriage. If his own choice proved to be Arabella Swinley, then all the better, but it would be *his* choice.

She, herself, had married so young, at sixteen, a man her parents had chosen; though Lord Leathorne was kind, he was not clever. Never had she been able share with him her deepest thoughts and wishes without him frowning in perplexity and requesting her to speak in plain English. It had made for a lonely life in many ways, for she had never been fashionable enough to take a lover, but she could not repine. She knew she was fortunate that George was kindhearted and lacking in the most distressing vices. He did not drink to excess or gamble, and he was discreet when satisfying his sexual needs. What more could a wife of her rank expect?

Love, perhaps? A companionship of the mind, a mate of the soul? Those things were not thought to be necessary or even desirable by parents looking for a husband for an eligible daughter in her day. And, yet, what could life be if one was so blessed? She thought she would leave Drake to run his life for himself . . . or she would try to, anyway. It was so tempting to interfere, for his own good.

The leaves were starting to turn from green to gold as the days shortened. There had been a few days of steady rain and the house party had felt dull, but finally a day dawned sunny and bright, and now, after luncheon, the young people had gone into the nearest village to visit the library there and make some frivolous purchases. Lady Leathorne had had one of the footmen drag a couple of chairs outside on the terrace and she sat facing the sun, allowing her skin, for once, the full force of sunlight.

"You will get spots, Jessica."

Lady Leathorne opened her eyes to see Isabella, Lady Swinley, standing by the other chair, bonnet firmly tied and shading her white skin. "And what does that matter at my age?" she returned, with a smile. "Sit with me, Isa. There is no one else here today, and I find I am enjoying the quiet."

Lady Swinley took the other chair but sat stiffly, as though she had never learned to relax. "I am glad to find you alone, I must confess."

Lady Leathorne gazed over at her old friend, at the concern on her pinched face, the worry on her brow. "What is wrong? Has anything happened?"

"No, of course not," Lady Swinley said. "I do have some concerns, but it is nothing that cannot be worked out."

"Out with it, Isa." She had a feeling she knew what Isabella was going to say. It had been coming on over the last week, as Lady Leathorne allowed the house party to devolve into a relaxed gathering feeling strangely family-like. Of course, Isabella was one of her oldest friends, and Arabella her daughter. Conroy was like a son to her, he had spent so much time in their home when Drake and he were boys. His parents were not a comfortable sort of couple, and he seemed to prefer Lea Park to home. Miss Becket she had just met a few weeks before, but there was an oddly peaceful quality about her company that Lady Leathorne appreciated. In short, it was not the sort of formal "engagement party" visit Isabella had perhaps envisioned.

"It has been weeks, Jessica. We came here, Arabella and I, to match her to your son. I expected your help—thought we had agreed on tactics, even—but you have given up!" Isabella's voice was harsh, with an unattractive note of desperation.

"I have not given up, I just think the children should choose for themselves."

"Jessica!" The woman looked shocked. "I had thought we felt alike on this subject. We did not choose our husbands, and we did just fine."

"Did we?" Lady Leathorne glanced up at the house. Her husband, she knew, was writing a letter in the library, or was when last she saw him. It was half past two, or thereabouts, so he would be consuming his midday port at that moment. A creature of habit was her George. Then he would look at the accounts—though he *had* never and *would* never understand them—and meet with his steward.

They had been married for over thirty-five years, and yet never had she felt more than a kind of irritated affection for Leathorne. And she had been mightily glad when he had stopped coming to her bed, for his fumbling attentions were wearisome at best. It was rumored that he visited a plump, complaisant barmaid in the village on his rare nights out, and that was just fine with her. "Would it have hurt us to look around and decide for ourselves?"

"That is just the kind of thinking that leads to trouble. It is what I allowed Arabella to do in London. Three seasons, and she could not decide on anyone!"

That was not strictly true, and Lady Leathorne knew it; Isabella forgot the letter she had written to her old friend worrying over her daughter's apparent determination to wed Lord Sweetan, a mere younger son. Isabella had put an end to that, and considered that she was doing her duty. And yet, it would not have been a bad match if the girl truly loved the young man.

Lady Swinley continued. "We always said that if Drake came back home unwed, and if Arabella had not decided on a husband, that we would marry them off to each other." Isabella was leaning forward in her chair, her narrow face grim. "Do you not want grandchildren?"

There was a sharp edge to her friend's voice that Lady Leathorne did not like. They had not in years spent this much time together, and she could not help but wonder if their friendship was just habit now. What did they have in common besides unwed children of a certain age? They rarely spoke of anything beyond fashion or London society, neither of which interested Lady Leathorne in truth. She really knew little of what her friend thought or felt. Was there something more to Isabella's determination to see the two wed besides a wish to see her daughter comfortably settled?

"You know I want grandchildren. More important to me, though, is Drake's health. I had not realized how badly he was wounded at Waterloo, and it went deeper than that awful saber cut to his leg. He has been so very troubled. I want him well."

"He looks perfectly fine to me. Certainly, he still

walks with a limp and needs that cane when he is tired, but he is fully capable of walking down the aisle and fathering a few children. He *is* capable of that, is he not?"

Isabella's inquisitive expression reminded Lady Leathorne of a ferret, nose twitching, beady eyes fixed. The frightening realization came to her that in truth, if she was ruthlessly honest, she did not like Isabella Swinley any more. And the more time she spent with her, the more she found to criticize. And this was to be her son's mother-in-law? All her joy in the bright and beautiful fall weather was quickly fleeing in the face of her friend's adamant refusal to understand her.

And so she would have to take the tone she took with subordinates and her husband. "I will *not* coax, cajole, trick or wheedle my son into marriage. It is a miracle of God that he is alive at all, and if he wants to spend the rest of his days as a bachelor, I will . . . I will be unhappy, but it is his life. Marriage will be his *own* choice, and will occur when he is ready." Lady Leathorne stood.

"My daughter turned down perfectly good offers of marriage with the understanding that your son was hers!" Isabella Swinley leaped to her feet. "You cannot back out of our agreement, Jessica. It is not right!"

"That is not my concern. My understanding was that if she found someone to her taste, she was to feel free to accept him. We had no agreement . . . or at least, I have come to think that we did not have any right to make an agreement when it concerns two young lives. Drake is a man—his *own* man. I could not force him into this marriage even if I was of a mind to." Lady Leathorne turned and walked back through the glass terrace doors and into the blue saloon.

* * *

The drapes were drawn in the music room against the evening darkness, and Arabella moodily leafed through the selections available. Lord Conroy, as always, was hovering nearby to lend her support if she needed anything. Lord Drake was quietly reading a paper, his gaunt, handsome face somber at some news he was reading. He had had another of his nightmares the night before, she was sure of it; she had heard screams, and then silence. His nightly perturbations were supposed to be a great secret, but Lord Conroy, or Nathan, as he had begged her to call him, had told her that Lord Drake had the most frightful dreams in which he was dying on that awful battlefield.

While one could not help respecting such a man, a man who had risen to his ranking of major general at an astonishingly young age—there were only one or two in Wellington's army who had attained the rank younger—it did not mean that she thought she could stomach lying with such a man as he thrashed and screamed. It gave her the cold horrors. And yet, what choice had she? Her mother's announcement a few nights before had left her dazed, but with the knowledge that her future was plain. She either coaxed the recalcitrant viscount into marriage, or dwindled into poverty-stricken old age, unmarried, unwanted . . .

It was just too much! It was all very well for someone like True to be a spinster, but she, the Honorable Miss Arabella Swinley, most beautiful diamond to illuminate the ballrooms of London in years, had seemed destined for a brilliant marriage. It was all her mother's fault! She tossed the music aside. She had been very willing to marry the gay, amusing Lord Sweetan the previous spring, but he, poor fellow, was merely the youngest son of the Duke of Brefort—a prolific papa of seven boys and four girls—and had little money, or at least little in her

mother's estimation. *She* did not think 7,000 pounds
a year was so very near poverty. Her mother had put
a stop to it, though, with the reminder that she had
very much liked Viscount Drake, and that he was
hers for the asking.

And truth to tell, Lord Sweetan's glory paled in
comparison to her memories of Lord Drake, so she
had not been so very hard to persuade.

Unfortunately, the viscount she had met the previous year, late spring of 1814, had little in common with this brooding, disturbed and wounded
ex-soldier. In his regimentals, and with a fund of
amusing stories and dashing adventures to tell, he
had seemed the perfect beau, the *beau ideal*, in fact.
Now he was positively frightening, or at least the
thought of his nightmares was, and she could not
picture being tied for life to a man like him.

She glanced over at True, who sat in the lamplight at Lord Drake's side and sewed. Lord, but
they looked like an old married couple! He reading the paper and she sewing a hem. Arabella
tossed her blond curls and selected a piece at ran-
dom. Such boredom was not for her. Perhaps she
would marry Lord Drake after all—with their financial situation she supposed she did not really have
a choice—but if she did, she would make him take
her to London, and buy her jewels and a high-
perch phaeton with four white ponies, and they
would stay at Leathorne Place in Mayfair. That was
her destiny. And if she had to marry the gloomy
Lord Drake to attain her rightful place in the
world, then so be it. She would do as her mother
wished, and at night she would . . . she would
close her eyes and think of plumes for her ponies.

"Will you walk on the terrace with me? I have
something I wish to ask you."

We'd Like to Invite You to Subscribe to Zebra's Regency Romance Book Club and Give You a Gift of 4 Free Books as Your Introduction! (Worth $19.96!)

If you're a Regency lover, imagine the joy of getting 4 FREE Zebra Regency Romances and then the chance to have these lovely stories delivered to your home each month at the lowest price available! Well, that's our offer to you and here's how you benefit by becoming a Regency Romance subscriber:

- 4 FREE Introductory Regency Romances are delivered to your doorstep
- 4 BRAND NEW Regencies are then delivered each month (usually before they're available in bookstores)
- Subscribers save almost $4.00 every month
- Home delivery is always FREE
- You also receive a FREE monthly newsletter, which features author profiles, discounts, subscriber benefits, book previews and more
- No risks or obligations...in other words, you can cancel whenever you wish with no questions asked

Join the thousands of readers who enjoy the savings and convenience offered to Regency Romance subscribers. After your initial introductory shipment, you receive 4 brand-new Zebra Regency Romances each month to examine for 10 days. Then, if you decide to keep the books, you'll pay the preferred subscriber's price of just $4.00 per title. That's only $16.00 for all 4 books and there's never an extra charge for shipping and handling.

It's a no-lose proposition, so return the FREE BOOK CERTIFICATE today!

Say Yes to 4 Free Books!

Complete and return the order card to receive this $19.96 value, ABSOLUTELY FREE!

If the certificate is missing below, write to:
Regency Romance Book Club
P.O. Box 5214, Clifton, New Jersey 07015-5214
or call TOLL-FREE 1-888-345-BOOK

Visit our website at www.kensingtonbooks.com.

FREE BOOK CERTIFICATE

YES! Please rush me 4 Zebra Regency Romances without cost or obligation. I understand that each month thereafter I will be able to preview 4 brand-new Regency Romances FREE for 10 days. Then, if I should decide to keep them, I will pay the money-saving preferred subscriber's price of just $16.00 for all 4...that's a savings of almost $4 off the publisher's price with no additional charge for shipping and handling. I may return any shipment within 10 days and owe nothing, and I may cancel this subscription at any time. My 4 FREE books will be mine to keep in any case.

Name _____

Address _____ Apt. _____

City _____ State _____ Zip _____

Telephone ( ) _____

Signature _____ RN061A
(If under 18, parent or guardian must sign.)

True's heart thumped, but she put aside the first ridiculous thought that had sprung into her foolish brain at Drake's whispered words. He had discarded his paper some time ago, and sat gravely listening to Arabella's dramatic performance on the piano. Her cousin was really a brilliant pianist, as good as many professionals. It was the one ability True envied Arabella, but had never been able to learn. The vicarage piano was old and out of tune, and that must be her excuse for her inability. Arabella had just started another equally difficult piece when Lord Drake had whispered his request to her. She slipped out onto the terrace after him, away from the evening gathering in the music room. All eyes were on Arabella, as Conroy turned the pages for her. The music room was next to the blue saloon, and so it opened out onto the terrace, too, through large glass doors.

Her first thought at his words had been "He means to ask me to marry him!" but of course that was impossible. Ridiculous! What could have entered her brain to think such a thing? Never, by word or gesture, had Drake given her any reason to expect that he would repeat his impetuous offer of marriage, an offer spurred only by his sense of honor and feeling that he had compromised her. It had been a week since that afternoon by the river, and in that time they had often walked together, talking about anything and everything, as Lord Conroy and Arabella amused themselves.

True was puzzled that Arabella did not make more of a push to attach the viscount, but she seemed to almost fear him sometimes. She had confessed to True that Drake's nightmares—his screams had awoken the household more than a few times in the night, including the night before—frightened her. And yet, still, she seemed determined to have him.

When they were together, she gave every indication of finding him fascinating and irresistible.

True caught up with him by a large potted plant at the low wall at one end of the terrace. "What is it, Wy?"

"Will you go for a drive with me tomorrow? I want to show you something."

His voice was eager, boyish, and utterly irresistible to True. But still . . . "I—I don't think that would look good, Wy. What excuse could we offer? Would it not look peculiar?"

His gaze was fond, and he reached out and caressed one curl, letting it run through his fingers. "Just a short drive in an open gig, my dear. I would not compromise you; you should know that by now. Have I not asked you to marry me?" he teased.

"You did not ask me, sir," she said, laughing. "You reluctantly said that as I had been compromised, you supposed we *must* marry!"

"I did not say anything in such an unchivalrous manner, I hope. But about the drive. . . . Have you not been wanting to see the countryside? I know you are an avid naturalist."

True rolled her eyes. "I pick weeds and wildflowers, Wy, nothing so grand as a 'naturalist,' please. At home I find herbs that I need to brew healing potions." She paused. "I—I will go with you, if you think you can explain it to your mother. I would not have her think badly of me."

"How could she? You are the sweetest of girls, and no one with a brain could think ill of you."

He chucked her under the chin as he said that. If only he meant it, she thought, or at least, if only he meant more by it than just that he was fond of her as a friend and sister. She had acknowledged the danger to herself. She was in love with him, or could be, if she allowed herself, and she was not going to do that.

But still, the chance to be alone with him, driving through the English countryside in autumn, was irresistible. "All right. Take me driving tomorrow, sir!"

He put his arms around her and gave her a smacking kiss on the cheek, but he did not release her immediately, as he should have. He stood gazing down at her in the circle of his arms. True heard a rustling sound behind her, but was lost and dazed in Wy's moonlit eyes, golden like a cat's. It was like there was a spell on her when he surrounded her with his strong arms, holding her close to him, a spell that kept her motionless. But then he released her and smiled.

"It is settled then. Tomorrow morning at eleven."

Drake tossed and turned in his bed. Not once since that afternoon with Truelove by the river had he slept for so many hours unbroken. He longed for that sleep, the oblivion of it, the sweet release. He had been able to snatch a few more hours here and there, but only by remembering the feel of her arms around him, a soft bosom under his cheek, a small hand stroking his hair. If he could just recapture that feeling, that utter peace and contentedness, he could sleep, he was *sure* of it. He turned over on his back and stared into the blackness.

But the memory, or at least the sensory part of that memory, was fading. He needed a repeat of that afternoon to refresh his recollection, but he doubted very much if True, even as kindhearted as she was, would agree to slip away with him to the riverbank so he could sleep in her arms again. He snorted at the idea. Ridiculous, no matter how enticing the thought.

Well, he knew one thing after all these months.

If he had had any intention of marrying, it could not be soon. He might recover from these awful nightmares, but it would take some time, years perhaps. How could he inflict his sleepless nights on a wife? He knew that they would have separate chambers as all in their sphere did, but their rooms at Thorne House would be side by side, and she would know of his sleeplessness. Inevitably they would spend some part of the night together. If he should fall asleep after lovemaking and descend into one of his nightmares . . . how horrible! He tried to imagine Arabella Swinley cradling him in her slender arms, bringing him to his senses gently and gradually, as True had, stroking his hair, murmuring sweet words to him.

No. Couldn't picture it. She would likely kick him out of her bed, and who could blame her?

He hoped he had begun the journey back to health, but he was a long way from arriving at his destination. Until he did, he would not even think about marriage. He willed himself to sleep, finally, but again, the nightmare field of Mont St. Jean surrounded him with all its bloody horror, and the weight of his dead horse and poor Captain Lewis pressed down on him and he awoke screaming to find Horace bending over him, shaking him awake.

"Wake up, sir. Another narsty night, it be. I shall get your breeches."

True glanced over at her companion as he handled the ribbons of the small lightweight gig with easy skill. As a sop to propriety, they had a tiger up behind them, as they would had they been in London. He was really just a small stable boy, but he seemed to be enjoying the ride as much as True was, a grin on his not-too-clean face as they trotted along the country lane at a spanking pace.

At home she had a pony cart, for some of the calls she had to make were a ways away from the vicarage. But the speed did not compare to this lovely gig, and her skills were not those of a top sawyer, as Lord Drake evidently was.

With the thought of home came worries. She hoped her villagers were not missing her too much. Mrs. Saunders, a plump, tidy widow and member of her father's congregation, had promised to look after things for her, and Faithful would take care of what she could, but True worried anyway. It was not just that it was her duty; she truly liked visiting the shut-ins and elderly, for they often, despite illness and deprivation, were less complaining than they had a right to be. And the older ones told marvelous stories of village life back in the middle of the last century. It always seemed to her to be a more colorful time, more vivid and lively.

But every one of her "special friends," as she called them, had urged her to take this holiday, just as her father had, saying yes, they would miss her but that she was entitled to a bit of fun like any girl. Girl! She was a spinster of what was called "uncertain years," meaning no one was unkind enough to remember her true age. She had meant this to be a time of serious soul-searching, a time to make her decisions about Mr. Bottleby and the rest of her life, but she had come to no decisions.

She glanced again at Wy. She had awoken in the night to the sound of echoing screams and had gotten up, alarmed. How she wished she could go to him! How precious to have that right and tender obligation, and to be able to give the gift of comfort. But minutes later she had glanced out the window and seen Drake striding down the steps toward the stable. In the last week his nightmares had not decreased in number, but most times he had not left the house after, and she assumed he was able to go back to sleep, or at least she hoped he was able.

But not last night.

He looked remarkably cheerful, though, for the kind of torment he was going through. Perhaps he had decided that what could not be conquered must be endured. He was a soldier, and had likely been through worse than nightmares in his many years. He would overcome eventually, she had no doubt of it. But on this lovely autumn day, with the sun shining and the leaves brilliant and golden around them, she was not going to concentrate on gloomy thoughts. It was a day for happiness, just to be beside Wy and bowling along a country lane in such a well-sprung vehicle.

"Tell me where we are going!" she said. "I am dying of curiosity."

"When we get there." His grin was sly. "I will give you a hint. Do you remember talking about Stanley, and how much he seemed to enjoy his job, and the country?"

She nodded. "He said he had lived in Bristol all his life, but that he had fallen in love with the countryside—or words to that effect, anyway."

"Well, it has to do with that." He snapped the reins, and Dancer, recovered from her twisted ankle, and Juniper, a bay matched in size and speed to Dancer, picked up the pace.

They trundled along in silence for a while. Again, True's mind wandered and she worried at the problem of what to do about Mr. Bottleby. One day she would think she should marry him, and the next she would be sure she could not. She *must* make up her mind!

What was wrong with her? He was handsome enough; not like Wy, but not repulsive. Not that she should even be considering looks, but those thoughts would intrude, especially when she looked at Wy. Mr. Bottleby was not dirty, he had no bad habits or vices, did not smoke, gamble or drink. He was Godly, forceful and energetic, hardworking, sincere, but . . .

And that was what it always came down to. A feeble "but." It was almost as though her mind was stalling, refusing to make a decision, because she knew that yes or no, she would have to leave Lea Park once she decided, to let Mr. Bottleby know in person what she was going to do. She would not refuse or accept his generous proposal in a letter. Already she had been a guest at Lea Park for a month, but leaving meant she would have no excuse to come back, no excuse to see Wy's dear face again.

And that was the root of her indecision. She did not want to leave his side. She worried that if she left, Arabella and Lady Swinley would find a way to cajole him into marriage, and she thought that he was not ready for that yet, not ready for such a life-changing occurrence. Given time—time to heal, time to find peace in his heart—he would make a wonderful husband, maybe not for Arabella, but . . .

Who was she trying to fool? Arabella would make him a good wife, for she had many admirable qualities and talents, and he would be the man who could tame all of her unhappy quirks. He could possibly turn her into the woman she had the potential to be—good, loving, sweet. A lesser man would let her rule the roost, and that would be disastrous for her. It was not that True felt women needed to be tamed or subjugated, but Arabella had a tendency to pouting and selfishness. The sooner she was out of her mother's clutches the better, and marriage was her only way away from Lady Swinley. With the right influences—Wy and his mother, to name two good ones—she would be a brilliant viscountess, and countess, some day, and more importantly, a good woman.

"We're here," he said, pulling up on the road outside of a large, vacant, rambling house. It was enormous, with numerous outbuildings and stables.

The tiger ran around to hold the horses and Drake jumped down from the gig, wincing as he hit the ground. He reached up and swung True down to the road, then took her arm and walked her down the lane toward the building, opening the gate for her, guiding her through, and shutting it behind her.

"What is this?" she asked, looking up at him. "Why are we here?"

"This, my dear," he said, motioning with a grand sweep of his arm, "is the Drake School of Carpentry and Animal Husbandry!"

Eleven

"The Drake . . . *what*?"

He laughed at her look of puzzlement, and took out a key. "Come inside. I'll show you around."

The door was sheltered in a stone alcove that protected the entrance from wind. Tangled masses of vegetation climbed the stone and wound around the pillars, giving True the feeling that this house had not been inhabited for a very long time. It was brick, two full stories plus an attic. The first floor consisted of a drawing room, library, parlor, and a large back kitchen, all with the musty smell of disuse. Drake threw back the draperies in the drawing room, and was rewarded by a shower of dust. They exited quickly, laughing and sneezing as the cloud of dust filled the room.

"This house needs a good turn out!" True said, coughing and brushing her skirts.

The second floor had eight bedrooms of varying sizes, as well as a couple of dressing rooms. The attic, Drake said, had servants' quarters. True explored, her "houswife's" eye taking in the furnishings that remained, what would need to be repaired, the condition of the wall-coverings and floors, all the minute details her companion said he had not noticed when he had looked at it with the agent in charge of the property. He lounged against the door frame and watched her with laughter in his eyes.

"I was here the other day," he said, "and I swear to you, I did not even notice that the wallpaper is moldy, as you have so kindly pointed out, and that half the bedrooms are missing wardrobes."

"But you must notice, sir, you must!" True rattled a cupboard door and it fell off in her hand. She shook her head, propped it against the cupboard and stood, dusting her gloves off. "A house is not just the walls and the grounds, but every stick of furniture, and the linens and the plate and the—"

"Stop, stop!" he cried, his hands up in mock surrender. He took her arm and they descended to the first floor again and went out the kitchen door that faced the stable in back. "Before I decide to purchase this place, I shall consult with you, for you clearly have a much steadier head on your shoulders than mine. If I start talking about moldy wall coverings and wormy furniture to the land agent it will help me get a better price, I warrant."

True pulled her arm out of her companion's grip and put her hands on her hips. "I am going no farther until you tell me what you are talking about."

Drake laughed. He put his arm around her shoulders and stood with her, gazing out from the back stone steps over the outbuildings; besides the stable there was a chicken house, a barn, and a couple of sheds, one of them leaning at such an angle it would not survive the next strong wind. It was perhaps a shabby scene, but it was gilded for her by the amity between her and her companion. True sighed and laid her cheek against Wy's chest. This felt much too nice, being held in the circle of his arm.

"You gave me the idea for this when you marveled

at how much Stanley knew about carpentry, and how it was a pity he could not pass that knowledge along. Do you know how many men went into the army because they were trained for nothing else? And do you know how many others there were who were experienced craftsmen? A good carpenter, farrier, blacksmith, whatever, could always name his own price. I thought that some of the fellows out of work since Waterloo might like to train in one of the trades. And I further thought that some of the men, like Stanley, could train them."

True pulled herself away, with difficulty, from the comforting rumble of his voice, reverberating in his chest and against her cheek. She gazed up at him with admiration. "Wy, what a perfect idea!"

"It won't solve the problems of the world, but it might help a few fellows support their families, or just make a living. I know old Nosey said our army was the "scum of the earth," but a lot of the men are decent enough fellows given half a chance. We wouldn't have won the war without them. I sent a message to my steward about it, and he sent me the key to this place. It is about halfway between Lea Park and Thorne House."

Impulsively, True threw her arms around Drake's waist. "I think it is a marvelous idea, Wy, truly marvelous, just like you."

She felt his hesitation, but then his arms settled around her, and they stood gazing out at the humble stable yard and farm buildings, while he talked about his vision of a school for teaching the trades, employing ex-soldiers as the teachers, housing the students and teachers there, too, and hiring some ex-soldiers and their wives to look after the physical needs—cooking, cleaning, and more.

Drake felt a curious calm overtake him as he held True close. With her, he could talk of anything; he never needed to worry about witty chat,

or that he bored her. She already knew more about
his war experiences than any other person outside
of those who were there.

In short, he could say anything to her but what
was in his heart. He suspected that he might be a
little in love with Miss Truelove Becket, which was
funny because he had thought he would never fall
in love with anyone, but what did he have to offer
her outside of material things? He was half of a
man, emotionally if not physically. He had a terror
of marrying and then finding that he would never
get any better, never be able to sleep through the
night untormented by nightmare visions of his own
death, or of the faces of the men he had killed.
What kind of future was that to offer a lovely
young lady like Truelove? She deserved her wise
and good vicar, who would value her and give her
a life of toil, yes, but honest work that True would
thrive on.

He held her close to his heart, breathed in her
essence, and wished things were different.

"Shall we walk?" he said, determined to be
cheerful at all costs. He would beat the demons
that plagued him one way or another. "There is a
little wooded area with a brook running through
it. I can like no place that does not have water
access, you know; a brook or a stream is essential
to me. I would like you to see it. I thought some
of the fellows might like to fish while they are staying here."

He whistled to the stable boy and called out to
unhitch the horses for a while, and he led True
through a field. It was some time before they made
their way back to the house.

The next morning Arabella determinedly cor-
nered Lord Drake in the breakfast room as he

helped himself to eggs from the covered chafing dish. She took a plate and spooned on a tiny helping of eggs and a slice of ham. And she would have to be careful that she did not eat even that. Despite what he had said at the inn, she was sure that Lord Drake would approve a dainty appetite. It was time to steel herself to necessity, and set all her efforts to the task at hand. "I must say, my lord, that your . . . your infirmity appears to be healing!"

He scowled at her, but then saw her motioning toward his abandoned cane with her fork. "Er, yes. This last month, the exercise of walking with you ladies has done my leg good, I think."

She dimpled up at him as he pulled out a chair for her. "Soon you will be as good as new! One would never know you were in that awful battle."

"On the contrary, Miss Swinley," he said, taking the seat next to her. They were the only two in the breakfast room at that early hour. "I wish no one to forget about that battle. I was lucky enough to be given an injury that will heal. Many of our poor soldiers lost limbs on the battlefield."

She nodded, determined not to scold him for bringing up subjects unfit for a lady's ears. If he wanted to talk about the dreadful war, then she would do it. If True could, she could. With the determination of a field general planning an attack, she took a deep breath and said, "Why, I think our gallant soldiers injured in the line of duty should be given a pension for their work for our country."

"There is some provision for the injured, Miss Swinley. Chelsea Hospital is for the care of elderly and severely disabled soldiers. It is pitiful, but it is something, I suppose."

"Why, then, they are taken care of!" Arabella was pleased that she had finally engaged the dour viscount in conversation. It was going well, she thought. She stabbed at the piece of ham, then remembered herself and cut a minuscule portion and popped it in her mouth.

"Not really. Not when one considers the sacrifices made. I still believe we could be doing more—much more." He glanced over at her curiously. "Are you genuinely interested in the welfare of our returning soldiers, Miss Swinley?"

She swallowed. 'Oh, Lord,' she thought, 'I hope he does not have some dreary society he wishes me to join!' "I am," she said, nodding vigorously. "I cannot think of anything more fascinating!"

Drake smiled, and over coffee told her much more than she ever wanted to know about military life, and the dilemma facing those concerned about the plight of returning and injured soldiers. And that was just the beginning, she found. That afternoon she walked with him on the terrace, and he told her all about the Peninsula campaign, Ciudad Rodrigo, Badajoz, Salamanca. . . . By the end of the day, her head was whirling with dates and names and facts and figures.

But Lord Drake no longer avoided her company, she saw, with triumph. He sat with her at dinner, even, and they had another "stimulating" discussion. Her mother was right, she found; as long as one listened, nodded and agreed, the gentlemen considered you a brilliant conversationalist. Later, she could not have said just what it was they talked about; something about parliamentary reform, she seemed to remember. After dinner, they gathered in the more intimate confines of the rose parlor for coffee.

Drake had been pleasantly surprised by Arabella. Really, the girl was not such a bacon-brained lackwit as he had first thought. The afternoon had been much more pleasant than he had imagined one spent in her company could be. She had listened and asked intelligent—well, mostly intelligent—questions.

It had seemed a good idea, after the day before, to stay away from True for a while. His feelings were confused, tumultuous, in fact. He and True had walked down to the stream on the property he was buying, and, well, he had taken advantage of her. There was no other way to put it; he had compromised her terribly. He had kissed her again, and they had reclined on the bank of the stream in the most improper manner—improper, and yet it had felt so right!—just holding each other for the longest time until they both fell asleep.

Sleep. In her company, he could sleep without dreams, or at least, without nightmares. For he *had* dreamed, actually; he had wandering, misty dreams of Thorne House, and a golden-haired child who called True "Mama," and always he was holding her, touching her, even when the child clung to them both.

What on earth had it meant? Likely just the gibberish of the unconscious mind. He had awoken from an hour's sound sleep to find that True slumbered in his arms, and the calm he had felt was such as he had never experienced since coming home. And, yet, when she awoke, Drake could feel her embarrassment in the way she avoided his eyes and apologized for her "unseemly" behavior. *Her* unseemly behavior! It was all *his* doing, *he* was filling her with the hideous burden of guilt.

It was not right to involve her with him in this way, when she was virtually betrothed to her vicar. Yet, if that was the case, why did she allow such trespasses? Could she care for him? Or was it the pity he had seen in her eyes the first time, when he had awoken from a nightmare?

He needed to think and he could not do that in her presence. And so that was why he had devoted himself to Arabella Swinley that day. He needed time away from Truelove. He needed to understand himself before he compromised her beyond rescuing, an outcome that seemed almost tempting sometimes, when he thought that his dilemma could be resolved that way, at least. He would have a wife, and she . . . she would have no choice. And that was wrong. He *must* leave her free to choose or reject her vicar!

That evening, emboldened by True's positive reaction to his radical idea and Arabella Swinley's interest in the ex-soldiers' plight, Drake summoned his courage as the household gathered after dinner for coffee, and cleared his throat. The rose saloon, much smaller than the blue saloon, was also more conveniently furnished for conversation, with a grouping of chairs and sofas gathered near the hearth. He was standing by the fireplace, which was lit for the first time in the season, as a cold wind had come up; autumn was advancing. Conroy, who had been talking eagerly to Miss Swinley, was the first to glance up.

"What is it, old man? Looks like you're ready to make a speech."

"Make a speech? Drake? Ha!" Lord Leathorne, his red face split in a wide grin said, "He'd no more make a speech than I would."

"Actually, Father, I do have something to say."

Arabella colored, and Lady Swinley leaned forward, her eyes gleaming as she shot significant glances at her daughter. Lady Leathorne saw the looks between mother and daughter, and, not sure if she was pleased or alarmed, fastened her gaze on her son.

"What is it, Drake?" she asked. "Do you have an announcement to make?"

"I do." Drake paced in front of the fireplace. The room filled with tension.

Drake stopped and let his gaze drift over the collected company. His mother was watching him, and he could see that she was troubled about something. He was not usually so noticing of that kind of thing, but between his mother and him there had always been a strong bond, a kinship of mind as much as of heart. It had not escaped him early in his youth, that his mother's intelligence far outstripped her husband's. He had always wondered if that disparity of understanding had made her unhappy, but she had always seemed contented enough.

True was sitting quietly just in the shadows, her sewing resting on her lap. Lady Swinley and Arabella sat on matching chairs near the window, with Lord Conroy on a footstool by Arabella.

Drake frowned. Lady Swinley had taken her daughter's hand, and shot her a look of—of what? He could not guess at the meaning of a look that seemed almost triumphant. Miss Swinley was pale but composed. Ah, well, it was nothing to do with him. Maybe Conroy, poor chap, had proposed or something. He certainly seemed badly in love with the girl. It would not be a terrible match for his friend, not as bad as he would have supposed before spending the day talking to Miss Swinley. She appeared to have a brain and a heart after all, though she would lead poor Conroy a merry dance, no doubt.

He cleared his throat. His father had drifted off to sleep in the silence. Oh, well, he would not understand what his son was about to talk about, anyway, so let him sleep.

"I have been thinking of the future. I do not want my time on this earth to be wasted in morbid self-recrimination. It did not come upon me at once when I entered the military, but over the years I began to feel that as a soldier my purpose in life was destructive, and I do not want that to be my legacy. I want to give something to the world." He paused and shook his head, wryly reflecting that he sounded like he was running for political office. "Oh, Lord, that sounds so very pompous."

"No, dear, I understand," Lady Leathorne said. He offered her a smile.

"Go on Lord Drake! We are all most interested to hear what you have to say! About your future plans?" That was Lady Swinley, and she clutched her daughter's hand with a firm grip.

Drake wondered why she was so interested. She had never shown the slightest bit of interest in anything to do with the war before. Even True had looked up by now, and she was pale, but composed. Drake felt there was an undercurrent in the room that he was not privy to the source of. They all waited for him to go on.

"Well, I . . . I just wanted to announce . . . that is—" Drake felt a sweat break out on his forehead. Infernal fire! Who needed a fire on a mild autumn evening? He had not meant to make a speech out of a simple statement of what he was doing with the school! "Miss Becket and I went for a drive yesterday afternoon, and I came to a decision."

A gasp came from somewhere in the room, but he was determined not to let it stop him. He forged ahead. "She, more than anyone else, is responsible for the decision I have come to." Oh, God, worse and worse. Now all eyes were turned to Truelove, and he had not meant to place her in an awkward position.

All right. He must marshal his scattering wits as he would his soldiers.

"I have purchased a property, and am starting

a . . . a school for ex-soldiers, to learn a trade. That is it."

At that exact same moment, Arabella Swinley gave a ladylike scream and fell into an elegant swoon.

Twelve

"Do you know how close we came to disaster tonight, my temperamental young miss?" Lady Swinley's voice was a hiss as she followed Arabella to her chamber.

Forced to withdraw from the parlor after her disastrous attempt at a bit of drama, Arabella was not in the mood for one of her mother's lectures, but she was also badly frightened. Her mother was more angry than she had ever seen her. She closed the door behind them and turned, her hands trembling at her sides. Somehow she thought this moment would determine her course for the rest of her life, and she did not know if she could face it. Better to plead a headache or a chill, and retire to her bed.

But no. She had never run from anything or anyone in her whole life, and this was her *mother*, the woman who had given her life. They were the only real family each of them had. She squared her shoulders.

"Mother, you must tell me the truth. How far in the soup are we? Are we badly dished?" Arabella took a deep breath, trying to calm her erratic heartbeat. It was the only reason she could think of for her mother's unwarranted anger. She sat down at the vanity table while her mother paced.

Her faux swoon had been calculated to give her a few moments to think if Lord Drake's announcement had been that he was to marry Truelove. Thank the Lord it had not been that! How would she face the humiliation of her country cousin plucking a prime plum right out of her hand? But her faint had also ended the evening, and so it was not that late; still, she was so tired! The effort of keeping up with Lord Drake all day, and of walking with him, listening to his dreary conversation about soldiers and battles and death! It was enough to put a lady off male companionship for life.

She glanced up at her mother, when the woman did not answer. A gnawing fear in her stomach made it growl, though the lack of food that day had probably as much to do with it. She had merely picked, mindful of her "ladylike" appetite, until Lord Conroy, concerned for her health, demanded that she eat a biscuit. He had been much impressed when she had been "unable" to finish even that. Why could Lord Drake not be so easily impressed? Why did capturing his interest require listening to long, desperately boring lectures about the war and the sorry state of all the old soldiers?

But she must not get distracted from the matter at hand. "Mother, tell me the truth. How bad is it?" She had imagined a little financial distress, but her mother's anger seemed to portend something much worse.

"We are . . ." Lady Swinley paced to the window and stared out into the gloom. "We are badly in need of financial aid, I will admit."

"But what happened? I thought Father left us well-provided for. There is no entail, since there is no legitimate heir, and so Swinley Manor stays with us. And Swinley Manor farms are prosperous; the steward has sold off some of the timber, and . . ."

Lady Swinley strode over to her daughter and

glared down at her. Her eyes were hostile and her mouth pinched into an unattractive grimace. "Yes, but do you think that will pay for three seasons for a foolish daughter who will not settle on one of the rich beaux her loving mother has paraded before her? I cannot believe the ingratitude, after all my hard work, and you will not so much as lift a finger to do what you are supposed to do."

The attack left Arabella breathless. "But you said . . . you said I need not marry, because I had Lord Drake in my pocket, and then you would not let me marry Lord Sweetan when I wanted to, and—"

"Lord Sweetan had no money! I wanted you to marry Sir Richard Fosdick, but you turned your nose up—"

"Sir Richard is ancient!" Arabella cried, leaping from her seat. "I accept that I must marry, but I will not marry a . . . a fossil! I want a *man*, not a dried up old prune! I want a man who can take me in his arms and—"

Lady Swinley's hand flashed up and the smack across Arabella's cheek echoed in the quiet chamber. Arabella held her hand to her cheek and stared down at her much shorter mother. "How could you do that?" she cried, tears starting in her eyes.

Eyes wide, pinched face bleached a ghastly white, Lady Swinley covered her mouth with one shaking hand. "I . . . oh, Arabella, my darling girl, I am sorry. I am overwrought." She collapsed on the chair near the vanity table. "I cannot face being poor! I cannot! I am too old to live in poverty, forced to rely on the charity of the church. The manor is mortgaged to the hilt and if we do not show signs of turning things around, or if you do not marry well and *soon*, we shall have to leave it and . . . and . . ." She broke down into tears, burying her face in her hands and sobbing.

Arabella, stunned to see tears coursing down her

mother's lined cheeks and through her fingers, felt
a moment of tenderness she had never experienced before. With all her faults, her mother was
still her mother. She approached the woman many
damned as cold, and put her arms around her
shaking shoulders. "Don't worry, Mother, you will
not have to leave Swinley Manor. I shall marry, and
marry well. I promise I will take care of you."

And she would start her campaign that very
night. Because first, she must eliminate the competition.

A book propped on her lap, True tried to read
by the flickering light of her candle. It was impossible, though, when her mind kept going back to
the scene in the parlor. She could not get out of
her mind how Drake had made his innocuous announcement after such a build-up! What had he
been thinking? It was guaranteed that more than
one person had thought there was an announcement of marriage in the offing.

And then Arabella had swooned. Was it genuine
this time? She had appeared insensible for a good
three minutes or more.

But what kept True's mind off Maria Edgeworth's *The Absentee,* was what she, and evidently
others, had thought Lord Drake was going to say.
The way he had started, and then bringing her
name into it—it had held every appearance of an
announcement that he intended to wed *her!* Was
that why Arabella had swooned when the real announcement turned out to be something so very
different?

Perhaps. Bella and Lord Drake had spent the
whole day together talking and walking, and maybe
she had discovered all there was in the viscount to
love and value. He was gentle and thoughtful,

good-natured and intelligent, gallant and . . . and she had no business cataloging his virtues. Had Bella fallen for the handsome lord?

True shivered, laid her book on the bedside table, and pulled the covers up over her shoulders, staring at the paneled walls of her elegant chamber. Her mind returned to the afternoon before. They had walked down to the brook and sat down to talk. The sun had been warm and she had felt sleepiness overtake her; before she knew it he was tilting her head back and kissing her with such gentle, persuasive passion, that she had found herself responding, unable to resist. But she could not fool herself. It was not as if she was out of her mind, or anything so ridiculous. She had *wanted* him to kiss her, had been hoping for it. Ever since the night at the inn when he had kissed her in the hallway, she had been wishing for a repeat of that caress to test her memory of a sweetness singing through her that she had never felt in her life.

But what had possessed her to lay with him on the banks of that brook, in his arms, reclining as if she were inviting him to . . . Her mind turned away from what her actions were an invitation to. He was too much the gentleman to take advantage of her that way. Instead, silence had fallen between them, as if the moment was too precious to spoil with words.

And they had slept together in the golden sunshine like two children, their arms wrapped around each other. Later—it must have been an hour or more that they stayed in that scandalous pose—she had awoken to find his fond gaze on her. She had been hideously embarrassed, her modesty finally awoken from a slumber deeper than her body's. She hardly remembered if she said anything, but she had scrambled away from him with flaming cheeks at the memory of her lax behavior. She was indeed lucky he was a true gentleman.

He had escorted her without comment back to the gig—they found the little stable boy dozing under a tree near the horses—and they had returned to Lea Park with Drake chatting happily about the school. Nothing had been said between them of their odd lapse from propriety.

But the next day he had devoted himself to Arabella. He had smiled at True, and had not avoided her company at any time, but his companionship was solely for her beautiful cousin. True had watched them walk away, golden heads together as they talked and strolled, making a gorgeous matched couple. Had he decided that he needed a helpmeet in his path? Was he intent on giving his mother's choice a fair trial?

There was a light tap at her door, and True said, "Come in."

Arabella slipped in, her long blond hair down around her shoulders. She looked hesitant and so very young. She stopped just inside the door, shivering and with an unhappy expression on her pretty face.

"What is it, Bella? Do you want to talk? Are you recovered?" True patted the bed beside her and Bella crossed the room and climbed on the bed as she had when she was a little girl, and in True's charge.

"Oh, True, what am I going to do?" she cried, snuggling close to her cousin and taking her hand.

Surprised but pleased by this return to the intimacy they had shared as children, True smoothed her cousin's blonde tresses away from her high, pale forehead. There were worry lines there, and True gently smoothed them, too. "What is it, love?" This was the cousin she remembered, the cousin who would come to her with her troubles.

When Lady Swinley had descended on the vicarage on Bella's seventeenth birthday and informed her daughter that they were to go to London, and this was likely the last vacation she would ever spend at the vicarage, Bella had wept on True's shoulder and promised that no matter what happened, the vicarage was her home. She was afraid of her mother she said, and what the woman had in mind for her.

No matter what, True had told her, she would always have a home with her cousins. She had meant it then and she still felt that way, no matter what divided them. Bella held the place in True's heart of another sister, just like Faithful.

"Sweetheart, what is the matter?"

"I—oh, True, what am I going to do? I have fallen in love with Lord Drake, but he does not love me, does he? Oh, what shall I do if he does not love me? I shall go mad with sorrow! I shall kill myself!"

Shocked but unwilling to let Bella see that she was, True enfolded her in her arms. She swallowed a lump in her throat, and said, "Hush, love, hush. Everything will be all right."

After her sobbing confession and a tormented torrent of tears, Bella slept in True's arms. True had shed some tears herself, but now was calm as she stroked her cousin's silky hair and stared into the dark. The candle had long ago burnt out, but sleep would not come to True for a very long time, she feared.

They were both in love with Lord Drake. Yes, she had finally admitted to herself her feelings. She loved the man, though she had intended to stay heart-whole. But Bella loved him, too, with the powerful love of one surprised by the emotion.

But what, or whom, was best for Drake? Should he marry at all? It was up to him, of course, but on the whole, True had started to think he would very soon come to the conclusion that marriage was his next step. Just the way he had phrased his announcement in the library showed that he was thinking of the future now, not the past. His mind had turned, and he could now look ahead. That was good and right, as it should be. He would make a superb husband and was capable, True thought, of great love.

His inherent sweetness had been displayed every day to True, in the little gestures of affection and preference toward herself, gestures that she saw now could be construed as, well, *brotherly*. He had kissed her, yes, and at least one of those kisses had been passionate. But that was the night at the inn; he was a little drunk and it was the first couple of days of their acquaintance. The kisses of the previous day, as sweet and lingering as they were, could have been intended as affectionate, friendly, she supposed. All of the other constructs she placed on them could be her own treacherous, feminine whimsy, seeing love where it was wanted so very much. She was inexperienced in such matters, and reluctant to jump to conclusions.

But one thing she did know; Drake was a decisive man when he wanted something. Look at how quickly he had acted on his idea for a school! If he had fallen in love with her, or meant more by those caresses than simple gestures of affection, he would have offered for her.

And she was meant for other things, was she not? She was meant to marry Mr. Bottleby and do God's work in the north. That was what her would-be fiancé believed. He felt that he had been called by God, and that she had been indicated as his suitable helpmeet. Granted, the fervor in his eyes had made True uneasy as he said that, but it was just the fervor of a God-fearing man, a *good* man.

What to do?

Bella stirred and mumbled. "Drake, oh, Drake, how I *love* you," she murmured.

True sighed, feeling a shaft of jealousy and pain lance her heart. If only there was some sign of what was right, of what she should do. "God, please send me a sign," she whispered. "Tell me what to do and I will do it, gladly and with my whole heart. I love him, but I will give him up forever if it is Your will."

Drowsily, Bella shifted. "Did you say something, True?"

"No, dear. Go back to sleep."

"Miss Becket, there is a letter for you." Lady Leathorne, sorting the mail as the ladies sat at the breakfast table lingering over coffee, handed a letter sealed with ivory wax over to True.

"It is from home," True said with a smile. "I have written my father several letters since I have been here, but he is a poor correspondent. I did not expect a letter in return at all."

"Feel free to read it, Miss Becket," the countess said. "We do not stand on ceremony here."

"Ah, it is not in my father's hand, but in my sister Faith's writing." She perused the contents. "Oh, no! Father has been asking for me! Faith does not say it, but he must be ill!"

"I am so sorry to hear that, my dear." Lady Leathorne laid down the letter she was reading.

At the same moment, Bella said, "Poor Uncle!" He was not her uncle, but her affection for the old man had given him that courtesy title. "Is he all right, True?"

True laid her hand over Arabella's. "I do not know; Faith does not say, but he hasn't been perfectly well for some time and he has been asking Faith when I am coming home. I can always make

him feel better. My sister does not know exactly
what helps his gout. They do not say what is wrong
this time, but sometimes his feet are so bad he
cannot walk. Poor Papa!"

"Perhaps you should go home for a time," Lady
Swinley said. She wore a frown of concern. "If
Becket is ailing, he will need you. You may use our
carriage if you like, True."

It was an unexpectedly generous offer, one that
had even Arabella looking at her mother in surprise, but True was grateful. And if she was wanting
a message from God as to where her rightful place
was, there could not be a stronger one than this.
Not that she thought that God had exacerbated
her father's poor health as some kind of sign, but
it surely was an indication of where True belonged.
"Thank you, Cousin. That is so very kind of you!"

She turned to her hostess. Her heart was leaden,
but at least she was clear about where her duty lay.
"Lady Leathorne, your gracious hospitality has
been . . . has been the most generous that I have
ever known. I have been overwhelmed by your and
Lord Leathorne's treatment of me, and Lord
Drake's kindness, but my father needs me and I
think I shall take my cousin up on her kind offer
of a carriage home. I will leave tomorrow."

Thirteen

True wandered the meadow that afternoon, thinking of all that she had experienced since coming to Lea Park. She had never truly been in love before, she realized. Her love for Harry had been the love of youth, and if they had married, she would have been a good wife to him, but she did not know if the kind of love she felt for Drake would ever have been theirs.

And that was a dangerous way to think, she knew. Especially after Bella's sobbing confession the night before, of her own love for Lord Drake. Between the two of them, it was clear who would make the better countess. She had feared all along that if Lord Drake had deigned to ask her to marry him, her own misplaced passion for him would have persuaded her that she should say yes. She could not have borne it if over the years her own inability to rule a household like Lea Park had turned Drake's infinite kindness sour, or if he had become bored by her prosaic nature. Arabella was more talented, more beautiful, and better trained for the role of countess. It was not false modesty, just realism.

So, she was in the unenviable position of having to hope that his feelings for her truly were of the brotherly sort. And she knew that she would have

to forget that hers had ever been anything more
than sisterly if she wanted to live happily and without regret.

The river lay before her, sparkling in the autumn
sunlight. The lush grass was yellowing and the
leaves were dropping off the trees; in the distance
she could see how a breeze tossed the treetops, a
harbinger of the colder weather to come, of winter.
Life moved on, changed, progressed, and she must,
too. She threw off her bonnet and sat at the base
of the big oak tree, the scene of precious memories
for her. It was going to be difficult to forget about
her love for Lord Drake, but she must, especially
if he and Bella came to an agreement. He would
be her cousin, then, and married.

"I thought I would find you here."

The shadow cast over her was a big one. She
looked up and smiled, her heart gladdened by the
sight of the viscount, tall and handsome, his stance
easier than it was when first they met. "This
seemed a good place to say good-bye to Lea Park."

Drake sat down beside her. "Yes, I have heard
you are leaving. I hope your father is not too ill?"

"I hope not," True said, with a worried frown.
"Faith, my sister, did not say exactly what his com-
plaint is, just that he wants me to come home. I
am hoping it is only his gout, as it usually is. But
the doctor was in some apprehension that he
would be unable to walk before long, and I pray
that is not the case."

Drake took her ungloved hand and kissed it, re-
taining it as they sat. "I will keep you in my
thoughts. Will you let us know how your father is,
and how you go on?"

True blushed. She looked down at their joined
hands, his long fingers curled protectively around
her smaller ones. "I will write to Bella."

"Bella . . . ah, yes, Arabella. Is that what you call her?"

She nodded. "Since she was a child. I was fourteen the first time she came to stay with us, this frail, sickly child of eight years. It was my mission in life to fatten her up. I never really succeeded in that, but she did become a radiant young woman."

"She is lovely," Drake said, squinting down at the river. He shaded his eyes with his free hand. "Look down there; a fish just jumped. I should have brought my pole and I could have taught you to fish."

"Bella knows how," True said, pushed on by some martyred little demon in her soul to try to advance the match between her cousin and the man she loved. She must be mad. "You would not know it to look at her, she is so elegant and beautiful, but she is up to every rig, you know. She can even play cricket. Bested the boys in our village at batting. They would not play with her after that."

"Ah, cricket! Hampshire is famous for our cricketers, you know. Yes, I saw her at battledore and shuttlecock; beat Conroy, and he is considered a fair hand at games. She is a sportswoman, to be sure."

Silence fell between them. True was uncomfortably aware of his hand engulfing her own, the heat from his palm, the way his thumb moved, caressing her fingers. They would have to curb this physical closeness they always fell into if he were to marry Bella. It would not be appropriate; it was inappropriate now! She tried to slide her hand out of his grip, but his hand tightened.

"Will you come back?" he asked, still staring down at the river.

"Come back?"

"Come back to Lea Park. Or are you so glad to

get away from this brooding, glum old soldier that you will forget about me entirely?" He chuckled, but the laugh broke and died. "Will you promise to return once your father is better?"

True thought about what he was asking. He said nothing about his feelings, nothing about love, he just liked having her around. Exasperating man! What did he want from her? What did he expect her to do, hang over his shoulder and help him woo her lovely cousin? Tears started in her eyes, but she determinedly blinked them away. "I think . . ."

"You will. I know you will." He pulled her close and cuddled her to him.

Contentment stole through Drake. Since his and True's afternoon at the new school, he had slept two whole nights with no nightmares, no wakefulness. There had been no furious faces in his dreams, no bloody corpses. It was strange to feel almost whole, and it was taking some getting used to. He glanced down with affection at True, tucked securely under his arm. When she came back, he thought that he might have a question to ask her. Let the vicar find another woman; this one was his. She had become as necessary to him as sunshine and fresh air, and now it appeared that she had healed his heart. For the first time he looked forward to the future.

Her cheeks were rosy with the sunshine's glow, and he could not resist. He stole a kiss. And then another. He turned her to face him and pulled her even closer, gazing down into her breathless face and searching eyes, as blue as the sky reflected in the river. He could not be mistaken; he was in love with her, and he was full of the hope that she returned his feelings. But it was certainly not appropriate to divulge his newly understood emotions, nor to ask her to marry him while she was

fearful of her father's health. It would have to wait
until next they met.

But he *could* taste those luscious lips once more.
He pressed a kiss to them, lost in a delirious delight that coursed through his body, savoring her
sweetness and allowing himself to experience fully
the dizzying feel of her body pressed to his, soft
breasts pushing against his waistcoat. He wanted
her so badly—he allowed himself to admit it now—
wanted her in every way a man could want a
woman. But he must not dwell on what marriage
would mean; how he could have her in his bed,
under him, loving him with her sweet, womanly
body. He released her, thinking that for his own
sanity he must leave her alone until she returned
to him. Standing abruptly, he said, "I must be going back up to the house. This afternoon Conroy
and I are riding over to Thorne House to see how
the renovations go on. I am—" He swallowed and
thrust his fingers through his hair, determined to
calm his racing pulse. "I am suddenly anxious that
the house should be habitable very soon. *Vaya con
dios,* as the Spaniards say, Truelove, until we meet
again. I pray your father is all right."

He turned and stalked away, up over the rise
and toward the house.

At first during the long journey home, True,
with only a quiet little maid for company, was lost
in contemplation of Lord Drake and their last moments together. Dazed by the experience and his
abrupt departure from her, she had sat a long time
staring at the river with unseeing eyes. What had
it meant? He had kissed her in a way that was *not*
brotherly; there could be no mistaking that. Was
he unsure himself? Was he torn between her and
Bella? He had stayed away from her the whole day

before and devoted himself to her cousin, and then the next day kissed her like that!

It was lucky that fate had decreed she was to leave Lea Park and Lord Drake, because she did not think she would have the strength to leave the field open to her compet . . . no, not her competition, her *cousin,* whom she loved very much.

By the time she had gone back up to the house an hour or so later, he was gone; as he had said, he had ridden with Lord Conroy over to Thorne House to stay the night. They were going shooting the next day in his own woods near Thorne House, and would not be back until late that next night, or even the day after that. She had dreamed of that last kiss all night long, it seemed, and could not help wondering what it meant. She needed time to think.

But the last half of the long journey—many hours on the road, even traveling post—saw her worries for her father increase to the point that she feared the very fact that Faith had not told her what was wrong was an indication that things were very bad indeed. What would she find when she came home to the vicarage? There had been influenza among some of the poor families; had he taken ill after visiting them?

They dropped the little maid off at her family's home in a nearby village—Lady Leathorne had pointed out that this was a way of giving True a chaperon, while letting little Betty go for a long-promised visit to her ailing mother—and continued on, arriving in the early hours of twilight. True directed Lady Swinley's driver to the nearest inn, where the stable would house the carriage before it returned to Lea Park in the morning, and then she dashed to the door, leaving her baggage by the roadside for their manservant Jem to pick up.

The light was on in the parlor. True let herself

in and raced into the room, looking wildly around for her sister. "Faith? Faith?" she called out. "What is wrong? Where is Father?"

"I am right here, my dear."

True turned to find her father in the doorway, pulling off his glasses. "Papa," she cried, and flung herself into his arms. "Papa, I was so afraid for you, and I pictured all kinds of terrible things, and when Faith did not say what was wrong with you, I imagined the worst. . . ."

Her father enclosed her in his arms and rubbed her back. "My dear little girl, I am not sick. What did Faith say in the letter? I did not want to alarm you. Come, let us sit down and you can tell me all."

They sat together in the homely small parlor off the main vestibule, and True glanced around. Home. This was home. The grand saloons and parlors of Lea Park did not have the warmth of this small shabby room, with furniture frayed at the edges, a pool of yellow lamplight spilling across tables littered with books and papers and material, and Patch, her father's elderly springer spaniel, sleeping on the hearth near the fire. Cook came in just then with the tea tray, and True presided over the flowered porcelain teapot.

"Faith is at her friend Alison's this evening," Mr. Becket said. "I think there is something in the air between her and Alison Wentworth's brother, but no one ever tells me anything."

"But Father, what is wrong that you asked Faith to call me home?" True curled up in her usual chair, a cast off from Squire Jacob's manor house and chewed in one corner by his old hound. "I thought to find you ill."

"Well," he said, looking just a little guilty. "My gout has been acting up, and there were two days when I could not walk, but Widow Saunders has been very attentive. In fact, I was thinking, True, that if you should marry young Bottleby, and things work out between Faith and her young man, I have considered asking Mrs. Saunders to throw her lot in with me."

"Throw her lot . . . Father! You think to marry?" It took a major adjustment in the way she viewed her father and the widow Saunders, but she could see now how the woman's solicitousness could have another meaning than just the natural kindness of a good and motherly woman. Were they . . . were they in love? For some reason the thought was heart-warming, that one could fall in love even in old age.

"Only thought about it, my dear." He slid his glasses back up his nose, then tilted his head and gazed over them at her in a familiar and much-loved gesture. "She has become an important part of my day, of late."

"Is that why you wanted me home? To tell me this?"

"N-no."

His hesitance was unlike him and True gazed at him shrewdly. He was evading the question. "Papa, you know you will tell me eventually what is bothering you, so you might as well tell me now."

Mr. Becket, instead of answering, got up and left the room, coming back a few minutes later with a letter in hand. He squinted down at it, pushed his glasses back up his nose again, read a few lines, and then handed the letter over to True.

Frowning, she read it through. "Of all the . . . I cannot believe . . . she had the nerve . . . OH!" She could not even speak, she was so furious, and she felt an angry blush mount in her cheeks.

"Is it not true, dear? What is she talking about? *Who* is she talking about?" His lined face sagged with worry, and his eyes behind the glasses held all the love and concern he could feel for his eld-est daughter.

True, mortified to have her private life and feelings put down on paper and made to sound so . . . so *tawdry*, put one hand to her scarlet cheek. She reread the letter. Lady Swinley wrote, *Dear, sweet True is being seduced by a nobleman with no motive but to pass away a few pleasant hours with a willing young lady. She has become most unguarded in her behavior, and has displayed her preference for everyone to see and remark upon. Trust me, my dear sir, I know the ways of the ton. He is dallying with her. I saw them kissing and holding each other with my own eyes, and I trust that you will do whatever is necessary to rescue poor, sweet, gullible True before it is too late!*

"Well, my dear? Is she lying? I cannot help but think that she must be, and yet I would lay that terrible accusation at no door unfounded. But I could easier believe she is lying than I could believe that you had forgotten yourself so far as to be kissing a man willingly. Did he impose himself on you? And if he did, why did you not come directly home?"

Oh dear. What could she tell him? For she had a feeling her cousin had witnessed the embrace on the terrace the night Drake asked her to go for a drive with him the next day, and so in good conscience she could not accuse Lady Swinley of lying. She had heard a rustle as of skirts that night, but had been lost in her own feelings and had not turned. And she had done so very much more, had gone so *very* much farther than even her cousin knew. Such was the price of moral laxity, she feared; the coming revelation would undoubtedly damage her in her father's eyes.

"Well, my dear? Does she lie?"

True stared down at her hands. "No, Father. She did not lie. I have kissed Lord Drake."

It took a lot of explaining, for in her father's mind feminine virtue was a fragile thing as much of appearances as of reality. A woman must not only *be* virtuous, but *appear* to be virtuous. He was sorely disappointed in her for allowing a trespass upon her person in such a way, especially since it was not followed by a proposal. Eventually, though, True talked him into believing what she was trying to accept herself, that Lord Drake's caresses were in the nature of brotherly affection. Finally, when her father was more comfortable in his heart, she kissed him on the forehead and retired to her bedchamber, tired to the bones from the emotional turmoil of the day.

But of course, sleep would not come. She was not fooled by Lady Swinley's insincere expressions of concern for True's virtue. The only thing that woman was concerned about was to trap Lord Drake for her daughter, and to remove anything or anyone she saw as an impediment to that goal. At first, anger toward her cousin burned. She acquitted Arabella of any part of the trick. Her young cousin did not have a devious bone in her body, nor would she stoop to alarming True with worries about her father. It was the mother.

But on reflection, she began to think that the woman had actually done her a favor. If Drake was torn between True and Bella, unhappiness for all concerned would be the sure result. With only Bella there and his mind healing, turning toward the future, he would soon fall in love, if he was not already there.

She had known she had to come home, if only to settle her own future with Mr. Bottleby. Poor man, he had been waiting long enough. Her father said that he was on a trip up north to see that his cottage was fit for habitation, and had left a message for her that he awaited her answer, still, and hoped to receive it when he came home, which would be in a week or ten days. They could be married by license, he said, for they would not have time for the banns. If there was reproach implied in the message, True could hardly blame the man. She had kept him waiting long enough, and he was kindness himself to be so patient.

And, so, her answer would be yes. If love was meant for her, it would come with Mr. Bottleby—Arthur; he was a good man. He must take up his duties in his new parish very soon, and she would be by his side eager to meet her future, a partnership of service to God and man. She heard Faith come up the stairs and hastily blew out her candle. Somehow, she did not want to talk right then.

Fourteen

"I say, Drake, should we not be getting back to Lea Park?"

Conroy fidgeted around the library as Drake shelved books in the new bookcases Stanley and his team had now finished, relishing the rich look of the scarlet and indigo and olive bindings against the dark wood. He wondered if True would like it. He had planned the new shelving and had contacted a London bookseller about some first editions he wanted, but that was before he had met Miss True-love Becket. He would want to consult her about her preferences once they were married, for this was a family library he was building, *his* family library. She was a reader, he knew that, and they had talked of books they had enjoyed and those they wanted to read. He advocated Scott's adventurous stories while she preferred the domestic tales of Miss Maria Edgeworth and the author of *Pride and Prejudice*. What a capital wedding present that would make to her! A first edition of . . .

"Drake! Should we not be getting back to Lea Park? It is terribly rude to leave Miss Swinley to cool her heels while you muck about with a lot of old books." Conroy stood glaring down at Drake and nudged a pile of books with his shiny boot toe, sending them spilling in a tumble over the carpet.

Exasperated, Drake righted the pile and said, "They are my parents' guests, Con, old man. If you are so set on it, why do you not go back alone?"

Through gritted teeth, Conroy said, "But, Drake, *old man,* Miss Swinley was invited because you evidently made a cake of yourself over her last year and raised everyone's hopes for a match."

Drake sat back on his heels on the blue-and-tan Aubusson carpet and stared up at his friend. Whatever had gotten into Conroy, usually the most even-tempered of fellows? "I did no such thing! Have you ever known me to make a cake of myself over some flighty chit?" He felt a twinge of guilt over his denial, but still! He may have flirted with her a little, but it was doing it up too strong to call it "making a cake of himself."

"She is not a flighty chit," Conroy said, angrily. "She is a respectable young lady, and has every right to be treated as such."

Standing slowly to stretch out his sore leg, Drake gazed at his friend with a speculative gleam in his eyes, and said, "So that is how the wind blows, eh? You fancy the pretty Arabella for yourself, and want to get back to Lea Park to cut me out of the running."

"Not at all, old man," Conroy sputtered.

Drake smiled to himself. If he was not mistaken, his friend was badly smitten with the fair Arabella. "All right, then, we have been here three days. We have hunted and played billiards and I have ordered new renovations, starting with my suite, for Stanley and his men to start. There is no real reason why we should hole up here any longer. We shall return to my parents' home."

Besides, he thought, as he climbed the stairs to give Horace the news that they were leaving, there might be a letter from Truelove to Arabella. He had thought of nothing but Truelove for the three days he and his friend had spent at Thorne House, wondering how she was, hoping her father was all right, wishing he had said something before she left of how he felt. There was a nagging dread somewhere in his mind, a superstitious twinge that not telling her he loved her had been unlucky. It was strange, for he was not a superstitious man. Some of his fellow officers in the army would not sleep without performing lucky rituals, or would not go into battle without saying certain words, and he had always scoffed at their irrationality, but now he would give anything if he could just go back three days and say "I love you" to Truelove. What if her vicar presented himself to her? Would she have him?

No, he could not believe that with the intimacy they had created between them, she would not know his feelings. She must! If she did not come back to Lea Park soon enough for him, there was nothing stopping him from traveling down to her home and posing his question. If she did not return within a week, he would do just that.

Lady Swinley paced up and down the carpet of the rose parlor.

"Mother, you will wear the carpet out with your constant pacing." Arabella glanced up from a letter she was writing on the small table near the fireplace.

"I cannot help it," Lady Swinley said, stopping and frowning at her daughter. "Where is the man? Why is he not back here?"

"If you are speaking of Lord Drake, I suppose he will come back when he feels like it."

"Ho, my girl, do not act as if this does not concern you." She approached the table, leaned over and shook a finger in Arabella's face. "It is almost November! How long do you think we can linger here with no engagement between the two of you and no sign of one in the offing? And with True out of the way, I thought you could be making some headway with the viscount."

"It is not my fault," Arabella sulked. "I did my best. Is it my fault if the great idiot takes this time to repair to his estate?"

Lady Swinley pushed away from the leather-topped table with a swift, inelegant movement, betraying her agitation. "You should have secured him before he departed! He was showing you the most particular attention before True left, and her leaving should have secured the deal. Once she was out of the way I thought you would have the freedom to pursue him properly, without her interference. Who would have thought your spinster cousin could cut you out of the running?"

Arabella glared up at her mother, who stood before the table with an ugly sneer on her face. "She has not cut me out of the running. Lord, but you make it sound like a fox hunt, like I should have Lord Drake's brush by now."

Lady Swinley once again planted her two hands on the table and leaned across it. "I do not think you are taking this seriously enough, my girl. We shall be the talk of the *ton* this coming spring, and not for desirable reasons, if you do not secure that "great idiot," as you call him, and his thirty thousand a year. How would you like those Stimson chits to wed before you? I hear that Charlotte has accepted Sir Richard Fosdick, and that Caroline is expected to be betrothed before the start of the new season. But you, with your looks, have not secured even—"

"My lord," Arabella said, rising and speaking loudly, trying to drown out her mother's strident voice before Lord Drake should hear her complaints. "Welcome back. I hope your time at Thorne House was pleasant."

Lady Leathorne presided over the tea table, dispensing cups of Bohea and plates of cakes with her usual aplomb. It was good that Drake was back, and he looked fine, really. But the first question he had asked when he arrived after a three day absence was whether there was any news of the vicar Becket, Miss Becket's father, a man he had never met! He was doing the pretty to Miss Swinley at that moment, while Lord Conroy talked to the earl, but still, the countess could not help noticing that he gave Arabella only half his attention. And in all truth, the girl was a vision in a pale plum day dress with dove gray ribbons, her silvery-blonde hair shining in the weak daylight that still came through the open curtains. She had begun, with a mother's fierce loyalty, to think that Arabella was perhaps not good enough for Drake, but they had spent some time together over the last few days and the girl was remarkably sensible, well-spoken, and no one could fault her breeding or bloodlines. She had not absorbed Isabella's crassness, it seemed, yet.

Drake caught her watching him, and came over to her with a murmured word to Arabella. "Mama, you look worried. What is wrong?" He sat by her and captured her hand.

How strange, she thought, as she ran her fingers through his mop of tawny golden curls. It seemed only yesterday that he sat beside her with his feet not touching the carpet, his legs were so short, and she did not have to reach up to ruffle his curls. And yet he would be three and thirty on his next birthday, at the end of December. "Nothing, my dear. Are you . . . are you sleeping well these days?"

His expression sobered, but he answered her. "Better. I have been a little restless, but . . . that is why I stayed at Thorne House. I want it to be ready—" He did not finish his sentence, but left it hanging in the air between them.

"Ready for—" No, she would not push it. It was as close as he had come to stating a future plan, and she would not push him. "I see Lord Conroy has taken advantage of your defection to sit by Arabella."

Drake glanced over and chuckled. "I fear he is besotted. She is fetching, isn't she?"

"She is beautiful. And really a nice girl, I think. She improves upon acquaintance. What say you?" She shot her son a sideways glance.

"Very nice. More intelligent than I at first thought, spirited, reasonably good-natured. A man could do far worse."

Lady Leathorne's hopes soared. Was he really looking seriously at Arabella Swinley with marriage on his mind? Oh, if he only would!

Lady Swinley swept into the room that moment. She waved a cream piece of paper that was crossed and recrossed with writing, around in the air. "Marvelous news!" she crowed. "Our little cousin, Miss Becket, has accepted her vicar and is to marry him within the fortnight!"

The mud, always the muck squishing up under his scarlet tunic! And the pain from the damned saber thrust shot through him. He was going to die. Andromeda's ponderous weight was burying him alive on the muddy field of Mont St. Jean, and all he could see were the faces of the dead, screaming out for his blood, shrieking like Valkyries for him to join them in hell.

He couldn't breathe! Another few minutes and he must perish, suffocated with the hideous guilt of a thousand deaths, those of the enemy, and those of his own men, men who would never see sweethearts nor babies, aged mothers nor frantic wives, again. Faces twisted in pain, crabbed hands clawed at him, dragging him . . .

"Sir! Major! You're right bedeviled again, sir, an' ya must wake up."

Drake awoke gasping and striking out with his fist, his pillow over his face, the case rent from his desperate clawing to escape the suffocating mud of the battlefield. Abruptly the night demons fled, leaving him shaking and weak with horror. "Oh, God, Horace! I thought I was back there; I thought I was dying again!" He sat, but doubled over and buried his face in the silky counterpane, pounding his fist into the mattress. "I cannot do this anymore! I thought this was over! Merciful God, I thought I was cured."

" 'Pears not, sir. 'Pears like you're not quite over it yet. But ya had a good run o' nights, sir, and that'll happen again."

Drake flung the covers back and slung his legs over the edge of the bed. "I don't think so, Horace. I don't think I shall ever sleep peacefully again. Get me my shirt."

"But there's a rain's set in, sir . . . my lord. You'll catch yer death, an' that's a fact."

"I don't give a damn," Drake roared, his fierce eyes blazing in an unusual show of temper. "Get my damned shirt and breeches, or I'll report you for—"

"To who will you be reportin' me, sir, beggin' yer parding. Her ladyship?" Horace stared at Drake, sadness in his brown eyes.

"Just get my breeches," Drake said, wearily.

Lady Leathorne, awoken by the angry roar of her son's voice, watched out the window, fretting. Yes, there he went down to the stable, and clad only in his shirt and breeches and boots! There was a steady, cold drizzle coming down; what did the foolish boy think he was doing? She laid her face against the cold pane and watched as a few moments later Drake galloped from the stables on Thunder, his favorite gelding. No more sleep for him that night, she guessed. Nor for her. She put on her wrap and went downstairs to wait.

"And so Miss Stimson said to Andrew Fetterly, 'Sir, you have ruined my train, and I would be very grateful if you would refrain from ruining my joke!' Isn't that delicious?"

Drake stared off into space, his handsome face, which in the last month had lost some of its gauntness, spoiled by a brooding expression. Arabella gazed up at him desperately, wondering how one charmed a man who did not even know one was there. No one had ever prepared her for that skill.

"Lord Drake," she said, hearing the angry edge to her voice but starting not to care. "Have you been attending?"

"What? Huh? Oh, I beg your pardon, Miss Swinley. You were speaking of a delicious, uh, a delicious . . ."

They walked together along the riverbank, near an enormous oak tree, and Lord Drake had stopped to caress the weathered bark as if it were the softest of skin. Arabella, bewildered, watched him. What was wrong with him? Was he mad? She had heard his screams the night before; they had awoken her from a sound sleep and a dream of the sparkling London season and a ball to end all balls. She shivered. And this was the man her mother wanted her to attach herself to for all time?

He had seemed better for a while, but the last few days had seen him lapse into his dark moodiness. Nathan, or rather, Lord Conroy, as she should call him, said that Drake had had several good nights at his own estate, but the nightmares had resumed at Lea Park. Perhaps that was the key. Once they married they need never stay at Lea Park, or if he did, she did not have to come.

His handsome mouth turned down into a scowl, Lord Drake slammed his heavy fist against the tree and turned back to her. "Does your cousin. . . . Does she ever change her mind, say one thing and do another?"

Arabella, her eyes wide at the unwarranted ferocity of Lord Drake's actions and the pain in his eyes, stuttered, "My c-co—True?"

"Yes. Miss Becket."

Arabella frowned and stared at the viscount. It was dreadfully disconcerting to find that all this time, it appeared the man had been thinking of True. Disconcerting and infuriating. "No. She is most decisive. Once she has made up her mind, she rarely relents."

"I was afraid of that."

Narrowing her eyes, Arabella crossed her arms across her chest in a most unladylike stance and stood in front of Lord Drake. She took a deep breath, her chin went up, and she said, "Sir, what is the meaning of all this?"

"All this? What do you mean?"

Arabella just glared. The viscount had the grace to look abashed.

"Uh, Miss Swinley, would you sit down by the river with me?"

He swept off his jacket and laid it on the long yellowing grass. Gingerly, careful not to tear the exquisite lace of her best walking dress, Arabella sat and neatly folded her gloved hands on her lap. Drake collapsed on the ground beside her and reclined lazily, a piece of grass in his teeth. Scandalized by such ungentlemanly behavior, Arabella refused to look his way, and thus was startled when he grasped her hand.

"Sir?" she gasped.

"Miss Swinley, please relax. I do not bite." His tone was sardonic, and he retained her hand in his.

It felt like a prison, she thought, regarding his large hand engulfing the fawn glove. "I did not think that you bite, sir. I was just taken by surprise."

"Have you never had your hand earnestly pressed by one of your London suitors? Has no one ever stolen a kiss from you before?"

Arabella stared down at the brooding man as though he were a snake in the grass rather than a viscount. "I really do not think that is any of your concern, sir," she said.

"Kiss me," he commanded.

Arabella jerked her hand away from Drake and stood, brushing at her skirts in case any errant blade of grass lingered. "I will not stay to be insulted, sir." Head held high, she stalked away, leaving Drake watching her with a bemused expression in his mud-brown eyes.

What had come over him to be so appallingly rude to a girl who had done nothing to merit it? he wondered. It was unpardonable, and unlike him. Disgusting and distasteful the depth into which he had sunk. He had become slovenly, even more so than usual, and exhaustion was wearing him down. But he missed True. He missed walking with her and talking with her, and . . . yes, he especially missed stolen hours kissing her and incidentally sleeping in the autumn sunshine, feeling her small hand tangled in his hair. Every moment they had spent together, sleeping and waking, seemed precious now, doubly so because there would never be more. The memories he had of her were counted and numbered. He had taken stock like a careful shopkeeper, and they would have to last him the rest of his days.

She was to marry her vicar. He had seen her words with his own eyes, had it thrust at him in triumph. The damned letter Lady Swinley had been waving around was one written to Arabella, but the baroness had evidently read it before it ever got to its intended recipient. Then she had shoved it in front of Drake's eyes and bade him read it as "he had been so concerned about the vicar, and it contained news of Mr. Becket, too."

He had not been fooled about her intentions, but neither could he resist being sure she was not lying. She would do that as surely as she would manipulate people to her own ends.

Her father was fine, True reported; his illness was just his gout flaring up as usual. Some days were bad, some good. It went on to prepare Arabella for "some very good news." She had decided to marry Mr. Arthur Bottleby. There was no time to invite her cousins to the wedding, as they were to be married by license as soon as was possible, and then they would travel to his northern parish as their honeymoon. She was very, very happy, she said, and Drake had no reason to disbelieve her. All his presentiments of dread had come true then, and she was lost to him forever.

That evening a headache started, and he had known that he was headed for a nightmare. Sure enough, two hours after closing his eyes it had begun, and then he had flung on his clothes and gone riding in the frigid drizzle. He shivered, feeling the ache behind his eyes. He dare not lay his head back on the ground, not even in this place that was precious to him, the oak tree where she had held him for the first time, for the nightmare would come again as it always did, and he would die once more in his dreams.

Wearily, he heaved himself to his feet and limped home.

Fifteen

"Drake, dear, you look feverish. You have been out in the pouring rain riding again, haven't you, last night? That makes two nights in a row." Lady Leathorne gazed across the table at her son, noting the two high spots of color on his sharp cheekbones.

"Don't coddle the boy, Jess. He'll be right as rain." Lord Leathorne plowed through his plate of mutton, while the others politely averted their eyes. Watching Lord Leathorne eat was too much like watching wild dogs pull apart a sheep's carcass, if any one of them could have seen that sight to make the comparison.

Lady Leathorne held her own counsel, and did not reply to her husband.

"I am fine, Mother. Nothing a good night's sleep wouldn't cure." His tone was wry, but Drake realized the justice of his mother's concern. He really did not feel well. It probably had been foolish to go out the night before to ride after his usual dream, but nothing helped him work off the horrors like riding hell for leather across the dark fields, and a little rain had never stopped the war, had it? And he was in his thirties; it was time his mother stopped worrying over him like a child.

Lady Swinley, eyes glittering almost as if she were fevered, too, said, "Arabella, dear, you should make your special nighttime tisane for his lordship, and I'll warrant he would sleep like a lamb."

Miss Swinley's expression warned that the tisane was more likely to guarantee an eternal sleep for the daring drinker, for her eyes glinted like jade, hard and cold. She glared at her mother and shook her head almost imperceptibly.

"Drake should go to sleep with a calf's foot beneath his pillow. That's what m'mother swears by. Makes the nightmares just trot right by you," Conroy said.

Since no one at the table had mentioned nightmares, Drake shot his friend a disgusted look.

Conroy reddened. "Didn't mean to imply. . . . I say, anyone up for whist tonight?"

Drake lost the rest of the conversation, as all entered to cover the awkward moment. As if everyone in the house did not know, by then, that he had nightmares, Drake thought, what with his howling and screaming down the house. The night before had been especially bad, thus the long ride in the rain once more. And this day the rain had continued, so they had all been forced to stay inside and pretend to be a merry company of friends. Conroy had devoted himself to Arabella Swinley, as usual, and Drake had wandered the house, not quite knowing what to do, but too restless to just sit with a book. There was scads of preparation to putting together the Drake School, but somehow he had lost enthusiasm for that project. He would see it through, but perhaps he would delegate some of the work to Horace, who was wholeheartedly for the idea.

He was lonely, he realized, since True had left, despite being surrounded by family and company. He had fallen into the habit of talking things over with her, anything and everything. She would sometimes listen, sometimes offer her own opinion, and sometimes flat-out contradict him. But that was what he liked. She asked questions, she debated, she disagreed, she never, *ever* flattered; in short, there was no one else to equal her.

Lady Swinley and her daughter would agree with anything he said; a pair of fortune hunters, the two of them. His mother—well, one did not confide some things to one's mother. He had a feeling it gave her the cold horrors to think of him in the kind of danger he was in on the battlefield. And forget his father. Sometimes he felt as though they didn't even speak the same language. Conroy, the best friend of his youth, frankly did not want to hear about it. Drake had come to believe that his friend thought that he exaggerated his tales of the war. He never came right out and said it, but it was in the rise of his elegant eyebrow and the tilt of his head.

Or maybe he, Drake, was just getting too damned sensitive. He wanted True back, but that chance was gone forever. She had made her choice and by her own words was happier then she had ever been in her life. He had to believe that the spark he had felt between them was one-sided, that she had merely been a polite listener and a concerned friend.

He tried to believe it, but he couldn't. *Damn* her for throwing her life away before he ever got a chance to offer her his own, whatever of it she wanted. He could not be angry, though; she had what she wanted, he hoped. She would be happy. And was that not what he truly wished for her?

"True, can I come in?" Faith stood at the door of the room they called the library, though it was more like a closet with shelves than anything resembling the grand rooms at Lea Park and Thorne House.

"Of course, widgeon," True said to her sister, with an affectionate glance. Faith had been tiptoeing around her for days, asking to join her, watching her when she thought her older sister didn't know. Somehow, in a way only sisters would understand, Faith had divined that something had happened at Lea Park, something extraordinary. But as True would not—*could* not—confide her feelings to her younger sister, Faith was left worried and cautious.

She sidled into the small room and perched on the arm of the only other chair, a heavily carved, oaken Stuart monstrosity. True met her gaze. "What is it, hon?" she asked, setting aside her pen and paper.

"Do you really mean to accept Mr. Bottleby?"

"If he is still of a mind to take me as his wife, yes." True tried to subdue the faint queasiness and panic that accompanied that statement.

"Do you love him?" Faith's eyes were wide, and they sparkled the same blue as True saw when she looked in the mirror.

"No, I don't love him, or at least not in a romantic way," she said, calmly. "He knows that. We have spoken of it, and he believes that it is enough that we like each other, respect each other, and want to work together to help people."

Faith slid down into the chair, looking about five years old in her pale-blue dress and white apron, her dark curls tied up in a blue ribbon. She had evidently been in the kitchen making pastries, because a dab of flour adorned her nose, adding to the impression of extreme youth. She was one and twenty, though, and not nearly as naive as her gaze led people to think. "I don't think you should marry him. I think you should marry the other gentleman."

"Faith, what are you talking about? There is no other gentleman!"

Rosy lips set in a stubborn line, Faith said, "Tell me about him, True. You have never kept anything from me before, and I think it is simply dreadful of you to start now, just when there is something interesting to tell."

"Honestly, honey, there is no other man who has proposed to me."

"P'raps not, but there *is* another man," Faith said shrewdly. She curled her feet up under her, and said, "I shall simply plague you until you tell me about him. Or I will write to Bella. She'll tell me, if you won't."

"Don't you dare!" True gasped. Wouldn't that make things awkward, if Faith took it into her head to question Arabella as to the identity of "another man"? True gazed down at the paper in front of her for a moment. She had been composing a list of things to take away with her to her new home, and things to leave. She had spoken with the widow Saunders, and that good woman was ready and willing to help with the housekeeping at the vicarage any time it should overwhelm Faith, which it was likely to on any given day, as Faith had a tendency to go off on a whim if she thought of something she wanted to do. True had spent a good deal of time over the past week with Mr. Wentworth, the man Faith was "walking out" with, and liked him. He was steady, a barrister and a good ten years older than Faith, but very much, from all signs, in love with True's little sister.

Their father approved, and True did, too. With both the girls gone, their father would finally feel free to marry the widow Saunders after his lengthy spell as a widower. True wanted that for her father, after seeing how the woman coddled and cared for the vicar. She was a youthful fifty or so, with married daughters and sons, and she had been spending more and more time at the vicarage; True now realized what the attraction was. It was mutual, apparently, a love match if ever there was one. She had seen it in both of their eyes when they looked at each other, and it touched her deeply.

And, so, life was changing for them all. And why was she keeping anything from her sister? She would trust Faith with any secret, and this one was really no different. It might help her to talk it over.

"If I could *choose* anyone in this whole world to marry," True said, absently, fiddling with the quill, "I would chose Wycliffe Prescott, Lord Drake. And not because he is Lord Drake, but because he is Wy; dear, brave, sweet Wy."

"Lord Drake!" Faith breathed. "How *grand* that sounds. Is he handsome?"

Closing her eyes, True smiled. "He is utterly beautiful, like the stained-glass window of Saint Michael in Papa's church. He has golden hair and golden eyes, and his face looks like it is carved; his very *bones* are beautiful. But he has suffered, and you can see it in his eyes when he doesn't know anyone is looking at him. When he is happy, they glow gold, but when he is disturbed, they muddy to brown."

"How has he suffered?" Faith asked.

"He was a soldier, a major general, though he is not above his middle thirties. But he has a sensitive soul, so the death around him, the death he was forced to mete out as a soldier—it has affected him deeply." True felt the sorrow in her own heart for her friend. She had thought about him often over the past week, and hoped he was still doing well. She saw no reason why he should not continue on the road to mending as he seemed to be, but somehow she was uneasy about him.

By the time they headed up to their shared bedroom an hour later, True had told Faith everything. She had cried a little, laughed a little, and sighed a lot over unrequited feelings she had done her best to suppress and would try to conquer before her wedding day. It all seemed unreal so far, since she had still not told Mr. Bottleby her decision. When he came back she would have to, and subdue any residual affection for Drake, but until then she could live in this state of suspended reality.

After they had donned night rails and True had blown out the candle, Faith spoke once more, drowsily, and as though from a distance.

"True? I forgot to tell you what I came in the library to tell you. A message came this evening. Mr. Bottleby is back, and will be coming to the vicarage tomorrow or the next day for your answer."

The day had started with wet, tired, desperately hungry troops awakening from restless sleep in whatever accommodation could be found, the rumble of their yawns and groans and voices like distant thunder. Men slept in cornfields, in the orchard of La Haye Sainte—this was a farmhouse that Wellington had ordered fortified as an outpost and one anchor of his battle area; the other two outposts were a farm called Papelotte and the chateau known as Hougoumont—in hastily rigged tents of standard issue blankets. Drake had spent the night with the select group of commanders in the company of an energetic Wellington. He took his orders from the duke, returned to the field, rallied his troops, and proceeded to move in the patterns decided on the previous night, all on no sleep and little food.

Now it was hours later, late afternoon, and La

Haye Sainte was at the center of the fight. All around the Belgian, Dutch, German and British forces the enemy cannonade pounded like thunder; smoke filled the air, obscuring even the burning sun. Then utter silence, and then, more frightening to the experienced among the troops, the insistent drumming of the *pas de charge* and shouts of *vive l'empereur* by tens of thousands of voices, followed by massive columns of French infantry marching on the allied positions.

Incredibly, impossibly, the inexperienced prince of Orange, too young at twenty-two to be Wellington's second in command but forced on the duke by virtue of the theatre of war, now Dutch territory, gave the command to the King's German Legion, a group of seasoned Hanoverian warriors, to advance. Advance! Christian von Ompteda, experienced and tough commander of the KGL, knew how enormous a mistake it was. There were holes in his line, but his men were in a good defensive position on the right of the crossroads behind La Haye Sainte, a position they could and would defend as long as there was one man left. They should hold fast. Everyone knew that. To move forward was the command of a young and inexperienced soldier, but the prince's pride would not let him back down even when shown his error.

There was nothing for Ompteda to do but obey his superior officer, for obedience in the army was the only way to ensure order and discipline. Once that broke down, each man felt justified in making his own decisions, and defections were inevitable. So Ompteda would lead his men to their death, and his own death, for honor would not allow him to live while his men died.

Drake, in command of the Kent Light Dragoons, watched in horror as the Germans advanced toward the French only to be slaughtered, all in five min-

utes, it seemed. He shouted an order and spurred
Andromeda into a gallop, leading his men in a
charge down the slope to try to save them, but it
was futile. The next seconds were a blur of smoke
and sound and thunder. The Germans were mostly
dead, but Ompteda, valiant to the end, leaped the
hedge into the garden of the farm, his sword
flashed, and then he went down. Drake's cavalry was
forced back, but not before Drake turned Andromeda, gallant horse as she was, to face a French
officer who raised his saber to cut Drake down. Instinct, pure and simple, enabled Drake to thrust with
his sword, spearing the Frenchman neatly through,
even as his thigh was being sliced open.

Drake saw the man's moustached face contort as
he was dying, and then Andromeda was falling and
Drake spilled from the saddle to be buried beneath
his horse as around him the battle raged on, with
shouts and artillery, and the screams of the
wounded and dying. And he was dying, too, suffocating, being pushed down into the muck and mire
of the battlefield by poor Andromeda as she
grunted and heaved, and then died from some unknown artillery wound that Drake had not even
seen her take. His own blood was pumping into
the gray-red mud of the field by La Haye Sainte,
and every breath might be his last.

His men, so many of them lost at Quatre Bras,
were valiant, but were driven back from that impossible battle. Brewster, Wayne, Williams, Connolly,
Stoddart, Andrews . . . so many young men in
Drake's company had fallen, cut to ribbons, slaughtered. But so many others fought on with a single-
minded determination that would win the day, or
die trying.

But for Drake the fighting was over. The day
turned into evening as he alternated between consciousness and unconsciousness, not knowing if the

English and allied forces were winning the day or going down in ignominious defeat. He was so very thirsty, as though he was in Hades and that was to be his eternal torment; a quick death was not to be his, he feared. The battle raged on and then seemed to drift away from that field, hell on earth for those who lay dying, their groans a chorus of tormented agony. Drake lingered in a hazy world between life and death, feeling his blood seeping from him, hearing people die, seeing only Andromeda's great flank and young Captain Lewis's dead, contorted, bloody face as twilight fell.

Time ceased to have meaning.

All around him the dead and dying were being looted by the French who had taken La Haye Sainte, and some who made a fuss about it were murdered where they lay. That barbarism was not confined to the French; allied forces did the same nasty work. The mercifully murdered were the lucky ones, Drake thought; no one would see him under his beast, and he would be forced to die little by little, his vision turning black as life dripped out of his severed vein into the mud. As the sun descended, he did not even have the blessing of unconsciousness any more, but heard every scream, every tortured last breath, every death rattle around him.

His long career had prepared him for death, he had thought. He had done what he was ordered as a soldier, and had done the best he could for his men as a commander. He had killed often, nearly died a couple of times, but nothing, *nothing* he had ever experienced, had prepared him for this agony. The pain was familiar, for he had been wounded at Badajoz, but this infernal waiting, *waiting* to die. He had always thought death would come quickly, with a musket ball or a saber slash. But now, the thirst and the horror, the utter futility and certainty of death and yet lingering life . . .

And then the dead began to come to him one by one, faces he had never forgotten, though he thought he had. The young Frenchman, his first kill as a raw recruit. *"Ne tirez pas,"* and then his shot, and then finding the miniature of wife and babe and the unloaded rifle. And him spending hours mourning for the woman and child who would perhaps starve without husband and father. And then other faces hovered over him, other men he had killed, one after the other, laying the guilt for their deaths at his door, all demanding his life in payment.

June 18, 1815 was a day without end for Major General Drake. Faces hovered, hands, claws of the dead, reached out and smote him in the ribs, tore at his clothes, pulled his hair, and he felt it before he heard it, felt the scream well up in his throat, and to his everlasting shame, erupt from him as though he were an untried ensign of seventeen, a boy not a man.

Suffocating; he was suffocating, and he would shoot himself before he would die like this, dribble by dribble. He was a man; he could not suffer this torment when his loaded pistol was in his tunic. If he could just reach it, he would hold it into his mouth and blast his way into eternity, rather than suffer with all the demons of hell clawing his face and tormenting his mind. The pistol! It was in his hand and he would—

"Sir . . . Major, I'm here. It's Horace, sir, let me have the gun, easy like, let me . . ."

Sixteen

Lady Leathorne stood and wrung her hands, gazing down at the sweating, twisting man who was her son. She put her hand to his damp forehead. "He is burning up! What must we do, Sergeant? What is best? I have never seen him like this."

Horace, who was called "the sergeant" by staff and family alike though he had never attained that rank, wrung out a cloth and applied it to Drake's forehead, only to have it flung across the room by his restless patient who uttered an oath more suited to the army barracks than a lady's presence. "I don't rightly know, milady. Ain't never seen him like this, neither, and that be fact, even at his worst, in the field hospital. Coulda knocked me over with a feather last night when I came inta his room like normal when he's a'screamin' and a'carryin' on, and he was crouched under that there bolster, with his pistol in his hand and raisin' it to his mouth."

That unusually long speech on his part was followed by more nursing, all of which was cursed roundly by Drake. Lady Leathorne, horrified by how close she had come to losing her son again, paced in the background, wringing her hands and feeling useless for the first time in all her years. The physician, summoned at dawn, bustled back into the room with a jar of wriggling, skinny black leeches.

"We have to bleed him," Mr. Jackson said. "We must bleed the fever off. I need a little sweetened milk to make the leeches bite."

Over the next hours Drake was cupped and bled profusely, but it did nothing to reduce his fever, nor his restlessness. The household was turned upside down as apothecaries, surgeons, other neighboring doctors, all were called in to give their opinion. All agreed that he had taken ill from a lack of sleep combined with his midnight wanderings in the rain, but not a one agreed on treatment. Their arguments were vociferous and lengthy.

Sweat it out, one said, as the medical men held a consultation in the library. He must sweat out the fever. Let him get as hot as he will, and burn the fever out of him.

Keep him cool, the other said. Cold water bathing, ice from the ice house, no covers at all. He must be allowed to cool naturally to get rid of the fever.

Still another said a plaister of herbs was needed, and the gloomiest of them all predicted a quick decline and death for Drake. He, poor fellow, was physically attacked by the apothecary, who had a long-standing grudge against him for stealing away a patient and curing him.

Finally, the butler expelled the medical men and the household was hushed. Arabella crept around the house, frightened by the reports she had heard of Drake, who, in his ravings, had attempted to kill himself. Annie, the Swinleys' maid, had heard it from a scullery maid, who had overheard the housekeeper and butler talking. It was said the butler had it from a footman, who had been summoned by Horace Cooper when he needed help subduing the viscount.

And this was the man they all wanted her to

marry? Her mother was urging her to demand to
stay with the fevered Drake, to prove to Lady
Leathorne that she was wifely material. Arabella
had a sneaking suspicion, though, that her mother
intended to complain that her daughter had been
compromised by staying with the viscount while he
was ill, and thus force the marriage on the
Leathornes. It was a despicable tactic, and one to
which she would never sink. If only True was there!
When she was ill as a child it was only ever her
cousin who could make her feel better.

Among the household, only Lord Conroy went
on as before. He was certainly disturbed by his
friend's illness, but did not seem to think it necessary to visit him, and had no opinion of whether
the man would survive or not. Arabella thought
him cold, but still, he was soothing company for
her jangled nerves and so she spent most of her
time with him.

By the second day of Drake's illness, Lady Leathorne
was beginning to despair. It was very early in the
morning, well before dawn, and at the very least he
was quiet, though that did not offer her any hope.
She would rather see him fighting his illness than
succumbing and lying still as death. She had sent
Horace off for a few hours rest, but she had had to
back up her recommendation with the information
that if he did not go and sleep, she would have him
locked in his room until he did. She was grateful
for the man's devotion to her son, and considered
him an honored friend for saving Drake's life at Waterloo, but he would be no good if he did not get
any rest himself.

And besides, she wanted a little time alone with
her son. She did not say it even to herself, but if
he should die, she wanted to be beside him.

She sat by her son's bed and smoothed his sweating brow with a damp cloth wet with an infusion

of chamomile and lavender. He moved, restless. His gaunt face was so very beautiful in the dim light from the candle, like an icon of some ancient saint, and Lady Leathorne found herself praying for direction, though she had never prayed for anything in her life, not even when she knew Drake was on the battlefields, though after he was home she quite often offered thanks for his deliverance. Quite simply, she did not believe in a God who had time for every human in His care.

But now she prayed. She prayed for some idea as to what to do, for the strength and wisdom to know good advice from bad and for guidance so they would not kill him before curing him.

He murmured something. She leaned forward, trying to catch the meaning. He had said nothing for two days but shouted battle instructions and horrible screams, as though all the souls in hell were dragging him down. But this was just a gentle murmur. She brought her ear near his lips.

"Truelove."

That was all. He said it again, and it was the name. Truelove. Miss Truelove Becket. Lady Leathorne remembered the serenity on Drake's face when he would come back from walking with the young woman; was it possible that Miss Becket's tranquil presence brought some kind of peace to her troubled son's mind? If there were even a tiny possibility that this was so, she could not ignore that hope, faint as it was. A mother's instinct had to count for something, and she knew what she had to do. Summoning her most trusted maid to sit with her son, a woman who had been a part of the household since Drake was a baby, she descended and called for the butler. The household being so upset with Lord Drake's illness, a haggard Marcot held himself available at all hours of the day and night. He stood stiffly before her, not allowing weariness to affect his erect posture one whit.

"Marcot, summon the driver and tell him I shall require the carriage—the fastest closed one we have. I need it ready and outside the door in three quarters . . . no, half an hour."

"Are you taking a journey, my lady?" As well-trained and disciplined as he was, he still could not conceal the surprise he must have felt at such a command, and at such an hour!

"I am. Do it. I shall be back down in half an hour. Have Mrs. Jones come to me in my chamber. I have instructions for the staff while I am gone."

True paced nervously around the tiny space of the library. It was twilight, and Mr. Bottleby was due any time. She was to give him his answer, and then she would have taken the irrevocable step that would lead her to her new life. Faith was out walking with her new fiancé. Mr. Wentworth had asked that very morning to speak to Mr. Becket, had offered for Faith, and had been accepted.

And now she would accept Mr. Bottleby.

She could hear a carriage outside the door and stiffened. Had he seen fit to make a formal call, carriage and all? Well, Penny knew to conduct her visitor into the library, so she would await him calmly. She folded her hands together, but found that would not do, for she gripped them so tightly, they hurt.

Despite having made the decision in what she believed was her own best self-interest, she felt a cold panic well up into her. There was still time. She could tell him *no* and send him away.

And what? Stay in her father's home for the rest of her life, a burden to him, keeping him from a marriage that was sure to be the sweet balm of his old age? For he would not marry if True did not.

With an overdeveloped feeling of delicacy, he did not believe he could ask either woman, True or Mrs. Saunders, to give way and let the other rule the roost. Truelove he would not ask because she was his daughter, and had been the lady of the house for so long, and Mrs. Saunders he would not ask because as his wife she could justly expect to be the female in charge. Perhaps, if True could convince her father that she did not mind Mrs. Saunders taking over her duties . . . but no, Papa would not . . . oh, what would she do? She had thought her mind was made up, her future settled, and here she was conning it over in her mind yet again, and with Mr. Bottleby just outside the door.

What was taking Penny so long to show him into the library?

There was a commotion outside the door, and True had just decided to go and investigate when the library door opened and Lady Leathorne swept in.

"My lady!" True exclaimed, curtsying. "What are you doing—I mean—"

Lady Leathorne, looking older than True had remembered her, her jowls sagging and her face deeply lined, came across the room and clasped the younger woman's hand. "Miss Becket. I gather from your maid's babble that you are expecting a visitor. I will be brief; the good Lord knows there is nothing to take time over."

"What is wrong?" True cried. "Is it Arabella? Is she ill? Or Lady Swinley?"

"No, they are well. It . . . it is my son."

True felt a constriction in her heart, but somehow she was not surprised. For the last couple of days she had had an uneasy feeling that she could not trace. As calmly as she was able she took the countess's hand in both of hers and said, "The nightmares? Are they back again?"

"Not just that."

Lady Leathorne collapsed in a chair and sobbed, covering her face with her gloved hands. True rang for Penny. "Tea, Penny, and quickly." True knelt by Drake's mother. "My lady, tell me what is wrong with him. What has happened?"

Lady Leathorne poured out her story in quick, jerky syllables; Drake, troubled sorely by his returning nightmares, had gone out one late night when it poured, and had not come back until morning, drenched and exhausted. It was the second night in a row he had done that, but this time his health was affected. That day he had gone from bad to worse, a hectic flush overtaking him about dinnertime. He retired at his usual time, but the household was awoken by his screams a couple of hours later. He had barricaded himself in his room, screaming in the midst of a kind of waking nightmare. His valet, Horace Cooper, had found him cowering under a bolster with his loaded pistol in his hand, ready to shoot himself in the mouth. He was convinced that he was on the verge of death and had decided to end it all more quickly.

True was sobbing and clutching the countess's hands before the end of the story, but she swallowed her terror. "What can I do, my lady?" she cried, her voice thick with tears. "Why did you come here? I am not a doctor."

Lady Leathorne, her face lined with pain and fear, gazed down at True, holding her hands in her own in a fierce grip. "Drake has been incoherent for two days. Not one word he has said could be understood. It is all inarticulate screams of pain such as I have never heard and . . . and battle orders about advancing in aid of . . . of the King's Legion, or something like that. But last night he was finally calmed. I fear he is not better, though, and in fact might be slipping away. As I sat there, I could see him forming one word. I got as close to him as possible, and he whispered again, and I caught the word. Truelove. He said *your name.* Out of all the horror of the last two days, your name is the first thing I can understand from him. Truelove. I don't know what else to do. Will you . . . will you come? Please? He was calmer when he was with you. *Please* say you will come."

True, tears streaming down her face, gazed up at the older woman. "Of course I will come."

Lady Leathorne, unwilling to even wait as long as it would take for True to pack, left that hour. True was to follow in a hired post-chaise with fresh horses that Lady Leathorne had ordered and was sending from the village inn.

With a babbled explanation to Faith, and a slightly more coherent one to her father, True made ready to go. Her bags were just being brought down the stairs by their man, Jem, when Mr. Bottleby was shown into the hall by a flustered and frightened Penny.

"Miss Becket, what is going on here? I am expected, am I not? What does your maid mean by denying me at the door?"

Mr. Bottleby looked cross, but willing to be placated by an explanation. True could not believe that she had forgotten what just an hour ago seemed the most important visit in her life. But she could not linger. He must understand! She would believe in the goodness of his heart, though it was surely trying his patience after how long he had waited for her answer.

"Mr. Bottleby, I am so sorry. Will you come into the library for a moment? I am sure once you hear my destination and the reason, you will kindly forgive me." She led him to the library and, against all decorum, closed the door behind them. Surely, as they were almost betrothed, they could be allowed these few moments.

He stood rigid, waiting. True stared at him, wondering how to start, how to explain. His face, darkly handsome under a careless tumble of dusky hair many a lord would cry for, was stern. He said not a word, and she could see that he was angry by the jump of a nerve under his left eye.

She took a deep breath and rallied her courage. If they were to be married she must feel that she could say anything to him, and that he would trust her judgment. This was not a propitious start to their engagement, for she still intended to tell him she would marry him—she must make the leap of faith into her future—but there was no help for it.

"You knew I was making a visit with my cousins, Lady Swinley and Miss Arabella Swinley." He nodded. "Lord Drake, the heir to the Leathorne earldom, was Major General Drake of the Kent Light Dragoons." Oh, she would need to speed this up! Twilight was far advanced, but she would travel all night. There was a full moon, and the roads were dry. With luck she would be there by noon.

She squared her shoulders and gazed up at Mr. Bottleby. If only she could see some softening in that stern jaw or a light in those dark eyes! "I must go to a friend, who is very ill. He . . . his mother was just here, and she is frantic for him. I leave within the hour."

Bottleby frowned. "This friend, I take it he is this Major General Drake?"

True nodded.

"He is ill, you say. Why did his mother come here?"

"He . . . he apparently said my name. It is the first coherent thing he has said for two days."

"Why would he say *your* name?"

True, stung by the disbelief in his voice, said, "We talked often while I was there. We became friends. He spoke to me of his . . . his dreams about the war, and how they troubled him. Perhaps he is harkening back to those conversations in his mind."

"Miss Becket, you are not a doctor, and they are not your family. I advise you to stay home and not jump at their behest simply because they are of the nobility." This pronouncement had very much the feel of the pulpit.

True stared at Mr. Bottleby, noting for the first time the pinched look of his features, and the hard glint in his eyes. She had witnessed many acts of kindness performed by the curate. It was what had first attracted her attention to him. He was undoubtedly a good man, and she must appeal to that side of him. She stepped close to him and looked up into his eyes. If only he would reach out and touch her, just her shoulder or her arm; could he not see that she was upset and worried for a friend? She steadfastly tried not to contrast his cold eyes with the warmth of a pair of tawny gold ones, but it was too late. She remembered the warmth of Lord Drake, the caring and fondness in his eyes. Could she live without that from a husband, a husband with whom she would need to be intimate, who would become her life partner and soul mate?

"Arthur," she said, softly. "He is ill and troubled, and his mother is worried. I cannot ignore their plea, not after the kindness they have shown me, and just out of simple human caring! I will disregard what you said about me responding simply because they are of the nobility, for I feel that was beneath you, and I do not believe you meant it. I *must* go."

"Miss Becket," he said, emphasizing the fullness of her name, in contrast to her daring use of his given name. "You are not a doctor. I believe you should send a polite note of apology, with your best wishes for the viscount's return to health. It is as much as should be expected of you."

"I have promised Lady Leathorne, and even if I had not, I would still go! Are we not to visit the afflicted? Is that not part of our religion?"

Impatiently shaking his head, Mr. Bottleby said, "Do not preach scripture at me, Miss Becket. It is not seemly in a vicar's wife to throw the Lord's words at him! Be directed by me and do not over-reach your usual humility. How can you possibly be necessary for this gentleman's recovery? Are we to believe that with all the money and doctors in the world at his disposal, only *you* can heal him?"

His words stung like a slap, a final blow to any hope she had of marrying and living peacefully with Mr. Arthur Bottleby. If they felt so differently about this, then other things would inevitably serve to separate them, and she must, at least, live in harmony with a man she would take as husband.

"I am sorry to appear disobedient, Mr. Bottleby. I have already spoken to my father, and he quite agreed that it was my duty as a Christian to do this. But even if he had said as you do that it is none of my affair, I would still follow my conscience." *And my heart,* she thought. She straightened and held her head high. "I am sorry, sir, but I am in rather a hurry. I hope you will not take it ill if I say now, without further ado, that I think we should not suit as husband and wife. You would soon be sorry you had wed me, and I could not live with a spouse who did not respect my need to do what I think right. Good-bye, sir. I wish you well in your new parish."

Seventeen

"I want to go home!"

"Arabella, do not be unreasonable," Lady Swinley hissed. They were in her chamber, and it was right next to Lord Drake's. "We came here for a reason, and if you would just cooperate, this could be a propitious turn of events for us."

"Lord Drake's illness?" Arabella stared at her mother, amazed at the twisted way her mother could view such a tragedy for the family.

"Yes, Lord Drake's illness! Do not look at me that way. If you would just push your way in, they would not turn you away! Be tender, be worried, be *womanly*! Be anything but yourself, in other words."

Disgusted and furious, Arabella turned on her mother. "How can you say such a thing, you who never attended a sickbed a day in your life? Where were you when I was ill as a child, and the school sent me away for fear of contagion? I went to the vicarage, and True tended me. *Hers* was the hand that bathed my brow, not yours, so if anyone is unwomanly, look rather at the woman who would not care for her own child!"

Lady Swinley's hand flashed up to slap Arabella, but she caught her mother's hand in her own grip, surprisingly strong for so slender a girl. "Do not *dare!* You would send me in there to catch who knows what illness, a fever, perhaps, and all to compromise me with Lord Drake so they will be forced to accept me as daughter-in-law? How—"

Her words were interrupted by a high, keening wail and a thump. Drake's batman, Horace Cooper, shouted out for help and footsteps could be heard thudding along the corridor. Arabella waved her arm and said, "You see? That servant of Drake's, even *he* needs help to deal with the viscount. What do you expect me to do, hold Lord Drake down?"

"Do not be vulgar!"

"Then do not be ridiculous! We should not even be here, if you had any decency, Mother!"

Lady Swinley raised her hand once more, but at a glare from her daughter, dropped it. Trembling, she stiffened her posture. "Lord Drake," she said, calmly, "will recover. If you could just show a modicum of concern for the man, his mother would advance the match, and you could take advantage of his recovery period to nurse him. Read to him, bathe his fevered brow. Men are children when they are sick. He would be as soft as custard, and vulnerable."

"And why do you continue to think that I still wish to marry him?"

"Because you *have* to, that is why," Lady Swinley muttered. "Arabella, you do not seem to understand. We cannot go back to Swinley Manor! I . . . I owe the moneylenders, and we cannot return without some assurance of future prosperity."

"But how . . . ? Father left—"

"Listen to me, once and for all. Your father left a mess," Lady Swinley said, glaring into her daughter's eyes. "A mess! He owed everyone, and had failed to secure your marriage settlement. He left me without provision, and three seasons in London have been horribly expensive! I have had to borrow against Swinley Manor, even."

"But you encouraged me to not settle for a younger son! I could have married Lord Sweetan! He was not as wealthy as Lord Drake, but provisions would have been made, and I—"

"We cannot afford for you to marry anyone less than Lord Drake! The moneylenders were willing to finance another season only after they learned your . . . your pedigree, and now we are so far in debt, only a very wealthy man will do."

Revolted, Arabella stared at her mother. "You borrowed on my . . . my prospects?"

"Yes. Would you have preferred to go to the sponging house? Think, Arabella! Think of all of the lovely clothes and jewels and trips we could have if you marry properly!" Her voice had changed and was wheedling in tone.

"But . . . but what if Lord Drake comes out of this mad? What if he always has those awful nightmares? I cannot live like that!"

Lady Swinley, sensing victory, was quick to say, "You will only be sharing his bed to breed an heir! You don't actually have to *sleep* with the man! He will visit your bed and return to his own to sleep."

"Is that what you and father did?" Arabella gazed at her mother with curiosity.

"Certainly. It is what any well-bred lady expects. Men know that gentlewomen must be treated differently than their doxies. That sort of thing—sleeping together—is done among the lower classes, but they have no refinement in their feelings."

There was nothing she could do, Arabella realized. Her fate was sealed. "I . . . I shall seek out Lady Leathorne and beg to be allowed to sit with Lord Drake," she said, with as much of an air of noble sacrifice as she could muster. If things were truly as bad as her mother said, then it did not really matter who she married, as long as they had sufficient money. She was born and raised with the expectation that she would live in comfort and luxury, without worry, her whole life. Well, it looked like if she was to live on in that manner, or any manner at all, it would have to be with Lord Drake.

Now she would pay the price of three seasons in London, three seasons of delirious pleasure, knowing that she had a bridegroom in reserve, so to speak. Lord Drake had always been there in the background of her mind as a not unpleasant destiny. But fate had dealt her a nasty turn, making her resort to that destiny just when it looked to assure a troubled future. Well, she would hope for the best. "I will convince Lady Leathorne that I am half dead with worry for him."

"Good girl," Lady Swinley said with satisfaction.

But on asking, Arabella found that the lady of the house was not there. She had departed in the early hours before dawn of the previous day, Marcot, the butler, informed her as he polished the silver in the dining room, leaving no word where she would be. It was most strange, Arabella thought, that she would leave her son at such a juncture, but she would go to Lord Drake anyway, and make sure his mother knew about it when she returned home. With any luck at all, it would be just as Arabella was bathing his fevered brow. She gritted her teeth and started back up the stairs to the family quarters.

Traveling through the night and stopping only to change horses and take a brief necessary break, True found herself at Lea Park by late morning of the next day. Marcot was evidently watching out for her, for the door was swung open and she was escorted up the stone steps and into the manse without delay.

"Marcot, is Lord Drake—is he—" She could not ask the question.

"He is still alive, but very feverish. Her ladyship just arrived an hour ago, in time to keep the physician, Mr. Jackson, from bleeding the viscount yet again."

That Marcot, normally the most unbending of servants, should be so forthcoming, was a good indication of the turmoil the estate dwelt in. As he escorted True up the stairs, the butler added that the earl had not come out of his study for two days, and was said to be drunk, while Lord Conroy and the ladies had carried on much as usual.

True stopped only to remove her bonnet, but even as she did so heard a commotion that burst into the hallway outside of Lord Drake's room.

"I will not stay in the same room as that madman!" Arabella screeched.

True raced into the hallway, stripping off her gloves as she went, to find her cousin standing outside the open door to Lord Drake's room. His voice was a hoarse shout from the depths of the room, and Lady Leathorne's exhausted voice cried out, "Hold him, Sergeant, I am afraid he will try to do away with himself again."

Arabella cried out, lifted her skirts and ran down the hall, stopping when she saw True. Her face was drained of all color. "He is mad! He struck out at me . . . he thought I was some dead captain, and that I was haunting him, and . . . oh! I will not marry him! I do not care what my mother says!"

"Bella, get a hold of yourself," True said, grasping her cousin by the shoulders. The girl was genuinely distraught, and True reflected that many people were not fit for the sickroom. She took out a handkerchief, gently wiped the tears from her younger cousin's cheeks, and said, "Go down and get yourself tea. You will make yourself sick if you get upset this way. Calm, Bella. No one is going to force you into anything, I swear it."

"Lord, True, I cannot help it! I just . . ." Arabella burst into tears and embraced her cousin. She sniffed, finally, and subdued her tears. "What are you doing here? We did not know you were coming back."

There was another cry from Lord Drake's room, and True broke away from Arabella. "I came to help Lady Leathorne with her son. I have to go to him, Bella."

She raced down the hall and was almost pulled into the room by the countess, who had heard her voice, it seemed, and was coming to fetch her. Arabella watched with a puzzled frown. What was going on? Why was True suddenly an indispensable part of Lord Drake's recovery? Slowly she went down the stairs, wondering just how far True's "friendship" with the viscount had progressed.

Lady Leathorne pulled True into the room and shut the door to the hallway. "He said your name again, just before this last fit."

True approached the bed, where Drake thrashed in a fevered nightmare as Horace held onto him, trying to keep him from falling from the bed. The viscount was sweating and flushed, his face gaunt and his eyes open, glittering with a hectic light.

"They . . . they want to take me to hell! Hell. *Hell!*"

His last word was a howl, and True felt desperate fear well up in her. This was far worse than she had anticipated, but as she saw it, the fever was the treatable part of this ailment. She unbuttoned her sleeves and rolled them up. He would not die! She had seen these same symptoms in her village in the last bout of influenza—the fever and thrashing—and God willing, she would treat Lord Drake

with the same remedies that had proved so effica-
cious for any who would allow her to administer
them.

"Lady Leathorne," she said, turning to the countess. "I brought with me two infusions that have
proved valuable for reducing fever among the people of our village. If you could have someone fetch
them out of my bag—they are in white pottery jars
and are labeled 'Feverfew' and 'White Willow.' "

The countess looked doubtful for a minute.

"I have experience with this, my lady. Please trust
me. I would do nothing to hurt Wy, you must know."

Lady Leathorne gazed at her steadily, the ghost
of a smile curving her lips. "Wy. I have not called
him that since he was a child. I will get them myself; white pottery jars you said? What shall we do
with them?"

"The infusions must be mixed with equal parts
hot water, and given to him as a tea. I have not
figured out yet which of the herbs is more effica-
cious, and it will not harm him to use both mixed
together. If you will bring them I will attempt to
induce him to take it." She turned from the countess without ceremony, alarmed by the moans that
emanated from Drake, moans as of deep pain.

She approached the bed, but turned back to see
the countess staring at her with hope mixed with
despair. The look on that mother's face was so very
similar to the look on any villager's face, when
their child was ailing. It was the first time True
had realized just how much the frosty countess
loved her son. "Go," she said, gently. "Get the
remedies and bring a kettle of boiling water and
a cup. I will prepare the mixture."

The woman hurried out and True turned back to
the bed where the gallant soldier, Drake's batman,
not much taller than herself, held the powerful viscount in a hard grip. He gave her a wry grin, and

said, "He's a mite restless, ya might say, miss. Don't want 'im to hurt hisself."

"I see." She approached the bed. The room was gloomy, though it was midday. Drake seemed to be settling down some, and she said, "Horace—that is your name, is it not?—will you open the curtains a little and let some light in? He has not been complaining of aching eyes, has he?"

"No, miss. It ain't the scarlet fever."

"I didn't think so. You are a good nurse."

The batman hesitantly released his charge and slid off the bed to do as True bid. Given her first real look at Drake's face, True felt tears well up. His eyes were glazed, his face gaunt, and his night-shirt soaked from perspiration. His golden curls were plastered to his head with sweat.

As she watched, he began to thrash and struck out with his fist at some phantom enemy. An inarticulate yell erupted from him and his body arched as though from some great pain. Horace galloped over but True held up one hand. "Go see what her ladyship is doing."

Horace looked doubtful. "He be headin' fer another bad turn, miss, an' I'll have to hold him down."

In the distance, thunder rumbled across the sky and a patter of rain started up against the window-pane.

"The guns," Drake yelled. "F-French artillery, boys, but we'll . . . we . . ."

"Just go," True commanded. Horace scuttled to the door, and with one last look, left the two alone.

Drake yelled again, this time for his gun, then a string of obscenities. True cautiously, her heart pounding, said, "Wy, I am here. Do you know me?" More incoherent, garbled battle talk. "Wy, it is me, Truelove. You asked me to come, and I am here."

Lightning flashed suddenly, thunder rumbled and

crashed and Drake let out a long, keening cry. True could not bear it and hopped up beside him, pulling him to her, rocking him in her arms. He struggled but she locked her arms around him with all the strength she could muster, more than she thought she possessed. "Wy, it is all right," she said, gently. "You are going to be all right. Please, Wy, listen to me; hush and listen, my love."

To her surprise the viscount stilled. His body was damp. She could feel the heat of him, his fever burning bright in his cheeks and through his whole body. He moaned, but then quieted, and nuzzled her neck.

"Oh, my poor dear," True whispered, pushing soaked curls off his forehead. "I would never have left if I had known. . . ." But of course, if she had it to do all over, she would have done the same. When she left, she had thought her father ill, and she would never have ignored that loving duty to her father. What had happened that had brought back the viscount's nightmares? He had seemed healed of them finally. Was it just the fever, or did the nightmares precede the fever? From what the countess had said, the nightmares came first, and it was his inattentiveness to his health as a result of exhaustion that had caused his problems.

When the countess and batman came back, True demanded clean, cold water, fresh cloths, a change of nightshirt for Drake, and she set about making the infusions of willow bark and feverfew into tea. It was going to be a long day, but True was emboldened by a feeling that perhaps Lady Leathorne had been right to fetch her. She had experience with fever patients, and no one could want him well more than her, unless, perhaps, it was the countess herself. Also, she had the feeling that Drake had heard her, that he was listening somewhere in there, behind the glazed eyes.

If that was so, if he could hear her, she would find a way to bring him back. Drake was strong; he would not succumb to a mere fever.

"It is scandalous," Lady Swinley muttered. "Utterly scandalous, and so I shall tell Jessica when she comes down, *if* she comes down! I have not seen her in days. I cannot believe she went away and came back, all without saying a word to her houseguests! Abominable treatment. And now this. She has shut my cousin in with that raving lunatic and has left them alone. *Alone!* Together!"

"Drake is hardly in a condition to ravish her, Mother," Arabella said, sulkily.

Lord Conroy entered the saloon just then and crossed to the two ladies. "I have heard a report I cannot but think must be false. M'valet says that your cousin, Miss Becket, has returned and is closeted alone with Drake!"

"Absolutely true," Arabella said. She sniffed into a handkerchief, daintily, then eyed the gentleman. He looked gratifyingly concerned. "I am so afraid for her! I tried to help, but he . . . he beat me!" She held out her arm to show a bruise she had gotten the day before when she had accidentally knocked against the bedpost.

Lord Conroy, his dark eyes wide with horror, swiftly knelt beside her and, taking the handkerchief from her hand, dabbed at her dry eyes. He daringly pressed a kiss to the bruise. "You poor, delicate child! What were you thinking? You haven't the strength for sickroom nursing!"

Lady Swinley turned from the window and gazed at the nobleman, appraising him from his polished Hessians to his immaculate jacket and breeches to his gold watch fob, gold seal fob, and gold quizzing glass fob, all dangling on display on his waistcoat.

"Of course not," she said, slowly. Then she came to a decision. "My darling girl is a delicate flower, and her bloom would soon be faded if she spent all her time in a house of sickness. And a place of such . . . such immoral goings on! To shut an unmarried girl like True up alone with a lunatic like Lord Drake! Anything could happen."

"But she went in willingly, Mother!" Arabella reminded her, with a side-glance.

"Yes, well, I always did say the minx had an eye for the main chance. No better than she should be, even though she is my kin."

Arabella felt a little queasy at the havoc her mother was wreaking with poor True's reputation. But her cousin had chosen her course knowing what it entailed. It was no longer any of her business, and perhaps True's betrothal to her dull vicar protected her in societal eyes. At any rate, she must start thinking what to do for her and her mother now that a marriage to Lord Drake seemed out of the question. "I am leaving tomorrow," Arabella announced, making a sudden decision. What was there to stay at Lea Park for? "With or without you, Mother."

"I shall escort both of you ladies anywhere you like, if I may be so bold as to offer. I would not rest knowing you were alone on the road."

Arabella dimpled up at him. "We would be delighted, sir," she said. She laid her hand on his arm and felt him quiver at her touch. How delightfully susceptible he was! And good-natured, and *rich!*

Lady Swinley smiled, too. "Delighted, sir. So nice to know true gentility still survives in this world."

Eighteen

Darkness had fallen, the storm had played itself out and a light rain fell against the window, and still True held Drake. Horace had changed his nightshirt, and a maid had brought a fresh bowl of water. The countess had helped prepare the tea of the infusions True had brought. Then, on True's orders they had all left, just as Drake was beginning to get restless again.

Once more he had started the downward spiral of nightmare visions and fevered delusions, but through it all True talked, calmly, about anything and everything. She told him stories of her childhood and her sister, and about her village. And all the while she held him, stroked his hair off his forehead and fed him, bit by bit, the herbal tea, dripping it down his throat with infinite patience whenever he would let her. She felt a tension ease out of him, draining like a bad humor from his body, leaving him limp in her arms.

Soon she knew every inch of his sleek shoulder and arm and neck muscles under the light linen of his nightshirt. Her own arms ached with the effort, but still she held him close. Once a maid came, at Lady Leathorne's request, to bring True some broth and toast.

"Her ladyship's order, miss. She does not want

you to be taking ill from your nursing," the girl
said, timidly advancing with the tray, eyes wide to
see True holding the viscount in such a close and
intimate way.

Drake started to toss and turn at the maid's
sharp voice.

"Thank you . . . Bess, is it? Bess. Tell her ladyship I thank her. It is just the thing. Will you bring
me some fresh water for his lordship and more of
the tea infusion? Lady Leathorne knows how it is
to be prepared."

Alone again with just True, Drake settled down.
He could not seem to bear anyone's voice but her
own. The evening wore on, with just occasional in-
terruptions from the maid, and once from the
countess looking in on the two of them.

"Has the fever broken yet?" the worried mother
whispered, putting her hand to his forehead.

"Not yet," True had to admit. "But it has had
enough time to take a fierce hold of him; it will
take some time to conquer. I have seen worse recover, though. I . . . I am so touched that you
trust me to nurse him. We were strangers just a
month ago."

"Quite frankly, my dear, I am desperate. We have
had all the medical men in the area to see him,
and they cannot seem to heal what they all agree
is a simple fever. My fear was that he did not *want*
to get well, and I have always thought that a necessary part of recovery. When he asked for you, I
knew that you would be his good angel. How could
I not trust you when Drake so clearly does?"

True was silent, not knowing how to answer.

The countess perched on the edge of the bed.
Keeping her voice quiet, she whispered, "I believe
he missed you, when you left. He expected you to
come back, I think. He asked every day if Miss
Swinley had received word from you yet. The night-

mares started when . . ." She stopped and shook
her head and looked away.

True thought she heard the woman say "Not fair
to do that to you," but she said no more.

"I—I never promised to come back," True said.
Drake shifted a little in her arms, and she rolled
her shoulders, trying to drive the ache from her
body. "I was silent when he asked, though. He may
have had the impression . . . but we were just
friends; I did not think—" She broke off, not sure
what she was trying to say.

"You were nothing more than friends? Are you
sure?" With a kind smile, and a caress for her son,
the countess left, saying, "Try to get some sleep,
my dear. I would not have you making yourself ill
nursing my son."

True thought about the woman's question. She
could not speak for him, but she knew that she
loved him. Drake shifted again, threw his arm over
her and pulled her closer to him. She smoothed
the damp cloth over his forehead and threaded her
fingers through his soaked curls, lifting them off
his neck and patting away the sweat.

She must have been mad to think that, loving
Drake as she did, she had a right to marry another
man. It would not do. It would have been unfair
to Mr. Bottleby, and even more unfair to herself.
Better to remain single. When the viscount recovered she would have to decide on her future, now
that she had refused the vicar, but for now she
must concentrate on helping her patient.

It seemed that for some reason she had a way
of keeping him calm. Not once since she had come
had he needed to be restrained, nor had he fully
descended into his nightmare world. His arm tightened around her waist, and for the first time she
realized how scandalous was her position, lying
with a man on his bed, alone in his room.

And, yet, she was among friends here, and all must understand the exigencies of this particular case. With her there he did not thrash nor suffer the awful nightmares that kept him from getting well. Surely no one would think indelicately of that which necessity demanded. Her patient murmured and shifted, and raised his face to True.

"Please get better, Wy! Please. So many people love you, and I miss the brightness of your eyes, the sweetness of your smile." Gently she laid a kiss on his lips and he murmured against them.

"Truelove."

It was just a faint whisper, but she was almost sure it was her name. "I am here, Wy, and I will not leave until you are better." She kneaded his shoulders and back muscles, for one thing she did know was that the sick suffered from inactivity. Muscles must be kept from stiffening. He lapsed back into the deep peaceful sleep that she hoped would break his fever, with the help of the herbal infusions she had been feeding him on and off through the evening.

Somewhere a clock sounded the hour, but time had ceased to have meaning for True, and she did not count the chimes. Hour after hour had passed, and she did not know if the household slept, or if somewhere they were gathered playing cards, or listening to Arabella play the piano. Her body ached from staying in one position so long, but as long as Drake slept, she would not move.

In the dim lamplight, True could see the door open. She expected Horace or Lady Leathorne, but it was Arabella who slipped in and shut the door behind her.

"Bella," she whispered, glad to see her cousin. "Are you better, love?"

The girl crept up to the bed and gazed down at the entwined twosome with a mixture of curiosity and censure. "How can you . . . how can you do this?" The distaste in her voice was sharp and clear.

Restlessly, Drake shifted.

"This? What do you mean?"

"Lie with him like that! Does he not become violent? What if he should take advantage of you?"

True felt a giggle well up in her throat, but suppressed it. She did not want to shake with laughter, for it would inevitably disturb Drake. "Take advantage of me? Bella, he is desperately ill! It would take some sort of miracle for him to 'take advantage' of me. I have spent days in the sickroom before, you know; perhaps not quite in this position, but at the bedside of men and women, children, even yours, when you were little, if you remember."

"I know that. It is not that I suspect you of any . . . any immoral actions, it is just . . . he is so very large and . . . and has such strange fits." Arabella eyed the sleeping viscount with distaste, but took a seat in a chair beside the bed. "I did not come just to visit. I— True, I told you an untruth before you left, and I want to get it off my conscience."

Gazing at her younger cousin, True thought what a combination the girl was of contradictory qualities. She thought she knew what was coming— she had pondered Arabella's profession of love for Drake, and something about it did not ring true— but she kept her own counsel. If Bella wanted to cleanse her conscience and confess, then True would let her. She wanted so much for her cousin to find happiness, but feared that was never to be as long as she let her mother guide her actions.

"What is it, love?"

Arabella gazed up at her cousin and held out her hand. True took it and squeezed.

"I—I told you I was in love with Lord Drake, but that was never so. I thought that you might be falling in love with him, and I . . ." She stopped.

Taking a deep breath, though, she started again. "Mother so wanted me to marry him and I had just found out—"

"Found out what, dear?"

Arabella colored, but shook her head. "Nothing, True; nothing important. But it is over. I have no intention of marrying him, no matter what happens. I do not love him, and never could. We—Mother, Lord Conroy and I—are leaving in the morning."

"Leaving? Where are you going? Back to Swinley?"

"No . . . uh, Lord Conroy has invited us to visit him at his father's home."

True smiled and raised her eyebrows. "Do I smell a romance in the offing? He is a very gallant gentleman."

Arabella shrugged.

"Your mother is not pushing you on Lord Conroy now, is she? Oh, Bella, do not make a mistake. Do you love him? Truly?"

"He thinks I am a pretty little widgeon," Arabella said, disparagingly. She drew herself up and took a deep breath. "But I *must* marry, and though he does not have pots of money like Lord Drake, his father intends to settle a small estate on him when he marries. Nathan has spoken of it already, so perhaps he does care for me in that way."

"But do you care for *him* in that way?"

"I don't know! I just don't know," the girl said, agitated.

Drake shifted and murmured. True released Bella's hand and stroked her patient's cheek. "Hush, Wy, shhh. It's all right." She glanced up to find her cousin's bright green eyes fixed on her. "He gets a little restless with other voices around, but if you talk quietly, it should be all right."

"You *are* in love with him, aren't you? I can see it in the way you touch him!"

True felt a blush coming to her cheek, but did not answer.

Arabella leaned forward in her chair. "I know you, True. Tell me it isn't so."

"It is a moot point, my dear. I never aspired to his hand, you know. I should make a miserable viscountess, and besides, Wy only ever treated me as a brother would treat a sister."

Arabella gazed at her incredulously. "A brother? Oh, Lord, True! It is a wonder God does not strike you dead as a liar! He looked at you as if you were the only woman alive! Like you were a delectable, juicy plum, and he was just deciding whether to devour you or save you for later. Every time you two would come back from a walk, smelling of April and May, I would wait for the announcement. Why else my fake swoon in the parlor? I thought an announcement was imminent, and was trying to stall so I could steal him away from you."

The girl's candor was one of the qualities she had had in her childhood, but that had been lost, True thought. It was good, if rather embarrassing, to hear her be so blunt, and True readily forgave her for scheming to eliminate the competition. It was obvious that Lady Swinley had been pushing her daughter relentlessly, and who would ever be proof against that woman's ruthless nature? "But he never proposed, Bella. If he felt toward me as you seem to think, surely he would have asked me to marry him, or . . . or given me some hint, despite the disparity in our positions! I wish you had just asked me, instead of wondering. You could have had him, you know, if you had just been yourself with him. He would have appreciated all your fine qualities and could have come to love you."

Arabella shuddered. "Ugh. I cannot imagine going through life with a man who has fits! I am not like you, True. I am selfish, not self-sacrificing."

"Do you think I am being self-sacrificing by being here with him? How little you understand, then. This is pure selfishness on my part, staying with him, being with him. I am indulging my every whim." True stroked his hair, feeling a swell of love overwhelm her. "If it was not for my fear for his health, I would . . . would be in a kind of heaven."

Staring at her in disbelief, Arabella shook her head. "Yes, well, so you say. What a strange duck you are, coz. As for me, I want a man, not an invalid."

"He is not an invalid, only fevered right now, and troubled. You sell yourself short, my dear. I think you have come to believe yourself the image of your mother, when you are not like her at all."

Her expression softening, Arabella said, "I wish I really were the girl you see when you look at me, True, but I am not." There were tears in her voice, but none in her eyes. She took a deep breath and stiffened her spine, holding her head up at a proud angle. "You see me that way because you love me, and I don't deserve it. I have been horrible to you; scheming to take Lord Drake away from you when any fool could see he was falling in love with you, and you with him. I would hope to see that same look in a man's eyes someday, but I fear that love is not for such as I. Perhaps when I am thirty and have borne my husband three sons, I will take a dashing lover who will adore me!" Her voice was gay, but hard, like flint. She stood, and said, "I have to go to bed. It is late, and we leave early."

"Bella," True said, reaching out for her cousin's hand. "If you really believe that about yourself, that I only see good in you because I love you— that is not true, but evidently you think it is—then you must see how powerful love is. Find it for yourself, and don't settle for anything less, my dear. You do deserve it, no matter what you think."

Finally, the tears started in Arabella's eyes, sparkling in the lamplight. "I wish I c-could, True. I wish I could wait for love, but I cannot. Pray for me!"

Fear clutched at True's heart. There was something her cousin was not telling her. "Is there anything wrong, Bella? Anything—"

"I have to go," the girl said, gathering her skirts and turning.

"Bella . . . write to me," True said, urgently. "Write to me, please. And remember, if you ever need me, you are welcome at the vicarage, or wherever I may be. You are *always* welcome. I love you, Bella."

Without a backward glance, Arabella fled the room, closing the door softly behind her. True thought about her cousin for long hours after she left, and then fell into a drifting sleep, to dream of the meadow and the river, and Wy sleeping on her lap in the summer sun.

When she awoke in the morning, as Horace came in followed by Lady Leathorne, it was to find that some time in the night, Drake's fever had broken. His forehead was cooler than it had yet been, and he slept a more natural sleep. His mother wept openly, and Horace could not contain his satisfaction.

"That'll be one fer the doctors, miss! Those old humbuggers'll be in some taking when they find out a slip of a girl knows medicatin' better'n them!"

But True cautioned them, "This is good, but he has lost a lot of strength, so do not expect him to be up and about too rapidly."

"But he is better? Truly?" Lady Leathorne gazed down at her son, who rested still in True's arms.

"I believe so. The fever is definitely abating. He will make a full recovery."

"God bless you, Miss Becket," Lady Leathorne said with a trembling smile, tears still shining on her cheeks. "If there is anything in this world you want, anything I can ever do for you—" She left it unsaid, for words did not begin to express the emotions that filled her eyes.

Over the next two days Drake continued to recover, spending most of his time sleeping, and was groggy at best when he was awake. At first, though, True insisted on staying by his side and feeding him still the herbal tea, as well as nourishing gruels and meat broths. She was taking no chance that the fever would return.

Lady Leathorne noted with concern that as her son recovered, so did the rumor and innuendo surrounding Drake and Miss Becket intensify. She blamed herself, and the short-sightedness that had led to her sending in that chatterbox, Bess, with food for True. And she could not address it head on, for that would only justify it in the minds of her staff. She knew as well as anybody that gossip had a life of its own, and ignoring it was one's only option. As long as Miss Becket stayed closeted with her son she was shielded from it, but soon, very soon, she would be faced with the knowledge that she was hopelessly compromised.

And they would handle that when Drake was better. She had wanted more for her son, wanted a woman of status and culture, social position and elegance, but Miss Becket, with no pretensions to elegance or status, had something much more important in the end, a good heart. She was the soul of kindness, and her son could do much worse. Now was not the time to make that decision, but soon. Very soon.

Drake watched True bustle around his room, fussing with some bottles, folding cloths. He had awoken just minutes before from what seemed like a long dream of burning desert sands or fiercely hot tropics, he couldn't decide which. And True was there, telling him all the while that they would get through it together. He had been sick, he supposed, and it seemed that Truelove had come back sometime during his illness. Why, he wondered? Had her cousins asked her to come back? And why was she in his room, alone? Surely his mother would not allow that.

"Truelove," he whispered, shocked at how weak his voice sounded.

She had just been opening the curtains to let the sun in, and she whirled at the sound of his voice. "You're awake!" she cried. "Really awake!"

"You sound as though that were a miracle," he said. He tried to raise himself, but found he had not the strength of a kitten. He slumped back on his pillows. "I have been ill."

She crossed the room and stood by his bed, gazing down at him. "You have," she said, reaching out and brushing back his hair. He felt a shiver go though him at her light touch, a touch so familiar it was as if he had felt it hundreds of times.

"How long?"

"Altogether? Six days."

"Six— I have been sick for that long?"

"You had a fever. You went out in the rain, riding, and took a chill, and came down with influenza."

Memory flooded back to him. It had been after a particularly bad night of horrid, torturing nightmares. Somehow, knowing True was to be married to her vicar, he had not given a damn about anything and so when the nightmares came back even worse than before, he had gone out riding and gotten soaked by a drenching rain. He had ended up at a hedge tavern with some very disreputable customers, had drunk for several hours with them, and then had made his inebriated way back to Lea

Park. He had done nothing so very irresponsible in a long, long time, since he was a boy, in fact. And the result, he supposed, was that he had been taken ill.

And nightmares! He remembered sweltering through some horribly vivid dreams of devils clawing at his innards, and hands dragging him down to the fires of hell . . . all manner of frightful apparitions. But then a voice had come to him, to tell him it would be all right. Could that have been Truelove?

"I . . . I think I remember. I was careless." He gazed up at her, her drawn, tired face, pretty blue eyes gazing down at him with some indefinable emotion. She was caressing his cheek, scuffing her fingers against his bristly beard, and he turned his head slightly to kiss her palm. "Did you . . . did you come back from your home just to nurse me?"

"I did," she said, gently.

"You look exhausted! True, you must take care of yourself."

"I will, now," she said, a serene smile on her face. "For now I really believe that you will be all right. I think I shall go to my room."

Nineteen

She slept around the clock, so exhausted was she. Life went on in the household; in that time Drake gained strength hourly, his former good health helping him, as well as a ravenous appetite that proved how well he was, and how rapid his recovery would be. Horace could hardly keep up with his demands. That night, Drake slept uninterrupted, deeply, a whole ten hours, and awoke the next morning again with an insatiable appetite.

At Horace's suggestion that he be brought weak tea and toast, he snorted. "Not bloody likely, old man. I have a feeling there are kippers and eggs and ham downstairs, and I mean to make my way through my fair share." He swung his legs over the edge of the bed and grimaced. "I am as weak as a drunken ensign! This will never do. I must regain my strength, for we will be moving to Thorne House in two weeks. We shall contrive to cheerily live amongst the renovations."

Lady Leathorne entered the room and gaped at her son. "Drake, you get back in that bed! You have no business getting up yet; you are still far from well." She bustled across the room and jerked the covers up over his legs, but he put one hand out to stop her.

"Mother," he said, gently. He knew how his illness

had scared her, but he was not about to let her coddle him forever because of that fear. "I am going to be fine. I am a little weak, but I am not going to regain my strength lying abed. I shall come down and rejoin the company and apologize for my prolonged absence."

"Lady Swinley and Miss Swinley have gone. Conroy escorted them . . . well, to his home."

"What?" Drake frowned. "Conroy took them to his home?" It was against his friend's nature to take any young lady to his family home, Drake knew, for that implied a relationship that could only lead to wedding vows. Conroy, a younger son, would marry someday, but was looking for a great heiress. The Swinleys must be comfortable, but he did not think them wealthy. Perhaps his friend had fallen in love. There had certainly been a partiality there, from what he could remember, but he could not swear that Miss Swinley had been equally interested. "I wish them well."

"You are not disappointed? That Miss Swinley did not stay?"

"No, Mama," he said, gazing down at her from the bed with an affectionate grin. "I am not disappointed or heartbroken, or anything else other than relieved. And now, I am going to undress, and since you have not been present for that event since I was a very young boy, I think we shall both be more comfortable if you leave the room."

With a gleam in her eye, Lady Leathorne reached up and ruffled her son's hair. "You will always be my 'young boy,' and do not forget that. I reserve the right to order you back to your bed if I see any sign that you are becoming overtired. I will not have you becoming sick again." She moved toward the door as Drake slipped off the bed.

"Mother?"

She turned back. Horace had come forward, and

was ready to help his former commanding officer should he prove to be unsteady on his feet. "What is it?"

"Is . . . is Truelove downstairs?"

"She is still sleeping, son. She went to bed yesterday and has been asleep since." She gazed at him with calculating eyes. "She wore herself out, and it is best if she sleeps as long as she needs to, to regain her own strength."

"She's very special, don't you think?"

"I truthfully think I love her as a daughter, Drake," Lady Leathorne said. Her smile was watery, but she sniffed and swallowed, took a deep breath, and spoke again. "I can never repay her adequately for giving me back my only child. Now, get dressed and I will see you at the breakfast table."

Everything, every dancing mote of dust in the sunlight, every stray scent of floor wax or toast or shoe polish seemed delicious and beautiful and heartbreakingly perfect to Drake. He wandered the household after breakfast—really more of a luncheon by the time he had bathed and dressed, resting between each ordeal while he got his wind back—and gloried in the perfection of everything.

How had he never seen before how truly beautiful something as simple as a single rose in a crystal vase was? He wandered through the house until teatime, and then followed the scent of biscuits into the rose parlor, where tea was being served.

His father was already there, helping himself to the buttered biscuits, spreading one lavishly with strawberry preserves. He stopped dead at the sight of his son, his rheumy eyes fixed on his progeny.

It was not the first time that Drake had wondered how two men so close in relation as he and his father could have so little in common as to seem almost strangers. When left alone in the same room they had virtually nothing to talk about. It should not be; this was his father. He had adored him as a child and had followed his strong, young, vigorous "papa" from stable to house and back again every day as a boy.

"Father," he said, approaching the tea table. "It is good to see you." Had his father shrunk, or was it just that he had grown so tall in the years he had been away with the army?

Leathorne looked up at him, putting the biscuit aside, brushing the crumbs from his hand, and thrusting it toward Drake. "Son, good to have you back in the land o' the living, I must say. Good to see you up and about." He took Drake's hand and pumped it vigorously, then clapped his son on the shoulder.

They stood thusly for a few minutes. Drake thought, for one brief moment, that he saw a hint of moisture in his father's eyes, but he could not be sure. "It *is* good to be up and about. I was very ill, I'm told. It all seems one long nightmare to me, until Miss Becket came, at least."

At the word nightmare, Leathorne dropped his son's hand and looked hastily away. "Not, er, not having the nightmares again, are you?"

"It has only been a couple of nights since my fever broke, I understand, but I don't think I shall, no. I think I have conquered the blackness and come out on the other side. I cannot be sure, of course, but I hope it is so." It was strange to speak of it openly, for he had tried to conceal the nightmares for so long that it amazed him his father was even aware. But then his mother had known, and she would have said something, perhaps. He was not going to hide from his own frailty any more, though. There was something to be said for an open admittance of weakness, for then one could truly be strong, rather than waste energy hiding things from people.

Leathorne cleared his throat. "Never said this, uh, son, but your mother and me, we're . . . well, we're demmed proud of you, *demmed* proud! I know you went through some kinda hell out there—Waterloo, dontcha know—and we're just glad to have you back safe and sound."

It was the longest speech his father had ever made regarding Drake's military career, and it touched the viscount's heart. "I did what I felt was right, but much of it I am *not* proud of," he said, honestly. He picked up a biscuit and layered butter and jam on it and took a bite. Ambrosia! He rolled his eyes at the utterly exquisite taste of Cook's strawberry preserves; it was like captured summer.

"How can you not be proud of yourself?" the earl said, his eyes squinted in puzzlement. "You're a hero! Got Wellington's own word on that, don't we?"

Drake knew well enough to leave it alone, and thanked his father with a smile. A hero. He had done what he had to do to preserve his own life and the lives of those in his company, and he had not always succeeded. So many good men had paid the ultimate price, and for what? Could victory have been purchased with no other currency than human lives? He did not know if he would ever become reconciled to the butchery he had witnessed, and yes, taken part in.

At that moment the parlor door opened, and True came in, a ready smile on her face. He was staggered by the emotions that raced through him pell-mell, and by the choking sensation in his throat. She was so very beautiful. Did she have any idea of how truly lovely she was, with that deep blue gown matching her eyes, and the baby-softness of her hair dressed in a simple style so that it caressed her neck in long soft curls?

She said something but he could not respond, he just stared. Fevered nights came back to him, and the feel of a cool hand on his brow, pushing back his curls, always doing just what he needed as he existed through a long nightmare of burning heat and an ache through his body that felt like someone was squeezing his very bones.

How much of his memory of that time was real, and how much was his fevered imagination? He would have sworn he felt kisses on his brow and his lips, and heard murmured words of love, unutterably sweet, keeping him sane, pulling him back from the nightmares every time they would threaten to invade his mind again.

She was chatting to his father and throwing brief, anxious glances toward him, but he could not speak, could not even swallow.

She turned to him. "I am so glad to see you are better, Wy," she said, her voice a low murmur.

His mother had come in, too, and was speaking to Lord Leathorne.

There were dark circles under Truelove's gorgeous eyes, and he prayed she had taken no lasting harm from what must have been days and nights of nursing. He must ask her, must speak before she thought he had been made an idiot by the fever. "I can never thank you, never repay you—"

"Hush," she said, and he could see her hand move as if she were about to reach out to him, but she restrained the urge and picked up a cup instead. "I did very little, really. It was your own strength that brought you through."

"You will minimize it, but I know. I was there, and I do remember. . . . I remember that it was only your voice that chased the demons away." He looked down at the biscuit in his hand. "I was being d-dragged to hell, but you—your voice, your words, your touch—sent them flying away. And every time they threatened to come back, you would just speak, and you would break through; all would calm in my mind." He did not realize he had remembered so much, but it was true. The nightmares had been the worst torment of the fever because unlike when he was well, he could not get away from them. When he was well he could wake up, get out of bed, and ride until they had fled his troubled mind, but as sick as he was they had taken permanent root in his fevered brain and until True arrived, threatened to drive him mad. He laid the biscuit down, his appetite gone for the moment.

This time she did reach out to him. Her small hand rested on his sleeve, and he imagined he could feel the warmth through the double layer of cloth. "Wy, you are better. Do not torture yourself with memories and remembered pain. I am so grateful you are better!"

He gazed down at her small tanned hand on his sleeve and covered it with his own hand. It disappeared entirely. Strange that such small hands should come with so much competent skill, and so much loving tenderness. He glanced up and smiled into her eyes. "I remember, too, some foul-tasting decoction that you insisted on dripping down my throat."

She giggled. "That, sir, was my willow bark tea, and a brew of feverfew. It played no small part in your recovery! So a little respect for my 'foul-tasting decoction,' if you will."

"I would gladly drink a yard of it to hear you laugh like that again," he said, and then shut his mouth, alarmed at the fervency in his tone and the way his voice had broken. She would think him a great looby if he started spouting such drivel. He had never been one to woo the ladies with fine words or tender sentiments; he just was not good at it. Poetry escaped him. Lovemaking was a foreign skill. And, yet, he found himself wishing he could compose sonnets on her eyes, like Shakespeare. *Shall I compare thee to a summer day?* That was Truelove Becket, all the warmth and beauty of a summer day.

She had quieted, and stood gazing up at him. She must have read his panicked expression, because a quirky smile lifted her lips. "Do not worry, sir, a little overemotionalism is the price one pays for recovery. I have long noticed that for a few hours or days, the patient, after recovering from a serious illness, finds everything and everyone beautiful and wonderful and unbearably perfect. It is almost overwhelming. You will regain your normal senses soon, I promise you, and all will fade into humdrum reality."

He laughed out loud at that. How like her to see right through him, and yet minimize her own attractions, the music of her laughter, in this case. "I do not think I will ever see you as anything but absolute perfection, True, for *that* is reality."

It could not be put off any longer, Lady Leathorne thought. She must broach the subject now. It was morning. Drake had gotten up after another sound and dreamless night's sleep and ridden off with his father to visit some of the tenants. His strength was returning, and his mother knew who she had to thank for that.

But that was not why she could not put off this conversation any longer. She had caught the maid, Bess, gossiping about Miss Becket's "nights alone with the young master," as she put it, and had threatened her with dismissal if she ever heard the girl saying such things again, but she feared it was far too late. In truth, she had known all along what would happen, for it was impossible to control rumor. It seemed to take on a life of its own. If it could have been confined to Lea Place it would not have signified, but that girl was sure to have a sister in service at some other house, and she would pass on such a juicy piece of tittle-tattle, and it would spread from there in the mysterious fashion of belowstairs gossip. She would protect Miss Becket from that. She would have no matter who the girl was, but Truelove Becket was infinitely precious to her, and this was the least she could do.

She found her in the small parlor, putting the final touches on a monogrammed handkerchief. "What exquisite work," Lady Leathorne said, as she sat down beside her guest. "I never had patience for such elegant stitchery."

True held it up to the light from the window. "This, for me, is relaxation. I have always had a pile of mending to do, so to be here with no sister poking holes through her gloves and no father wearing out his stockings, leaving me free to do embroidery, is pure luxury."

"Would you like to become accustomed to having that amount of time? To being wealthy enough that you would not need to worry about holes in gloves?"

True frowned and bit through the thread with her even, white teeth. "I never thought of it as a matter of wealth, my lady. Having a family entails a certain amount of work, and mending is just one of the things one does."

Lady Leathorne smiled. "Oh, my dear, not always. I have never mended a glove in my entire life. Why should I? When we wear through them we buy more."

Wondering where the countess was going with the conversation, True remained silent.

"You care about my son a great deal, I think. No

woman could look after a man the way you cared for Drake without feeling some tender emotion."

"I have nursed many, my lady—men, women and children. I have cared for every one of them." True felt her chest growing tight. She must not reveal her true feelings, especially not to this woman in front of her. It just would not do.

"Do not try to gull me, young woman. But that is neither here nor there. I . . . my son must marry some time. I want to have grandchildren. I think he is ready, now that he has retired from the army. Do you care for him enough to be a good wife to him?"

"My lady!" True exclaimed. She set aside her sewing and rose, pacing to the window. She turned, trying to conceal her shock. "Wy—I mean Lord Drake—does not feel like that toward me. His affection is the brotherly kind, and—"

"If that is true, it could soon be turned to the not-so-brotherly kind, if you put your mind to it. Men only require a little encouragement to go from affection to . . . well, to passion."

True felt the blood rush to her face, and knew she was likely an unbecoming shade of crimson. She covered her cheeks with her hands. "What are you suggesting, my lady?"

"I am suggesting that you would be a suitable wife for my son."

True was staggered. The countess's voice was so calm, so even. Was she offering her son as some kind of reward, out of gratitude? It was unheard of, and True was rather appalled, but she must conceal that, she knew. Perhaps the woman meant well, but she could not offer her son as some sort of prize for a job well done. "I would say, Lady Leathorne, that Drake is perfectly capable of choosing for himself a wife, if, and when, he wants one."

The countess rose, and stood in front of True. She took her hands in her own and squeezed them. "My dear, I see I will have to be blunt, for you have a natural delicacy that will not allow you to understand me, else. You spent nights alone with my son, in his room, on his bed. You were seen there by numerous staff members. I have tried my best to stem the tide of gossip, but have been unable to stop it entirely. It will spread, as it invariably does, and you will be . . . you *have* been compromised."

"And you th-think I would accept your son, that I would marry him, when he is forced to offer for me?" True pulled her hands away from the countess and clutched them to her bosom, horrified at the implications. She loved Drake dearly; loved him far too much to foist on him a marriage he did not choose, and become a millstone around his neck. His future countess should be everything he needed in life, including a hostess and his social equal. As for herself, how could gossip among the *ton* harm her? She lived a retired life, and none in her circle would listen to scandal concerning her anyway. That was the reward, she hoped, of a blameless life.

"Do not look at it that way," the countess said. "I am sure when Drake realizes, he will do the right thing and ask you himself. I just thought I should prepare the way. My dear, I welcome you as my daughter-in-law!"

"Because I have been compromised! And out of some mistaken notion that I require a reward for whatever part I played in restoring your son to health." Shock forced a bluntness that was not True's usual way. "Believe me, my lady, I did not do it for a reward! I did it out of human compassion. I would have done the same for anyone!"

"But it was you he asked for," Lady Leathorne said, and her voice was gentle. "It was your name he whispered in the depths of his fevered state. It was *you* he wanted, Miss Becket . . . Truelove. Is that not love? And do you not love him, too? Don't talk to me of what you would do for others. I saw how you were with him, and there was love in your touch."

Yes, she loved him. Loved him too much to trap him into a marriage just when he was well enough to start making his own decisions about life.

"Answer me, Miss Becket. Do you love my son?"

If she told the truth—if she said yes—Lady Leathorne would go to Drake and tell him that Miss Becket had been compromised and that he must marry her. And Drake would do it. He cared for her, she knew he did, but how humiliating to have him marry her to save her reputation. She could not stand every day of her life to look at him and know she was not his choice, that she was foisted on him to save her standing in society from being degraded. "Oh, yes, poor Drake . . . had to marry a Miss Becket, a Miss Nobody . . . compromised her, don't you know, on his sickbed of all places!" She could hear the ill-natured gossip, the tittle-tattle of vacant minds and spiteful tongues. She would hate it, every minute of it, and she would be in that circle, then, as viscountess and future countess, where she would hear it.

She straightened her shoulders and faced the mother of the man she loved. "I do not love him, Lady Leathorne."

The countess gazed at her steadily, doubt clouding her amber eyes. "Your cousin, Lady Swinley, read a letter of yours out loud to us. In it, you said you were betrothed to a vicar and were to be soon married. Is that true, then?"

True saw the danger. She had already lied by saying she did not love Drake, but that might not matter to the countess. Love did not come into marriage for many people. A prior betrothal would end her efforts on True's behalf. She swallowed. "Yes, I . . . I . . ." she could not say it, but the countess accepted it as said.

"I will not push the matter." Lady Leathorne gazed at True with kindness in her eyes. Her voice serious, she said, "But if your vicar hears the gossip and will not marry you, or if you change your mind, my son is yours to wed."

Twenty

Somehow, though she had determined she should leave the next morning, Lady Leathorne talked True into staying for a while longer. She said she wanted to show her appreciation, but somehow it was True who ended up feeling obligated—obligated to stay, obligated to acquiesce even though she feared her own feelings.

Because, like it or not, Lady Leathorne's offer of her son's hand in marriage was tempting. True loved him so much, and to look at him and know that just a word would make him her husband for all time was the stuff of sweet dreams. She could marry him, take his name, live in his house, have his children, love him forever.

But the cold, sober reality was, he did not love her back in the same way. It was obvious that he cared for her, and True was confused as to what that meant, for sometimes, in the past, he had kissed her as though he really loved her. Nothing was stopping him, though. If he really loved her that way, he would tell her, he would ask her to marry him.

Wouldn't he?

Reflecting on it, though, she realized that to a man of honor she must have seemed as good as betrothed from the beginning, as she was considering an offer of marriage. And then Lady Swinley had read aloud that foolish letter she wrote, the one claiming she was to marry Mr. Bottleby. Well, not foolish. She had thought she *would* be marrying him when she wrote it. So it seemed she was caught by her own lie to Lady Leathorne in confirming that letter. Even if Wy did love her she would never know, because his sense of honor would not allow him to say it to a betrothed woman. And, yet, if she had been honest when the countess asked, the woman would have forced a marriage of convenience, to save True's precious reputation. And so she was caught in the awkward position of regretting what was unchangeable.

She was walking in the garden alone two days after Lady Leathorne had made her incredible offer. It was late October, and the landscape was a palette with gold and gray and deep, conifer green squeezed on it in thick, vibrant array. Golden leaves had drifted to the ground to lay in puddles around the tree trunks, and blew into heaps against the sides of stone walls and outbuildings. Lea Park was on a prominence, and from the terrace one could see the whole park, long, jewel-green swards of grass broken by the river and the willows and the distant meadow.

There was a chill in the breeze as autumn rolled across Hampshire.

Drake strolled out onto the terrace and watched True, aware that she did not yet know he was there. What was this indefinable feeling of unbearable joy he felt just to be in her company? Just to see her slight figure, buffeted by the wind, her soft hair tugged into stray tendrils from under her bonnet, was like music in his ears, a sweet melody that filled his heart. She had been right; the unutterable beauty of everything about him had faded somewhat, but not the emotion he experienced when he looked at her.

He loved her.

And, yet, she would go away soon, back to her vicar, to her upcoming marriage and future life. When she was near he felt like himself, like the warrior he had been, strong and capable, sure of himself. He had ridden over that morning to Thorne House for the first time since his illness. Though still in the middle of renovations, enough was done that it was ready to move into. And the Drake School would be a reality; he had spoken to his steward and to Stanley, and both had sworn to help in the endeavor and were excited about the future of it.

But still, as long as True was at Lea Park he would not leave, would not move into his rightful home. He couldn't bear the thought of leaving her behind here, without being able to see her every day. What was it going to be like when she left for good?

He would survive. He knew he was over the dreams, the nightmares. But it was still as if some light in his life would go out when she left, never to come back to Lea Park again. He was deeply, completely in love, such as he had never thought possible; in fact, he had never known such an emotion existed.

He remembered before his illness that he had thought he would ask True to marry him. It had seemed a good idea, and since she was not *officially* betrothed, there would be no dishonor in asking. She liked him, he thought. She had responded to his kisses with a delicious, tender ardor that he had found entrancing, but some time after she left she had evidently decided on marriage to the vicar. So was he mistaken? Had she felt nothing for him, or was it just that she felt more for the vicar?

It was her rightful place. She deserved a man who could make her proud, who had spent his life helping people, not killing them. She turned, saw him and smiled, and his heart leaped. Almost against his own volition, he stepped down onto the terrace and walked toward her.

"What a glorious day," she said, making a sweeping motion with her arms to include the sky, the earth, everything around them.

"Breathtaking," he agreed, never taking his eyes from hers. She blushed, adorably, and looked down at her toes, peeping out from underneath the hem of her ivory-colored walking dress.

"I love this time of year," she said, her voice a little breathless.

"But it is the end of summer! The end of walks and warm weather and the garden!"

"Oh, I never look at a season for what it means or portends, but for what it is! The temperature is invigorating, but not freezing, and there are still flowers in the garden, and the leaves have fallen, giving everything a different vista, do you not think?" She swept her arm out, indicating the view of the park. "Does everything not look different now?"

Drake could not speak. He swallowed. Yes, everything looked different. He was completely head-over-ears in love with Miss Truelove Becket, and she was going to leave and marry another man. Forever gone. He would never see her again. He had known it all along, but had not acknowledged what it meant to him, personally. He would go on with life, but it would be bleak and empty. Some part of him would die when she left.

She turned and looked up at him, the sunlight brightening her blue eyes to the shade of bluebells. He longed to take her in his arms and kiss her, fiercely, and then put her away from him, asking her if her vicar could ever kiss her like that. Would the good vicar ever need her, want her, *desire* her that much? The longing to pull her to him hard, to punish her with rough kisses for deserting him, shook him, and he moved just a little away from her. She was too fine to use in such a vile way, too precious. He would break her with his need; he would clutch her to him too hard, want her too badly, and she would hate him for it. He finally understood all the poetry Reverend Thomas and his other schoolmasters had forced him to read; love was a cruel and bitter agony when unrequited.

"Wy, what is wrong?" she asked, and moved toward him.

He took another step back, bumping into a stone planter with a yew in it. "N-nothing is wrong." Nothing but a pain so wrenching as to rival the saber thrust he had taken at Waterloo.

She reached out and touched his sleeve. "You . . . you do not look well. You're not overdoing it, are you?"

"No, my little nursemaid. Stop worrying about me." He said it fiercely, grimly, but then softened his voice and attempted a wobbly smile. He would not, *could* not punish her for being unattainable. "I am as good as new, thanks to you. Better than new."

She smiled and relaxed. "Good. How are the plans for the school coming along?"

With such innocuous subject matter, Drake could relax, and he strolled with True around the gardens, sitting on a stone bench finally, when he could see her tiring. His old wound bothered him hardly at all, now, but he thought that nursing him had exhausted her, and she would need a few days to recuperate. They talked about the school for a while, and then about Thorne House. He was surprised at how much, from her brief visit there, she remembered. It hurt, surprisingly, because he

could see her in every room, giving light and life
to the place with her presence. He was renovating
it with a view to marriage and children, and had
even planned to have his wife-to-be's suite done
over in periwinkle blue, just for her, but now . . .

He fell silent and stared off down the walk, at
the boxy yew hedges and dying gardens.

True watched Drake's face, the shifting of emotion over it like shadows over water, ephemeral and
quickly changing. He was carefully maintaining a
distance between them and True wondered at that,
when they had used to be physically close as they
talked. She had never thought it meant more than
that they felt a natural kinship of sorts, but now
she wondered.

"What are you thinking about?" she ventured.

He turned toward her and she was caught, once
again, by the fierce golden light that shone from
somewhere within him. She had seen a captive
hawk up close, once, and the look in that bird's
eye was the same—untamed, proud, and yet humbled by circumstances. She had longed to cut its
bonds and see it soar free once again, but the
keeper had explained that the bird had been badly
injured and could not fly. It hurt itself with every
attempt, and so he kept it tethered, hoping it
would heal some day and be able to fly again.

Comparisons were inevitable. And yet, Drake was
healed. He should be free to fly, wherever he
wanted.

"Thinking? I—you know, I have not had the
nightmares since my recovery."

She laid one hand on his sleeve and felt a quiver
go through him. "I am so glad, Wy. You are reconciled to your past as a soldier, then?"

"No! That is the odd part. I feel just as deeply
that . . . that there is some taint in me, some deep
scar from all of the killing I did, all the men I

slaughtered, all the lives that were changed forever because of my actions, or inaction."

True sighed, but in her heart she honored him for caring about all of those lives. "Did you ever kill anyone who was not a soldier, Wy?"

"No! I only ever killed in battle. That was not true of everyone. That last day, on the battlefield, some soldiers killed those who put up a fuss as they were being looted. It was horrible. I heard it happening all around me, but I was trapped and dying—or thought I was dying—and I could do nothing. If I had not been so inaccessible, trapped beneath poor Andromeda, it might have happened to me."

Quickly, to shift his attention from that day, she said, "And was there ever any choice for you? What would have happened if you did not kill in battle?"

"I would have been dead very quickly myself. There was never even any time to think. It was kill or be killed."

"And was every one of those men beside you and opposite you there of their own volition? There was no impressment into the army, was there? Not like the navy?"

"No, every one of my men made the decision to take the king's shilling. Not all of them were sober when they signed up, but they went willingly enough." He smiled wryly. "I see where you are going with this. Yes, all my men knew, when they signed up, of the possibility of death every day."

"And you took that same chance alongside them, every day."

He nodded. "Maybe someday that knowledge will help."

True thought for a minute. "My father is a vicar, as you know. He has preached many a sermon condemning violence, and many a sermon praising the men who joined the army and navy. It took me a while to puzzle out the contradiction. We are

supposed to love one another and live in peace, but
not everyone follows that commandment. I think
that there are times when men have no choice but
to go to war to protect those they love. Napoleon
had every intention of overrunning our island, and
what do you think would have happened to all of
us? Your parents, your friends . . . me? Wy, you
fought to keep us safe; with every blow, you fought
for me!" Her voice shook with emotion.

Was she right? Was it true? Could he have just
stood by and turned the other cheek while his people were overtaken by the Corsican monster? No.
One way or another he would have risked his life
to defend his home, his people, his family, from danger. Maybe when he was seventeen he had joined
up for excitement and glory, but he had stayed because he was good at what he did, and he was performing a valuable service. He had felt needed.

But still, his hands were stained with the blood
of a thousand men. Nothing had changed just because she believed what he did was justified by the
threat to his home and family. Truelove had made
the right choice when she said yes to her man of
God. It was what an angel deserved, to have a man
unsoiled, clean. It was a hard burden to bear, but
he would have to do without her and find his way
alone.

The days passed quietly.

Drake sat alone in the library, his face buried in
his hands. It was getting tougher and tougher to
keep up a cheery front, but finally True had set a
day for leaving. It was a good thing, or he would
go mad with wanting her. He had sworn just the
day before to go and live at Thorne House, where
he belonged, but he could not force himself to
leave when True still stayed. Every day was becom-

ing worse torture; to see her and not be able to touch her, to talk with her, watch her pink lips move, and not be able to kiss them, to see her shiver in the chill of the breeze and not be able to pull her into his arms and hold her close.

He loved her utterly and completely, and he was a fool for letting her go, but what could he do? She was betrothed to a far better man than he had ever been or could ever aspire to be. He heard the library door open and close, but he felt absolutely no curiosity as to who it was.

"Drake!"

It was his mother. He pulled himself together and straightened. "Yes, Mother. I was, uh, resting."

She strolled into the room. She had been out walking, it seemed; walking and reading a letter, from the looks of the parchment in her hand. She strolled to the window and squinted out at the day. "It's warm outside, like August rather than late October. Last shot of summer-like weather, I shouldn't wonder, before the cold truly sets in," she mused. She turned back toward Drake. "I have become very fond of Truelove Becket," she said, without preamble.

Drake stared at her, wondering where she was going after such an odd opening. "I . . . I am fond of her, too. It would be impossible not to love, uh, be fond of True."

"I have been concerned for her welfare," Lady Leathorne went on. "I wished her to stay with us for a while, but I did not want her to feel obligated if it was keeping her from her marriage."

Drake felt a sour taste in his mouth. "Yes, her marriage."

"And so I wrote to her father. I expressed my fears, and he very kindly wrote back."

His mouth now dry, Drake remained silent. He didn't want to know if the saintly Mr. Bottleby was demanding his bride-to-be back. She would be his soon enough and for all time; could Drake not enjoy her company for just a little longer? Was his mother going to persuade her to stay a while, maybe through Christmas? What delicious agony that would be! And, yet, he must hope she would stay, even though he had just been congratulating himself that she was finally to leave.

Lady Leathorne held the letter up to the light. "Let's see, what does her father say? Ah yes," she read out loud, *'My dear madam, I assure you that from everything I have been able to gather from my former curate, there exists no engagement between my daughter and him. My younger daughter concurs. She says that Truelove broke off any possibility of that before she returned to Lea Park to nurse your son. I am delighted . . .'* and then he goes on to congratulate me on your return to good health." She refolded the letter and glanced at her son. "It is odd, is it not, that she has not spoken of this?"

Drake sat, staring into space. Truelove was not engaged?

Lady Leathorne strolled around the desk and put the letter in front of him. "It is a beautiful day out, Son. I have been walking and it is glorious weather we are enjoying. I especially recommend the river walk, down near the oak tree. I think you would delight in it."

Drake took his mother's advice and walked. A light breeze scudded across the tops of the long, yellowing grass of the meadow and it rippled like the ocean while clouds cast their shadows, drifting lazily across the blue heavens. It was warm, and Drake pulled his jacket off and slung it over his shoulder.

Truelove was not engaged. She had broken it off

irrevocably with the vicar; he had seen her father's words with his own eyes. But still, he was not fit to touch her. After all he had done and seen, he was changed from the idealistic young man he had been, marching off in his scarlet tunic, looking forward to glory on the battlefield.

But had the deeds they did in war ever stopped men from coming home and taking wives, loving them as their better selves? Was he shutting out happiness for them *both* by his scruples? She had loved once, and had sworn never to marry until she loved as much. She had rejected her virtuous vicar; perhaps she could not love him? Should he not just put it to her and let *her* decide if she could ever love him?

The sun beat down on his shoulders, the heat burning into him. He walked mindlessly toward the river, following his mother's suggestion without thought. He came over a rise and gazed down at the river sparkling in the autumn sunshine, glittering like a string of jewels. He strolled down to the bank, the lush grass dying now and turning to an old gold color, and then glanced over toward the oak tree, where True had first held him.

And there she was, sleeping in the sun on a yellow blanket of leaves, curled up on her side.

Somehow it did not surprise him. All paths led to Truelove. Somehow sleep—dreamless or nightmarish, sound or restless—had played some sort of role throughout their acquaintance. He stepped closer to her and watched her slumber, her face the picture of innocence, her cheek pillowed on her clasped hands.

Every moment with True was like a gift he gave himself. Was there anything he could give her in return? A light breeze lifted her curls and she moved, murmuring sleepily. He thought of the nights she had sat with him, held him, bathed his brow. Had he just imagined the kisses on his forehead, the murmured words of love? Her lips had been cool and her words like balm for his soul. He could not possibly have made them up.

Hope blossomed in his heart, and he tossed his jacket down and lowered himself beside her, brushing her hair off her cheek and kissing the sunwarmed curve. She smiled and turned, and he covered her lips with his own, feeling her quick response and her hands stealing up around his neck.

Miss Truelove Beckons. It had been like a prophecy, when he had first uttered those words. "True," he whispered, pulling her into his arms and onto his lap, glorying in the small bundle of feminine sweetness that he loved so very much. Her eyes fluttered open and she looked up at him drowsily. She touched his cheek and threaded her fingers through his hair.

"Wy! What . . . I must have fallen asleep. We seem to have a bad habit of sleeping in each other's company."

He gazed down at her in his arms and felt as though the world had shifted, and he had found the one place where everything made sense. "Truelove Beckons. It's as if I knew, the very first second I saw you." He had been talking to himself, but now he said, "True, I—I love you." It had rushed out, straight from his heart to his lips, and he felt fear clutch at him. What if she did not care for him that way? What if—

"Wy!" Her eyes were wide open now, the sun lightning their color to sky. "Do you . . . do you mean that?"

He felt a slow smile overtake him, and then he threw back his head and laughed.

True felt her body robbed of breath as she watched joy transform Wy's handsome face into the very picture of Apollo, the sun god. His golden curls, sun-touched and glinting with threads of bright silver, fell back off his face.

"Do I mean it? I have never spoken a word to you I did not mean, Truelove, my . . . my own true love. I love you. I have *always* loved you and I will never stop."

True reached up and framed his face with her hands, staring deep into golden hawk eyes. The were alight with joy and life and . . . and love. It was true! He loved her. He said he had always loved her, and perhaps that was the truth, but his heart had been so clouded with pain and guilt that he had not been able to release it.

His expression clouded. "Do you . . . True, you haven't said anything. Am I being presumptuous? Is there another?"

She shook her head. "No. There is no one else. I . . . I have loved you since . . . oh, since the first moment I saw you!"

"But you wrote that you were going to marry your vicar!"

"I thought I should. I was thinking with my brain and not my heart. But I let him go, and Faith wrote to me and told me that he has asked another girl to marry him, a girl I know who has been pining after him for a long time."

"But you love me," Drake repeated, anxious to establish that uncontrovertibly.

"I love you," True whispered.

He lowered his lips to hers again, and she felt love bubble up like springwater. But there was something else, too, something forbidden, some deep desire that threaded through her body. Every rational thought fled as he did delicious things to her with his lips, kissing her throat and under her chin and her ear and her neck. His breath was warm in her ear and she giggled, breathlessly. His hands traced the outline of her hip and her bottom, and she realized that she was sitting most improperly on his lap. She squirmed, but he would not release her.

"True, do not try to escape from me." He captured her chin in his hand and turned her face toward his. "While I have my courage, I need to ask you. Will you spend your life loving me as I shall spend my life loving you? Will you marry me?"

He was holding his breath, and she looked down into his eyes from her perch on his knee and was touched to see that doubt and fear still lingered, even after her shameless response to his kisses.

"Yes, Wy, oh, yes! I will marry you. I love you!"

On the prominence overlooking the river, Lady Leathorne gazed down at the distantly perceived scene of her son and her future daughter-in-law—more than "daughter in law," the daughter of her heart—most improperly engaged in pre-marital bliss. It was why she had sent him in this direction, with the knowledge that True was there, and not, as they had supposed, betrothed. Once she knew the truth about the girl's supposed "engagement," it had not taken her long to understand the reason for True's deception, and she honored her for not wanting to take advantage of so splendid a catch as Drake was, just because she was compromised. It ended any doubt the countess had entertained as to True's suitability.

How to manage an estate could be learned; nobility of spirit was ingrained. She would do as viscountess and then countess. But more importantly, Truelove Becket would love Lady Leathorne's son to the end of her days, and a mother could not wish for more for the child of her body.

She turned away to give them their privacy. They would be each other's sanctuary. They would love each other in ways Lady Leathorne had never experienced, but could envy. Truelove Becket was a woman to whom a mother could hand her son over, knowing she was worthy of him.

Drake was her son, would always be her son, but now he would have an attachment closer and more intimate than even the mother-son bond, and that was how it should be. She had been forced to watch her little boy march away and engage in a brutal war that had robbed him, for a time, of his happiness, and she had longed to restore his joy, but that was for his wife.

His wife. Soon to be her daughter, as much a daughter as if she had been born of her body.

With tears in her eyes, Lady Leathorne glanced one more time at the happy couple, and then turned away and walked back to Lea Park.

ABOUT THE AUTHOR

Donna Simpson lives with her family in Canada. She is currently working on her next Zebra regency romance, *Belle of the Ball,* to be published in November 2001. Donna loves to hear from readers and you may write to her c/o Zebra Books. Please include a self-addressed stamped envelope if you wish a reply.